PRAISE FOR THE
GOOD TIME GIRLS

Blakemore's rip-roaring action and lively characters capture the imagination. This series is off to a fine start.

— PUBLISHERS WEEKLY

Blakemore's madcap novel sparkles with scintillating wit, heartfelt warmth, and snappy repartee.

— HISTORICAL NOVEL REVIEWS

K.T. Blakemore crafts perfect characters and adds the right amount of action and a dash of suspense to create the ideal story to keep you entertained for hours. Five Stars!

— READERS FAVORITE

Magnificently written, *The Good Time Girls* is a tough, gritty and often humorous wild ride of danger, death, narrow escapes and yes, love. K.T. Blakemore owns the time period as if she had lived through it, and the characters as if she knew them personally. Open up the book, but hang onto your hat.

— JAMES ROBERT DANIELS, BESTSELLING
AUTHOR OF *THE COMANCHE KID*

Told in humorous, and sometimes touching, McMurtry-esque prose, this book will keep you entertained and glued to your chair far into the night. If you like bold women and stories of the West, you will love this literary adventure!

— KARI BOVEE, AWARD-WINNING AUTHOR OF THE ANNIE OAKLEY MYSTERY SERIES AND THE GRACE MICHELLE MYSTERIES.

Highly recommended if you like Westerns, road trips, great voice, and female friendship stories. I'm very much looking forward to the sequel!

— COFFEE & INK

THE GOOD TIME GIRLS
GET FAMOUS

ALSO BY K.T. BLAKEMORE

THE GOOD TIME GIRLS GET FAMOUS

THE GOOD TIME GIRLS SERIES
BOOK II

K.T. BLAKEMORE

SYCAMORE
CREEK
press

The Good Time Girls Get Famous

By K.T. Blakemore

Published by Sycamore Creek Press

Edited by Kerry Cathers

Book Cover Design by Hannah Linder Designs

ISBN-13: 979-8-9877480-3-9 (paperback)

ISBN-13: 979-8-9877480-9-1 (large print paperback)

ISBN-13: 979-8-9877480-2-2 (ebook)

First Edition November 2023

For good friends.
Life isn't much without them.
and
For Dana. Always.

WHAT HAPPENED
BEFORE, IN A NUTSHELL

Pip Quinn, my ex-dancehall partner and friend, convinced me to leave my thriving cigar shop to kill Cullen Wilder, her spiteful former lover and all-around bad man, before he could kill us. He said we took money from him, which we didn't (you can blame my ex-husband, the Damn Bastard, for that). Our pal Verna Rolfe had been threatened, too, so we thought we should find her and, if she was alive, save her. If she was dead, there wasn't much we could do.

We spent a good few days running around Kansas to elude Cullen's henchman, the Bible-selling and thoroughly immoral Barnabé Boudreaux, and trying to find Verna's speck of a town. Which we finally did, though it took travel by train, creek, automobile, our own feet, and a mule name Theodore, to get there.

Along the way, we managed to earn notoriety for shooting weapons in public locations, thieving, and attempted murder. Then we ended up with our faces plastered on Wanted posters from one side of Kansas to the other. I believe everyone accusing us of things was overreacting, as we just wanted directions.

We found Verna. Boudreaux found us. So did Cullen. He shot Pip so I shot him. A red Levantine leather Bible in Pip's shirt pocket saved her life. My bad aim saved Cullen's. Verna accused the bad men with criminal trespassing and had the gall to charge me seven dollars for busting a window.

Then the law showed up. Being sensible in dreadful situations, we stole some horses and fled. The mule and our new friend Martha Ruth came, too.

So we are on the run.

To Mexico.

To freedom.

I just wish I knew where the hell we were.

CHAPTER 1

AUGUST, 1905

A ROBBERY GOES AWRY—A DIRE SITUATION OCCURS

"Would you look at that." Pip Quinn pointed a black-gloved hand at the wanted posters papering the back wall of the mercantile we had stepped into. "That is an impressive line-up of criminality."

The owner, a mule-faced fellow in a wool suit and celluloid collar, stared from behind the counter. He tapped a rubber stamp against the wooden top with one hand while the other reached underneath to no doubt grab up a trusty firearm.

We were, after all, no one he knew. It didn't matter that Pip looked like a grieving widow, all in black with a heavy lace veil and a cane and a limp. I hung back near the door, my straw fedora low and collar up, looking like a sullen boy not at all happy to be out and about with his grandmother.

"I will be on the lookout for each and every miscreant posted above." Pip thumped the floor with the cane then swung it at me. "Cedric, let this wall of shame be a warning to you."

"Miscreants, Grandmama. That's what they are."

3

"Miscreants." She thumped the cane again, right near the counter. "Cedric. Come here. You need to see this. There is a woman on the wall who looks exactly like a chipmunk." She leaned forward as if her eyesight failed her. "Why she's wanted by the entire state of Kansas, this Ruby Calhoun. 'Attempted murder, Bible thieving, and general mayhem.' Huh. I did not know that was a crime."

I saw very well my own visage upon that wall, so did not come forward. It was a deeply unflattering photograph, having been taken on my last foray into the prison system, but Pip did not need to drive that home. I could very well have pointed to the next Most Wanted image and asked what demon spawned such an ugly face. Pip had never had a photograph of herself, but the artist's rendering got the scar right and that set of her jaw when she got mad.

Pip gasped and stepped back. "That other one, why she'd frighten me to death should I cross her." Her voice quavered. "That is the ferocious Pip Quinn, is it not? Even my failing eyes can see how ferocious she is."

The man's lips curled into a snake of a smile. "They got John Ward after them."

My heart thumped hard enough I knocked my fist to it. My skin went itchy and cold. John Ward's name did that to me.

"Word is…" The man shifted his eyes left and right, then leaned over the counter as if to tell a secret. "Word is he hangs 'em instead of bringing them in."

Pip went very still, except for her index finger rubbing the silver cap on the cane. "That is terrible."

"That's what I heard."

"This isn't the Wild West." Her laugh came out like a gurgle.

"'Act like a Dalton, you'll be treated like one.' That's what he said last week in the *World*."

"You got a copy of that paper?"

He shrugged and pushed the rubber stamp aside. "I did not hear you say where you've come from."

"Why, we just had a bite at the Fergusons. Bella is my cousin and—"

"Don't know a Ferguson."

"Really? I thought everyone knew everyone in these sorts of places."

"What sort is that?"

Pip gave a sharp little laugh. "The sort like your charming three-horse...I apologize. I am from the Little Rock area—that's in Arkansas —and all these prairies look the same to me. Bella lives two towns over that away. Cedric, where does our dear Bella live?"

I mumbled something, then stuffed my hands in my pockets and stared out at the empty street and the dirt gusting into spirals and curlicues. Pip's horse, Satan, chewed the post he was tied to and gave me the evil eye. Across the way was a single clapboard house with half a roof. An old man flapped a sheet about, losing the fight against the wind. Beyond him was a field of scrub grass and dust.

It was much like the other fields of scrub and dust we'd rambled through for too many days to count. We could have circled this hole-in-the-wall three times over and it was only happenstance we were standing here, with Pip ooh-la-lahing over her own Wanted poster and me tamping down my annoyance.

I glanced above the man's head at the clock. It was getting late and Martha Ruth still had not made her appearance.

"You got cigars?" I asked.

"You're too young to smoke."

"I'm old enough."

He ignored me and turned his attention back to Grandma Pip. "You leaving mail?"

"No, sir, I am not," Pip said. "But I would like to sample one of your butter cookies. My cousin Bella said I must stop at the Jaffa's mercantile for these very cookies. 'Little drops of heaven,' she says."

"Is that right? I didn't know they'd become so well-known."

"They are desired by many, sir."

"Well...the wife makes them." There was a scrape of glass and the scrunch of paper. "From her mother's mother's recipe."

"Better than better. And not to bother, but we would like a soap cake, some tooth powder, three toothbrushes and that box of Hidalgos —you wouldn't have a Peter Schuyler cheroot or two? No?"

She must've started in on the cookie as all I heard next were heavenly sighs.

The man took up the rubber-stamp and continued his rap-tap on the counter. He had added a cis-boom-bah rhythm to it and I had to stop myself from humming and throwing out a step-ball-change dance move.

Outside, a pretty girl in pink ribbons and flouncy skirts bobbed by the window. She slowed as she passed me, shifting a bunch of empty canvas satchels from one shoulder to the other, then crossed her eyes and rolled her tongue before continuing around the corner of the building. I spun from the window, sauntering and admiring the meager pickings. A single dusty rug hung on a couple hooks. I lifted the lid on a barrel of pickles but thought better of taking one and instead wandered by bins of garden seeds and tub tins and hoes. At the equine aisle, I picked up a hoof pick and held it aloft like a prize before pretending to set it down. Instead, I slipped it into my pocket.

The tapping stopped. "Did you just put that in your pocket?"

"Put what in my pocket?"

"You put a hoof pick in your pocket. I seen it clear as day." He stepped from behind the counter and strode toward me with a shotgun hanging from his right hand, which put a damper on my enthusiasm for our plan to rob the store.

I had told Pip it was too complicated a plan, but she wanted to try it. Never mind we could have soaked our feet in the muddy creek and left Martha Ruth to sneak into the back and get supplies. No, Pip wanted to see her picture. That's what she wanted, and I've never met someone with such vanity.

Now I had the barrel of a gun coming up at me, all over a little hoof pick we needed, as Theodore had a sore foot that required tending.

"Now sir..." Pip rushed the other aisle and came around the corner behind me. "I do not think a firearm is in order. The boy made a mistake. He'll put it back." She smacked my arm. "Put it back, Cedric."

"Grandmama..."

"He's a sensitive boy, and with his mama in the grave and—"

"Let go of me you godless sow." There was a loud shriek and

Martha Ruth tumbled through the curtain dividing off the storeroom, kicking to get free of the woman twisting her ear. Her red hair ribbons had come loose and flapped around.

"Look at the vermin I found, Henry."

"I'm being kidnapped. Someone help me." Martha Ruth took to keening and clawed at the woman's ample gut.

"You're a thief. Henry, she's a thief." The woman's spectacles hung off the tip of her nose. She tried to push them up with one hand as she kept a tight hold of Martha Ruth with her other.

"I didn't take a thing. I was getting in from the wind and asking for a small drop of water. You should be Christian about that."

Henry stalked over, gun to his shoulder. "Wilma, go telegraph the sheriff."

"You want me to let her go?"

"If you're going to get the sheriff then I expect you might have to."

Martha Ruth stood straight and still. "Please don't get the sheriff." Her doe eyes brimmed with tears and she let them drop pretty as a picture to her dewy cheeks. "I got nothing and no one. I just took a little bit of sorghum as I was wanting a sweet. As it's my birthday."

The gun barrel wavered. "Now, now."

Wilma dropped her deadly grip. "Well, I—"

"The sheriff, Wilma."

Her eyes slid to him, then her gaze shuffled across the floor. And that's how I knew there wasn't a sheriff anywhere near at all to call on.

"It's her birthday," I said. "You should let her go."

Three sets of eyes looked at me as if I had appeared from the ether. I forced myself to stare at Martha Ruth instead of Pip's rump as she snuck behind the counter and darted out the back.

"Who are you?" Wilma asked.

Henry hooked the gun over his elbow and glanced around. "Where's your Grandmama, son?"

"She's long gone. She doesn't like violence of any sort."

"I didn't hear the door."

"She's genteel that way."

Wilma adjusted her glasses and blinked a few times. Her white eyebrows dipped and raised. She looked at me, then swiveled her head to the Rogue's Gallery and back. I had but a split second to act before recognition clicked and hell and high water came to pass.

If I could come up with a story that put me and Pip here and Martha Ruth stealing foodstuffs from the back and then tie it all up with a ribbon like we were on our way to a funeral and needed a butter cookie for the road, then all this could be tamped to a reasonable level.

I took a breath. "Now see—"

My finessing was of no need. A polite knock came on the front door glass. The genteel widow leaned down from her shiny black horse, and used the Marlin repeating rifle she stole from a barn somewhere out by Langdon to push down the handle and urge the door wide. "Henry Jaffa."

He raised the gun to his shoulder.

"You shouldn't do that." Pip lowered herself to Satan's neck and kneed him so he clattered through the door, nostrils flared and stepping high and hard in the small space. Three canvas bags full of whatever Martha Ruth had stolen hung from the saddle horn.

"Get that horse out of here."

Pip sat upright, raising the repeater. Satan swung his rump my way. I stumbled into a stack of grain buckets, knocking them to the floor.

"It's them, Henry. I knew it from the minute—" Wilma tugged at her hair. "Shoot her."

"You can't shoot an old lady." I jumped between them, pushing at Satan's shoulder then at Pip's knee. "Put that thing away."

She shoved her horse right by me, crowding Henry and Wilma against the counter. Henry's shotgun was pressed against his chest, the barrel faced up to the tin ceiling.

"Hand that over." Pip kept her voice quiet and calm.

"I will not."

Martha Ruth turned from the back wall, the posters rolled in her hand. "I highly suggest you—"

A blast went off loud enough I clamped my ears tight. The clock above Martha Ruth's head was nothing but a big hole and a minute hand. Pip shifted the barrel so it aimed at poor Henry's head.

I scrambled around and took his gun before it hit the floor and caused someone irredeemable harm.

Satan clawed a hoof to the floor and danced around. He coiled up, and I knew he would kick out soon if Pip wasn't careful. She lay the reins across her lap, pulled the veil from her face, and glared down at the pair like she was center stage at the grandest opera house.

"I would like," she said, "four boxes of Marlin .25-20 cartridges. If you please."

"I don't have—"

"Winchester's will do just fine. We'll take that tooth powder and box of Hidalgos, too."

He swallowed hard, then side-stepped around the horse and gun and got the boxes and cigars down.

"Put them here." Pip gestured to a leather pouch on her saddle. "No jerky moves. My horse bites."

"This is outrageous. This is..." Wilma burst into a sob. Her glasses fogged up. She whipped them off, bending the frame, and letting out another sob at the state of them.

Martha Ruth rubbed the woman's arm. "That's a shame. It'll be days before the postman comes and you can order another pair."

"Weeks," she murmured.

"Well, sometimes the world looks rosier the blurrier it is."

That didn't give much comfort as far as I could tell. But it did give us some valuable information on the speed we'd need to ride. Which wasn't too fast, thank the Good Lord and the bad post.

"Ladies, I do think we have what we need, should you care to join me." Pip laid rein to Satan's neck, spun him around, and trotted pretty as you please out the door.

"Damn show off," I muttered.

Martha Ruth gave Wilma one last pat, plucked the eyeglasses from her hand, and darted for the storeroom.

I yanked down a rack of seeds and sprinted out to the hard-packed road. Pip grabbed my arm as I tucked my boot into the stirrup and swung up behind her. I shoved the shotgun in the rear rifle scabbard and then locked my arms around her waist.

Satan side-stepped and pranced. Across the way, the old man stared, arms to his hips and the sheet forgotten and flipping around the road.

"Was that all necessary?" I asked.

"Oh hell, no. But it was fun."

She gave a click of her tongue and we were off, Satan churning up dirt as we cut across a field toward a meager stand of willows.

We leaned low so the branches didn't whip our faces, but I felt them along my arm. Near the creek, Pip gave another whistle. Theodore lifted his head from where he was guzzling water, his mule ears flicking around.

"What about Martha Ruth?"

"Haw!"

Satan jumped the spit of a creek, his back arched up and all hooves tucked underneath him, for he despised water as much as Theodore loved it. I nearly lost my seat, grabbed tight to Pip to stay on, and spit out silt and grass that flew up as we took to the other side.

I pressed my cheek to her shoulder blade and turned my head to peer back, sure Henry Jaffa would be on our tail, and maybe the old man from the laundry, too. But there was no one following except Theodore who was exceptionally fast for being a smallish mule. The willows along the creek shrunk down to a thin line and disappeared, and the whole earth, no matter which way one looked, was flat and empty.

Pip pulled Satan up and let him blow. His sides expanded and contracted as he caught air. Theodore trotted up beside us and shook his head around before pushing his whiskery muzzle at Pip's thigh.

I slid off and dropped the canvas bag. Tin cans rolled out. I stared at the label of the one that landed near my foot. "Canned beets? You were going to get us killed over canned beets?"

She smirked. "I like beets."

"I like beets, too, but I do not think that's the best method to get them."

She slung her leg over Satan's neck and hopped down, giving him a pat on the neck. Then she watched the direction we came. "Huh."

My gut sank. The sun was near to setting, causing everything to glow with a strange yellowish tint. "She's got that little mare you stole over in...wherever."

"Yes, she does."

"She's like lightning. If you push her enough."

"Maybe I should've—"

"Not done what you did? That disguise took me three different sneak thievings to piece together. Hardest costume I ever had to sew. All for cans of beets."

We both waited. The sky went a wild orange and bronze as the sun made its way to rest. The plan had been for Martha Ruth to let loose the shopkeeper's nag, then cut out fast.

"She should've been right behind us," I said.

"Should've."

"We didn't consider the old man, Pip. He might have had a horse. He might've caught her."

Pip bent down to pick up the cans and shove them into the bag. "Did you see their faces? They won't forget me now, will they?"

"I thought the point was to be forgotten. How else will we get to your daughter?"

"We need to talk about—"

"Yes, we do. We get your daughter and we get to Mexico. That is the plan. New Mexico to Old Mexico. That plan does not involve you parading about and giving people every opportunity to remember us."

"That is still the plan. In general." She held the bag out to me. "Let's go."

"We can't leave Martha Ruth."

"Yes, we can. I'll give you a lift on to Theodore."

"We really can't."

"She got caught. We're not going to." Her green eye sparked. She took one look back and I saw a shimmer of regret in the brown one. "And if she didn't, she's already back at the hideout."

"Which the entire town of...where the hell are we?"

"Maxey. Colorado."

"We made it out of Kansas?"

"That we did." She cupped her hands for me to set a foot in.

Theo squirmed as I landed on his back. I grabbed up the halter rope and a hank of his mane.

She mounted up, skirts flying and settling like a witch's cape around her. "Ruby?"

"Pip?"

"How about I roast some of those beets tonight?"

"I'd like that."

"I knew you would."

She heeled Satan to an easy lope.

Theo took up his normal bone-jarring trot. Our shadows grew long as we followed a dry gulley south and then west, picking our way around prickly pear and sand sage. I tied a scarf over my nose and mouth to keep the worst of the dust from making its way in, for the wind was a dastardly thing, steady and moaning low and damn irksome.

I took one last look back into the dark, a sharp hope Martha Ruth would be pulling up behind. But she wasn't.

Theodore knew it, too. He stopped dead, laying his ears flat to his head and stretching out his neck.

I squeezed my heels to his ribs. "Come on, beast."

CHAPTER 2

The Hideout—Stewing on Old Bones—Bad Luck

We made the hideout as dark fell. It was nothing more than a crumbling sod house with half a roof sprouted with prairie grass. There were no trees around, not even a stick or two that at least showed someone had tried to make a go of a farm. Just dirt and more dirt and clumpy grasses and rotting melon upon rotting melon. Pip had found a bench amongst the rubble and set that up for our temporary comfort, and Theodore had found a little stream of clear water.

Our hideout would be impossible to find. Which was my fault, as I'd run out of timetables and maps, not paying attention to where we were or where we'd come from and surprised as hell we'd got through Kansas without being hauled to prison a multiplicity of times.

We had slept for three nights and four days, as we were all dog tired and lost and out of food. Hence the calamitous scheme to rob the mercantile that now left us here and Martha Ruth in the hands of the Jaffa's.

"I think we should go back, Pip."

Pip dismounted and lit a kerosene lantern we'd picked up along the way. She pulled the saddle from Satan's back. "It's too dark. We'll go at dawn and get her."

We took to tasks that had become as second nature as our routines on the Paradise stage. I made a fire with the stack of dried brush and a cow patty she'd kindly set out while she took care of the horse and mule.

She returned to the little camp, shrugging off the widow's weeds and putting on a loose camisole and pair of trousers.

I set the cans along the bench, so it seemed somewhat homey, then held up two tins. "Beets. And canned...something. The label's missing."

"We better heat it. Just to be safe."

⁂

We shared a fork and ate roasted beets and warm chunks of beef, both of which did the trick. I offered Pip the last of the beet juice, but she waved it off so I drank it.

We lay all three bedrolls around the small fire in case Martha Ruth had managed a way out and found the path back to camp.

Pip dropped her hat to the horn of her saddle, then settled back against it to gaze up at the sky. She stretched her legs and tapped the toes of her boots. "I think that's Orion."

"Good for it." I shook out Pip's disguise and sat cross-legged on my bedroll to check the seams and search for rips. "You are hard on clothes."

"I don't want to wear that again. It's too hot."

"Well, I don't see a dress shop nearby to get you another costume."

"I don't want a costume. I want to...be like this. It's easier to move in."

I glanced at her. "You'll be adding indecent exposure to your list of crimes."

"So be it."

The dress was dusty but did not appear worse for the wear, so I stood and took it inside the hovel. A couple bits of wood stuck out from the sod, evidence that at one time this area had been slightly more habitable. I hung the dress on one, then lifted the top of Pip's leather satchel hanging from the other and grabbed out a brush for my hair.

Pip lit a cigar and puffed it, blowing smoke rings and staring up at the sky. She was a beautiful woman, save for the ragged scar that marred her cheek and nose. It caused one side of her mouth to retain a smirking smile, and I think she enjoyed how that frightened people. She had spent many years having it drag her down and lead her to wander.

"I'm tired of wearing veils," she said.

"Well, you'll be more tired of prison should you *not* wear one in mixed company." I took the brush to my hair, sticking the handle in my mouth while I braided my tresses up. "Let me brush that mop of yours."

She scooted up so I could sit on the saddle behind her.

"You still have the damn prettiest of hair." I ran the brush along a thick strand.

"You can thank my mama for that." She leaned to the side to pick up a stone, and then drew a couple squares in the dirt. "This is Jaffa's. That barn sits catty-corner to the back storeroom entrance. If we cut in at an angle we can see if they've got Martha Ruth's horse in there. We'll get it out—ow."

I yanked at a tangle. "Sorry. Keep going."

"We'll head up the back stairs while they're sleeping, wake Martha Ruth up, and off we go."

"That's it?"

"Yeah, that's it. Is there something you want to add?"

"I just wondered. Most of your arrangements have other elements involved."

"I'll have the horses and mule ready, you go on up and get her. Take the shotgun, in case Jaffa hears something and has another piece of weaponry nearby."

"How about we switch those roles?"

"We could." She tossed the stone back and forth. "Maybe I could hide in the outhouse until Mr. Jaffa comes out, and scare him half to death because that look he had earlier was precious. Then I can conk him on the head to make sure he is unconscious and—"

"You're not going to conk anybody on the head."

"But he's awake. He could jump me and I might have the unfortunate situation of falling into the pit and where would we be? I'd be stinking of poo and you'd be stuck and he'd be hopping mad and calling for the wife. Maybe they got Martha Ruth tied up in a room, which is highly possible."

"How about we stick with the original set of actions?"

"You'll need to take the shotgun."

"All right."

I did not carry firearms as a rule, for they are deadly things and, as I am often told, I have miserable aim. As much as I worried on taking one up to rescue Martha Ruth, I worried more about Pip's horse biting my arm off and kicking me in the ribs.

"You promise, Ruby?"

"I promise."

"Wave it around if needed. I'm not asking you to fire it."

I TOSSED AND TURNED ON MY BEDROLL, KEPT AWAKE BY MUCH MORE than Pip's snoring. I was used to that now. But I could not stop the ruminations and regurgitations my mind stirred up.

I wasn't an outlaw. Not in the strict sense. It is true that I was wanted across multiple counties in the grand state of Kansas, though not one of the charges was accurate in any way. Pip's charges had the same inaccuracy. All she did was bust a farmer's nose. And steal an oil man's prize 1903 Winton automobile. And shoot at a Bible salesman.

These did warrant a wanted poster or two, I give you that.

"Pip?" I could not hold out any longer. "I'm having a bad spell."

Her snore cut off. "You did not kill him. If you did so, those posters would say murder." She rustled around, pounded her saddle pillow, and settled in with a squeak of leather. "Go to sleep."

"It doesn't seem much different."

"We have a job tomorrow, Ruby. Go to sleep."

"If you could—"

"No."

"I listen to you when you go on about—"

"Good night, Ruby."

I crawled over to her, shook her bare shoulder, waiting while she stretched and yawned and stretched again before opening her eyes and peering up at me.

"Are you on this again? You should be more concerned about the sheriff we're avoiding." She gave a shudder. "That's who should keep you up at night."

John Ward, the sheriff of Morris County, Kansas, had been after us since Emporia. He put our pictures in every newspaper, depot, post office, and lawman's lair in Kansas, then made a four state noose of them, too. We had never met him; his reputation was enough to keep us on the run. If he thought you were bad, you were so. Rumor was he didn't believe in juries, just a nice strong branch and a rope. Henry Jaffa had confirmed the tale so I considered it true.

"I wasn't thinking about Sheriff Ward. Now I can add that to my list. I appreciate your comforting words." I turned away. Something stuck sharp in my heel. I grabbed up my foot and hopped around, digging at a burr sticking in my skin. I got part of it out and hobbled about as it stung like a son of a bitch.

"Why are you dancing around?"

"I got a burr."

"Well, get it out, put your boots back on, and go to sleep."

"Fine." I thumped down on my bedroll. "If it's infected tomorrow, it's your damn fault."

"Fine."

"Go to sleep."

I squeezed my eyes shut and wrapped the bedding to my neck. "I'm sleeping."

She breathed out through her nose then got up and poked my thigh. "Ruby?"

"Pip?"

"You saved my life. You remember that."

"No, I didn't. The Bible saved your life."

"Who stole it for me?"

"Well, I did. All right. That makes me feel better."

"Good. Now go to damn sleep."

◈

WE COULD NOT TRAVEL THE NEXT DAY. BOTH HORSE AND MULE, who we'd tied to a pile of old wood planks, bit through the old ropes we'd found and wandered off. It wasn't hard to find them, as we could see miles out on the prairie. But it was damn hard to catch them. They both spooked when we came near, and pricked their ears to something they heard in the distance but we couldn't.

"Mustangs," Pip said.

"I don't see them."

"They're there."

She whistled until it was nothing more than air spit between her lips. The damn animals kept trotting west. Martha Ruth and Maxey lay out east.

"Go your damn ways, you fools," Pip called. Then she trudged back hideout way.

"We've got to get them, Pip."

"We've been out here all day. I need something to eat and something to drink, then perhaps I'll be in the mood to chase after them."

"They could get lost."

"We can see them. They can see us."

"You do realize they are our only transportation?"

"Find us a train. I'm done with horses."

I jogged after her. "There aren't any trains around. There's barely roads. There's barely people. I don't frankly even know where we are and that brings as much panic as losing Martha Ruth."

"I know where we are."

"No, you don't."

"Well, pretend I do. It'll make us both feel better."

I stopped cold. "That does not make me feel better."

The wind gusted, flattening the grasses and lifting my straw hat off my head. It flipped in the air like a kite. I ran after it, jumping to catch it, but each time the wind knocked it out of reach. The wind came stronger, no longer in puffs and gusts, but constant and with a low moan.

"Now I have no hat." I spun to yell at Pip. "You could have helped. This is all your fault." My braid flipped about and slapped my neck. "Pip. You are a selfish, good-for-nothing slackjaw turtle-faced pain in my—"

She kept on walking.

I leaned into the wind and followed. "Don't think I'm going to talk to you while you eat."

Luck has a way of bouldering downhill from bad to worse. The wind grew strong enough I was forced to crawl the last bit into our hideout. My eyes stung ever so from the whipped up dirt, and each time I blinked the grit scraped like a son of a bitch. Pip sat cross-legged, a blue scarf tied around her nose and mouth, holding onto both saddles by their horns.

Her eyes were puffy and red, closed to slits. She pointed at the sod house.

Only one wall still stood. The roof and what was left of a side wall had collapsed in a heap of dirt, burying our bedrolls and clothes and gear.

I took one of the saddles from her grip and set it on its side like a windbreak. Pip followed suit. It didn't do much good except it kept our spirits from shifting and blowing away with all the other dust. I ran my tongue over my teeth and spit out pebbles and plant refuse. Pip held her hat over her face with her free hand, the other hanging on to the saddle.

Kansas had been miserable. But these prairies were the hell-spawn of the Devil. One minute the land was waving golds of grass, sweet smelling like Eden on earth and then without any warning the Horsemen of the Apocalypse decided to ruin a person's life and clog up the lungs of anything stupid enough to stay standing. When they'd had their fill of vicious mayhem, off they went.

The gale ceased as sudden as it came. Pip uncurled herself, shook the dirt from her hat and set it back on her head. She tromped over to the hovel, picked up a sod brick and tossed it aside.

I brushed off my skirt and spit again. "I don't care about anything in that rubble. Except a toothbrush."

☙❧

We dug and shook things out and washed our teeth in the gritty creek water. Pip made a fire and we ate a can of plums and looked out the direction Satan and Theodore had gone.

"I'm going to bed. You tend the fire." Pip fluffed her bedroll and stretched out.

"It's barely dark."

"So what?" She put her arm across her forehead and let out a sigh. "So damn what?"

"Pardon me, but this is a precarious mess, and I do think we need to perhaps have a conversation about what to do."

"According to you, I'm a good-for-nothing slack jaw, so you just have a conversation with your perfectly capable and reasonable self."

"I am capable and reasonable."

"All right. You tell me what you come up with in the morning." With that she rolled over and gave me her back.

I tapped my thumbs to my knees and looked around. The widow's weeds and bridles and Pip's satchel had been secured to the ground with heavy rocks, as the wall we'd hung them on no longer existed. The bench had been turned aright, and I stacked the tin cans we had left and the box of Hidalgos underneath and shoved some of the sod bricks against them for safety. A smoke or two would have focused my thoughts, but we'd lost the matches along with one of the toothbrushes and Pip's favorite comb.

My heart started in on a distressing pattern. I needed a timetable to calm me. I hadn't seen one since somewhere near Garden City, for we'd tracked along the Santa Fe Rail Line and the Arkansas River for quite a while using the train whistle and my recall of stops. But every stop came with a depot and every depot had our pictures. We had turned south around Lakin. A few towns and then there wasn't a whistle anymore. Just grass and wind and creeks that promised they went somewhere before sputtering out.

"Paola," I mouthed. "Ottawa...no Osawatomie. Then something then Lomax." Yes. That was where Endicott and his sister Erline were headed. "Council Grove, Wilbey. McClaine." No. That was an entirely different line. My breath went funny. I could not remember. I smacked my forehead to dislodge the correct sequence of towns on the Missouri Pacific line.

I realized none of that mattered anymore. Any train I alighted on now would lead only one direction: a pair of handcuffs and a prison cell.

"Wilbey, Harrington, Hope—"

"Ruby—"

"Shh. Carlton."

"Be quiet."

"You be quiet. Carlton..." The crackling of grass stopped up my voice. Footsteps. Coming nearer. One set from the front and another from my side. "Animals?"

"I don't know."

"People, then."

Pip slid her hand to her Marlin and lifted it slow and steady.

"We don't want to kill you," I called out.

The rustling grew loud and frenetic. Pip got to a knee, aiming the gun one way and swinging it another and back again.

This was it. I put my hands to my ears, lowered my head and thought I should pray but couldn't come up with anything but "Dammit-and-hell, it wasn't supposed to end like this."

There was a burst of motion. Pip landed flat on her back, rolling out of the way as Satan stomped and spun around. I jumped up and put out my arms to wave him from the fire pit.

"Whoa, whoa."

Pip sprinted to grab a bridle, then slung the reins about his neck and held tight. He kicked up his front legs, threatening to rear.

"You don't need to do that, now do you?" Pip's voice was sultry. "No one's going to hurt you." She kept talking, her voice murmuring and singing sweet nothings as she stepped closer. "There you are, you big baby." Satan's skin rippled along his neck as she ran a hand down it, and without ado bridled him up. "You best see if Theo's around."

I shook my head from the hypnotics that had muddled it. "Theo."

"He's around somewhere. Get the bridle and go look by the creek. Slow and steady." All the while she kept rubbing Satan's neck and pulling at his forelock. She spoke sweet and soft, letting the reins stay loose. He stood calm as an angel by her side.

"How do you do that?" I asked.

"I understand them. It's people that puzzle me."

Theo was easy to find. Just steps away, lallygagging and guzzling water from the creek.

"You are a damnation of a beast," I said.

He swung his head up and pricked his ears forward. The water drizzled from the sides of his mouth.

He ambled over and pushed his big Roman nose against me, rubbing up and down. I looped a rein over his neck and scratched the white star on his forehead, which he particularly liked.

"Come on, mule. We got an early morning."

CHAPTER 3

RETURN TO JAFFA'S—ALMOST HELD FOR RANSOM—PIP MAKES AN
ENTRANCE

The Jaffa's barn was easy to sneak up on, for it backed on a stand of old willows that gave us cover and allowed us a tie up for both Theo and Satan. We hunkered down and slunk along the trunk of a tree that had fallen some time before, stopping in a spit of shadow to assess the next move.

A crow cawed above us. Pip gave it a deadly stare, but it didn't shut up, so she flipped a rock its way. That did the trick. It took off in a huff and we were able to concentrate on the job at hand.

"You got about seventy-five feet from here to the storeroom door," she whispered. "Stick to the side of the barn and when that ends—"

"Run like hell."

"Make it a dainty quiet run."

"It'd be easier without this big old shotgun."

"I asked if you wanted to take the Colt."

"This is fine." I did not wish to touch the Colt again. Looking at it gave me hives. It was the weapon I'd used on Cullen. "I'm not going to shoot it."

"You will if you need to, Ruby."

"Last night you said all I needed to do was wave it around."

"Things change."

A cock crowed but I could not see a chicken coop. Maybe it was the town's mascot and strutted around the streets, lording it over the population of three.

"Ready?" Pip asked.

"You go that way, I go this way, and we meet back here."

"That's right." Pip narrowed her eyes and took a sweeping gaze of the area. "You hear anything?"

The cock had stopped blaring out the time. The crow had long gone. The wind-wrecked barn was quiet and not a snippet of noise came from the two-story house that made up the Jaffa's mercantile and sleeping quarters.

"We best get on before everyone's up," I said.

"We best." Pip sprung up.

"Wait."

"What?"

"If we get separated and need to find each other—"

"Go back to the hideout."

"No, Pip, in general."

"I don't know." She pursed her lips up to think. "I'll meet you in the lobby of the Brown Palace Hotel in Denver."

"Why there?"

"They have a fancy afternoon tea."

"But it's the opposite direction we're going."

"So?"

"Is this meeting point meant to fool those who believe we are heading to Mexico?"

"Are we discussing this now?"

"I just want to know, Pip. No need to be curt."

"Now you know. Go get Martha Ruth." She darted to the barn, staying low along the side and giving a short whistle for me to move forward.

I lay the shotgun on the ground. The damn thing was too heavy anyway and was certain to trip me up. I sprinted out of the tree line, passing her and picking up speed across brittle grass that snapped so loud under my boots I thought it'd wake the state. A large yellow dog bounded out from the shadow of the cellar, loping straight at me. Its paws looked the size of my head. The cur gave a deep growl, sliding to a lock-kneed stop and blocking my way.

"Stay, dog." I held out my hand like I'd seen Pip do with the horses when she wanted them to maintain a bit of polite distance.

The dog tilted his head and panted.

"What a nice…" I took a peek. "What a friendly boy you are. Now I'm going to take very slow steps forward and give you a pat. Would you like that you perfectly friendly dog?"

He whined and took a step back. The bristle on his back lowered.

"That's right." I kept my voice a singsong, leading with an open palm to show him I trusted his inherent goodness.

His eyebrows danced as he looked from my hand to me. He panted again and yawned.

"You have damn bad breath, mongrel."

One more step and I'd be able to give him a good rub behind the ear, we'd be fast friends, and I could continue on.

"Psst."

I looked back to Pip crouched at the corner of the barn waving an arm for me to move on. "I'm going," I mouthed. Then I shook my head and turned back to the dog.

He'd rolled over on his back and wagged his stump of a tail in the dirt.

I scratched his burr matted chest then bounded the rest of the way to the storeroom door. He got up, shook himself, and trotted to the barn, no doubt seeking attention from Pip.

The door was ajar. Which gave me pause, as no one was outside the house to have opened it. I slipped in, letting my eyes adjust to the dark. The shelves were empty of foodstuffs. A long raw gash in the floor looked as if something heavy had been dragged across it. Staying light on my toes, I crept to the back stairwell that led to the living quarters. It was too quiet. So quiet my ears rang.

The dog bounded past me and clattered up the stairs, his big feet thumping on the floor above.

I slid under a shelf and stared at the door to the yard then mentally cursed myself for jumping this way instead of outside. Yet here I was. Canine toenails clicked from one side of the house to the other, stopping at each of the rooms.

There should have been noise upstairs, telling the dog 'Good morning' or telling it off for bringing its stinky paws inside. I crawled out and peered up the steps to the landing.

Nothing.

I peeked outside to give Pip a signal that something was strange in the situation, but she wasn't by the barn and I guessed she'd gone in to see if Martha Ruth's horse had been stabled. Then I crept up the stairs.

The dog nudged my hand with his wet nose and stuck to my leg as I took a look into each of the rooms. Two bedrooms. A parlor over the front of the store. A kitchen at the back. Nothing in the wardrobes. Not a speck of food in the kitchen. The front room had all its furniture but the side tables and cabinets were empty of the doodads and sentimentalities of a lived-in home. I turned in a circle where a rug had been.

"This makes no sense at all."

DOWNSTAIRS, THE MERCANTILE LOOKED AS IF THE OWNERS HAD abandoned the entire endeavor. There was evidence of a few items removed. The cash register draw hung open with a penny stuck in the seam. I scraped it out and pocketed it. A stack of old newspapers threatened to tumble along the back wall. I lifted the lids on the flour and oat barrels, surprised to find them full. The dog snuffled around, looking at me every so often but without an ounce of trepidation, such as filled me.

I tore off a square of paper that had been taped to the glass of the front door.

Gone to Springfield. Closed for good.

Across the street, sheets and long johns flapped on a line, though there was no sight of the old man.

The dog whimpered and scratched the floor.

"Dog, this is mysterious." I folded the note to my pocket so I could show it to Pip and hustled down the aisles to the back door. The dog nearly bowled me over as he flew by. I caught the edge of a shelf to steady myself, said a few choice words, and continued forward.

Straight into a solid body that was not Pip.

I landed on my ass and blinked up at a lumpy figure in calico holding a rifle crossways. "What in the hell?"

The woman bent low, her hair frizzled white and looking like the wind had set up shop in it. She squinted and ran her teeth over her lower lip.

The dog licked the side of her face, which made her snap straight up and take the back of her hand to her weather-beaten cheek to wipe off the slobber.

I darted forward, hoping to make the treeline and find Pip. But the woman swung that rifle down low and caught my feet from under me. I landed smack to the ground and even had I wanted to get up, I wouldn't have dared it. The dog took the chance to slather me with kisses but that did not negate the hard steel muzzle of the rifle pressed to the center of my back.

"I caught one!" The woman racked a laugh that ended up in a wheezy cough and the slurpy sound of spit that miraculously did not end up on me. "That man was right."

"Let me up."

"Keep your mouth shut."

A stone poked into my cheek. A trail of ants walked by, marching up and over a mound of manure. Beyond that, the barn doors swung open. No horse. No wagon. No Pip.

The dog lost interest in me and loped out of the yard. More ants toddled by, and then the original set returned, holding aloft their leafy treasures. The woman bent over and stared at me. A couple of ants trailed up her hair. "You're a bitty thing."

A pair of men's boots came up beside her. "Take that gun away, you damn woman."

She stepped back, though the rifle did still swing my direction. The man took her place, bent over and looking at me upside down. He smiled, his mouth more gum than teeth, and petted the top of my head. "He said you'd come back."

"Who? Who said?"

"Where's your friend?"

"It's just me."

His brows pulled together, creating a deep canyon, then they parted and smoothed out. "Are you hungry?"

"Hunger's not at the top of my list right now."

He stood and held out a calloused hand. "Well, I haven't had breakfast. Mabel fried up a prairie chicken and drippings."

"It's cold now." The apparent Mabel slung the rifle to her shoulder.

"It'll be all right." The man's smile went tense.

"It'll be inedible, Garvin. You know how their fat gets."

"Light the stove and give it a spin or two with the spoon. This little woman needs sustenance, she's looking peaked."

I fluttered my eyes. "I am very peaked, sir. It would help if I can sit up."

"Of course." Garvin graciously pulled me to my feet.

"Don't make any sudden moves." The rifle swung in an arc. Mabel planted her feet wide like someone very used to shooting things.

"Put that down, woman. She's worth more alive than dead. Isn't that right, Miss..."

"Calhoun."

"Calhoun." He slung a bony arm around my shoulders and moved us forward. "Let's go eat."

I squinted out to the distance, wondering how far it was to the hideout and if I could run the whole way without being picked off by Mabel the Sharpshooter.

The odds did not seem in my favor.

GARVIN USHERED ME ACROSS THE STREET FROM THE MERCANTILE, shooing off the dog and holding back the sheets that the wind whipped across the walkway. The house, if one could consider it such, consisted mostly of planks and twine, though the two rockers in the front looked of quality wood and the kitchen was bright with a red-check cloth on the table and a combination cast iron stove and oven. Mabel hung the gun on hooks over the back door, put on an apron and lit the fire under the pan of chicken.

"Sit." Garvin pointed to a bench against a rough white-washed wall. He took a plate from an open shelf and set it down in front of me. Two other plates had been previously set and, judging by the napkins slung haphazardly to the table, it looked as if my arrival had upended the morning.

Mabel huffed a bit as if she heard my thoughts and agreed. She scraped the wood spoon to the iron and narrowed her eyes at me. "Leg or breast?"

"I have no preference. Thank you."

I took the fork and napkin Garvin handed me. He ran his thumbs down his suspenders, looking pleased as could be, as if I were the Queen of Sheba gracing his humble abode. "I'll need to tie you up now, if that's all right with you."

"No, that is not all right with me."

"Tie her up, Garvin."

I slid around the table to evade him, but the room wasn't bigger than two coins rubbed together so all he had to do was stick out his arms to stop my escape either way.

"It's only until the man gets back," he said.

Mabel slapped some unknown greens into the pan. They sizzled and popped and she paid us no mind, intent on stirring them around so they wouldn't char.

I stared through the curtainless window between the stove and table, praying with all my might that Pip was outside. But she wasn't. It was me alone, stuck with the task of eating prairie chicken and figuring a way out of this.

"What man?" I shifted left to no avail as Garvin was light on his feet for being what looked a hundred-and-twelve years old.

"The one who took your friend."

"I thought the Jaffas took her." I flinched right then left but was caught out again.

"Jaffas went to Springfield."

"Without Martha Ruth?"

"Why would they have Martha Ruth?" he asked.

"Is that her name? They never talk about her in the papers." Mabel stabbed a piece of chicken with a serving fork and used a very large knife to slide it from the tines to a plate. She repeated that with each piece and upended the greens into a bowl. "Garvin."

"Yes, Mabel." He picked up the serving ware and set both plate and bowl in the middle of the table. "Sure smells good."

"I kept off the pepper, seeing as I do not know our guest's proclivity to spices." Mabel untied her apron and lay it on the counter. She took the chair directly across from me while Garvin slid his bony hip against mine, pinning me between him and the wall. I tossed up a prayer of thanks that ropes and/or handcuffs had been forgotten.

"What're you doing?" Mabel asked.

"I'm praying."

"Well, do it out loud, no need to be selfish about God."

I bowed my head and put my hands to my lap pretty as you please. "Dear Lord above, thank you for this exotic but certain to be delicious meal so generously cooked by my captors. If they could open their hearts and explain to me who the man is and where Martha Ruth— Yes, that is her name, though she used to answer to Candy Doll, you know that is a past she shed long ago, Lord—"

"Do you know how much you're worth?" Mabel leaned forward with bright eyes.

"I've seen the wanted posters."

"That's just a dollar and change. I wouldn't give two spits about that. Not after what the man give Henry for the girl."

Garvin took up a chicken leg and gnawed off a piece. He swallowed and waved the drumstick at me. "You know what a criminal's downfall is? Coming back to the scene of the crime. It's a dumb thing to do. And you did it."

"The man—he gave the Jaffa's a reward and took my friend?"

"Oh yes. A wad of cash, enough they packed right up—"

"Well, you know her sister is poorly," Mabel said. "They were waiting years for this opportunity."

Dread boiled in my stomach. The law, who we thought of only in abstractions, had been right on our tail. We been so careful at first, staying low during the day and riding at night. But the further we got from Emporia and Burdick, the more we let down our guard.

Mabel pushed a plate my way, the chicken cut up in bite size pieces and a spoon resting on the greens.

"Thank you." I scooped a bite of greens and puckered up. My stomach revolted, but I managed to get it down. "That was delicious." I glanced out the window again, but the same dust and desolation confronted me. "I take it this man is coming back. For me."

"He sure is. He said so plain as day." Garvin sucked the rest of the meat from the second leg he'd picked up. "'Keep those girls,'" he said. "'My job depends on it.'"

"He didn't say that. He said, 'If you see them, tell them I've got their friend and to find Dooley Corcoran at the El Otero. That it'd be worth their while to do so.'"

"I don't remember him saying that."

"Well, he did. Right before he rode off with the girl. He didn't look like much of a lawman," Mabel said. "Would you like more greens?"

She dolloped them to my plate.

"What'd he look like?"

"Not a sheriff," Garvin said. "Little too dandified for that, wouldn't you agree, Mabel?"

"It was that bowler. Or it was the flower he had in the button of his jacket. Of course, he could be detectifying, and had his badge hid away."

"Pinkerton." Garvin nodded to himself. "Only thing to account for that cash he gave over."

I half stood from my seat. "Pinkerton? Why would there be a Pinkerton?"

"No one said it was a Pinkerton."

"You just said so."

"I'm conjecturing. On account of that classified. It seems to me— where is that paper?"

"Last week's?" Mabel asked.

"The one we got yesterday."

"That's right, last week's. I cut it up for the outhouse. We were running low."

My head throbbed. "You wouldn't mind if I went out there and put it back together, would you?"

"Woman, I had not finished up the article on the governor…"

"You should have told me. How am I supposed to know? Half the time you tell me the newspaper is only good for the crapper."

"Well, this is the other half that isn't."

A movement outside the glass caught my eye. It was Pip. She passed by without stopping, pointing toward the back of the house.

"What're you looking at?" Mabel's head swiveled to the window.

"Nothing."

She got up and lumbered over to peer outside. "Something's out there."

She pushed her chair in and headed for the back door, grabbing the rifle from its rack as she pulled the door open.

I held my head and squeezed my eyes tight, expecting Pip to be standing there with her Colt and her dreadful smile.

But there was nothing but a lot of sun and the wind whistling in.

So I plugged my ears.

The bang from the Colt came from behind. I looked up at the new hole in the ceiling and watched the plaster drift down to the chicken bones and Garvin's head.

"You may hand me that weapon now, Mrs…?"

"Pearse. Mabel Pearse."

"Mrs. Mabel Pearse. My name is Pip Quinn. It is a pleasure to meet you."

Pip strode past, her Colt aimed straight at Mabel, her boots pounding the floorboards. She took the rifle from the woman's shaking hands. "Now you sit down with your husband."

Mabel put her hands up high, though Pip didn't ask her to, and sidestepped around Pip, sinking into the seat. "You cannot get away with this. That man will be back from La Junta and I'll tell him—"

Garvin gripped up the serving fork and slung it Pip's way. But it missed and went end over end out the back.

"You just tried to kill me." Pip's eyebrows rose up high. "Stand up so my friend can get off that bench."

"You're going to regret—"

Pip had that look about her that could cause all sorts of worries, so I squeezed Garvin's arm in apology and crawled over him.

"You damn women. Damn damn women." He started to hyperventilate.

"Put your head down," I said.

"Ruby—"

"This could be a serious medical issue."

Mabel made screechy sort of noises and reached across the table.

"Put your hands back up." Pip pointed the gun at Garvin. "And you. Put your head between your legs."

He did so, and the wheezing slowed.

"We are going to go out that back door," Pip said. "You two are going to sit here and count to one thousand and forty-one, do you understand me?"

"Why one thousand and forty-one?" Mabel asked.

"Because my bullet can still kill you from that distance." With that, Pip stalked out.

I held the Pearse's rifle in the crook of one arm. "Which way's La Junta?"

Mabel pointed an index finger.

"Thank you and I apologize for the hole in the ceiling." I turned tail and ran out to the yard.

Pip sat atop Satan. "Get up."

"Where's Theodore?"

"Just get on up."

"One minute." I looked back at the house. Mabel was counting aloud, and not very far into it, so I darted to the outhouse, grabbed up a stack of newspaper squares, and stuffed them to my pocket.

"What's that for?"

"We got Pinkertons after us."

"Damn."

I handed up the rifle to her, then got my foot in the stirrup and swung up behind her. "We need to go north."

She kneed Satan to a lope. The ground and a few cantaloupes churned up under us. I counted to one thousand and forty-one, and then to one thousand and forty-two to be safe.

Pip must've been counting, too, for she circled Satan around. She looped the reins to the horn. "Give me the gun." She emptied it, letting the shells drop one by one. "Hop off and shove it to the ground so they can find it."

I slid down, took the gun from her and poked it in the dirt. It looked like it might fall over, so I rolled a few melons over to prop it upright. Then I looked up at Pip who looked out at the sorry two-building town of Maxey. "I think you've grown a soft streak, Pip."

Her gaze snapped down at me. "Get the hell up, Ruby Calhoun."

Which I did. Then we dipped down a shallow dry riverbed and made away.

CHAPTER 4

On the Road—A Cigar and a Song—A Funeral Is Held

There was no Theo. I searched the landscape for him, thinking those big ears could be seen from here to Kansas City or at least at the next water hole.

"Pip?"

"What?"

"Where's the mule?"

I felt her back stiffen. "Maybe we should have this conversation with our feet on the ground, Ruby."

This did not bode well. She halted Satan and made me get down. Then she did, too, though she took a moment to fiddle with his bit and rejigger the saddle cinch.

"I asked you a question." I smacked her back to get her to stop picking a thumb and look me in the eye.

She straightened up and pulled at her belt and squinted at me. "He went with the herd."

"What herd?"

"The mustangs. From yesterday."

"The ones from—"

"Those ones."

"You have got to be..." I let out a breath. "I don't understand." I stumbled over furrows from old fields, stared out, and whistled. I whistled in each direction, but nothing answered save the buzz of flies.

"Ruby—"

"He had a saddle on, Pip. And you tied the halter line down and—"

"No, I took the saddle off. He was dozing and you were taking a long time looking for Martha Ruth in that mercantile and it was getting hot waiting around."

"I had been kidnapped, Pip."

"Yes, I did eventually realize that." She rubbed her eyes. "Now we got that out of the way we should go on."

"This is not out of the way. How in the hell is he going to survive?"

"The same way the other horses do. My guess is he'll be leader of the pack. Take them to the best lakes and rivers in Colorado."

"You sure?"

"I know so. I've been around horses my whole life—"

"Not mules."

"No, not mules, but they're close kin. I think Theo heard the call of the wild. Like a trumpet playing a song to come join those who are free of cares and worries—"

My heart hung heavy with the news. I waved for Pip to shut up with the nonsense. "We need to go find Dooley Corcoran."

"Who?"

"The possible Pinkerton. That's who they said took Martha Ruth."

"Well, he won't have her for long."

I trudged over to the horse. "We have no gear."

"The plan was to go back to the hideout. There's a couple tins of something in the saddlebag. You know how I like to be prepared."

"Do you?"

"Ruby..."

"Just help me up."

WE TOOK TURNS RIDING THE NEXT STRETCH OF THE WAY, FOR THE saddle was too small for two and caused chafing in areas not meant for such. The creek was a cruel one, a satisfying burble and sharp rocks in one place before disappearing down a mud hole in the next. Soon it disappeared altogether and neither of us rode, finding it more prudent to scout for the next spit of water along the bed.

The fields and grasses changed shape to a rocky land of shallow ravines. To the west, I saw the shadows of mesas with juniper dotting the ridges.

"We need to make camp," Pip said.

"You told me that twice already."

"Well, it'll be dark soon."

"You told me that, too."

Satan picked his way along the rocks, not helping at all, what with his aversion to all waterways. This made my heart heavy, for Theo would have figured this all out and given us a look showing his superiority to all humans as he did it. But he was not here.

I squeezed my eyes shut to erase the image of his run to the herd. "I would like to hold a funeral, Pip."

"For what reason?"

"We owe Theo a respectful sending off." My foot caught a rock that tumbled and sparked. "A small celebration."

"He hasn't died."

"I've been thinking on his odds. They are not good at all. There's plenty of grass now, but what's he going to do in winter? What about wolves? And mountain lions. And what's he going to do when all those water holes become skating rinks? The odds are he will not make it."

"The herd'll teach him how to handle all that."

"They may not like him. They may say 'Go away, you old mule.'"

"All right. We'll hold a ceremony."

WE STOPPED WHEN DUSK MADE IT IMPOSSIBLE TO KNOW NORTH from any other direction and all three of us got tired of tripping over all the loose rock at the base of the gulley.

"We'll stop here," Pip said.

It wasn't much of a hiding place, should one need to actually take cover. It was an overhang of white rock, but there was enough room to lay out the bedroll and a couple thin-trunk trees to tie the horse up. I stretched out on the roll. The papers I'd taken from the latrine crinkled in my pocket. I sat up and pulled them out, but wasn't of a mind to read them, so stuffed them in the saddle bag we'd set down as a pillow.

The fire crackled. Pip pushed at it with a stick. "We need to get to La Junta."

"Yep."

"Get Martha Ruth out of jail."

"That, too."

"That Corcoran fella may have already telegraphed Sheriff Ward."

A shiver went down my spine and right back up. "Maybe he's already on his way. Maybe he's going to make her answer questions for hours on end until she breaks down in tears and babbles every single damn crime we've committed. Which, by the way, we are stacking up too quickly for my liking."

"This Pinkerton—"

"Or bounty hunter—"

"Not much difference."

"That does not make me feel better about our predicament, Pip."

"This isn't a predicament. It's just a detour."

"You ever been to La Junta?" I asked.

"No."

"Do you know how to get to La Junta?"

"The old woman told you it's north."

"Oh. Well, that clears it up," I said.

"We'll pass someone along the way tomorrow and ask directions. You're stirred up now. We will get to La Junta, we will get Martha Ruth, and we will get back on the road."

"Easy."

"Easy as rye whiskey on a cold night."

I let out a breath and relaxed my shoulders. "We take one step and then another."

"That's right."

"We need another horse."

"We'll find another."

"The Santa Fe Railroad goes right through that town."

"I'll get you a timetable. It'll be the first thing I do."

"That would be immensely helpful for my nerves."

Pip walked over and crouched down. "That's going to be a tight bed."

"I was thinking you could go sleep with the horse."

"Don't be mad at me." She reached for the saddle pack and flipped back the cover. "What's all this?"

"There's some stories in there about us. I thought we might want to know what's being said."

"These might be more useful in the form they're in."

"Always better to know things."

"Fancy splitting a Hidalgo?"

"You left half our things and brought cigars?"

"I found matches at the Jaffa's."

I recognized she was trying hard to get my spirits up. It wasn't her fault that Theo had done a runner. Sometimes creatures, and people, want away and you've got to let them go. "Why, you have brightened my evening, Miss Quinn. I would most fancy sharing that cigar with you."

She knelt over the fire, puffed a few times to get it alight, then sunk back, crossing her legs and blowing smoke rings before handing it to me.

I took in a quick bolt and let it wiggle around my mouth so I could catch the full experience the Hidalgo offered. Then I blew it out. "This brings a bit of heaven to a miserable part of the world."

We smoked and listened to Satan nibble the wild grass. The sky gleamed with a million stars.

"You think that's the Milky Way?" I asked.

"Might be."

"Sometimes it makes me lonely. All that infinity. Kind of like windmills. Or an old cow in a field with not a soul to talk to."

"Cats in windows," Pip said.

"Yes, those, too."

Pip tilted her high crown Rough and Ready hat back off her forehead and rested on her elbows. She hummed a bit, then sang.

I'm dreaming now of Hallie, sweet Hallie, sweet Hallie
I'm dreaming now of Hallie, for the thought of her is one that never dies

She stood and moved her arms about as if she were parading in a diaphanous gown.

I picked up the next bit.

She's sleeping in the valley, the valley, the valley
She's sleeping in the valley, and the mockingbird singing where she lies

Pip warbled out. *Listen to the mockingbird, listen to the mockingbird*
Together, we finished the chorus with the tightest of harmonies.

The mockingbird is singing o'er her grave
Listen to the mockingbird, listen to the mockingbird
Still singing where the weeping willows wave

She stopped dancing around and took another toke on the cigar. "I remember that song being a tad brighter."

I clapped the top of my thighs and hopped up. "All right, then. I'm ready."

"For what?"

"The funeral."

Pip swiped off her hat. "I'll read from the Bible."

I peered down at the stone I'd picked up. "He was a good sort of mule, that Theodore."

"Thank you, Theo." Pip bent over to wipe some dirt off another stone then we both sidestepped to a larger jagged piece of white sandstone we'd found to mark Theodore's spiritual resting place. We balanced our rocks on the edge, as if setting down lilies or other such funereal flowers. Pip took her pocket-sized red Levantine leather bible from her back pocket, held it in both hands, and looked solemn as any minister.

"Will you be reading a final verse to speed him on his way?" I asked.

"Do you want him sped on his way?"

"Well, I don't want him suffering at the butt end of that herd."

"All right, then. Let's consider this both a wish for his well-being and if he can't have that, a worthy send off." She kneeled close to the little fire to get some light, licked her fingertip and thumbed through the pages. "Here." Her knees cracked as she stood, keeping the pages towards the glow. "*When thou sittest to eat with a ruler, consider diligently what is before thee: And put a knife to thy throat, if thou be a man given to appetite.*"

"I don't think that's right…"

"Unless they changed it."

"I always do wonder who 'they' is in this situation. Is there a granite temple somewhere with scribes who only see the light of day on Palm Sunday? Let me take a look." She handed the book over. "Why, you're in Proverbs. That's an easy mistake. Here. You read. I'm going to bow my head."

"*The Lord is my shepherd,*" Pip intoned. "*I shall not want. He maketh me to lie down in green pastures: he leadeth me beside the still waters.*

"*He restoreth my soul: he leadeth me in the paths of righteousness for his name's sake.*

"*Yea, though I walk through…*" Pip held the psalm to the fire and screwed up her face in concentration. She poked her finger into the bullet hole that saved her life. "There's a small bit missing here. "

I peered at the shredded pages. "I think we'd be safe with 'desert.' They did a lot of desert walking back then."

"Moses."

"Moses and Job and Jedediah and so forth."

She took a breath. "*Yea, though I walk through the God forsaken desert—*"

"That's a very good addition."

"There's room in the hole for it."

"Carry on."

"*I will fear no*...oh hell, this is all chewed up."

"Just start where it starts again."

"*Surely goodness and mercy shall follow me all the days of my life: and I will dwell in the house of the Lord forever.* Amen." She closed the book and rubbed the cover with her palm.

"Did you hold a service for Big Henry?"

Pip pursed her lips and shook her head.

I thought as much, being as her sentimentality tended toward nil and needed a small kick sometimes. "We could do that—"

"No." She tossed a cow patty on the fire and trudged to the shelter. "He's dead and that's that."

❦

THERE ARE GOOD HORSES AND THERE ARE GREAT HORSES. BIG Henry was a great one, Pip's pride and joy, a grand horse with a sweet temper who would move mountains if he could (what with his hooves) to do anything at all for Pip.

She had been a trick rider at one time, long before her career as a demi monde derailed that starry ambition. That's as far as she told the tale of those early days, and whenever I asked how Cullen Wilder knew Minnie DuBois and how Minnie DuBois tempted Pip from the rodeo stage to the dancehall stage and then again to a bed in a brothel, I was told those days were past and to mind my own business. That was generally followed by an hour or two of grumbling and grousing.

She'd kept Big Henry through heartaches and wanderings, and put the last penny she had into keeping him happy. No matter what the night before had brought, whether rough men or too much whiskey, she'd most days get up at dawn, put on silver-trimmed doodads and take herself from China Mary's down to Matteo's Livery. She and Henry spent the mornings happy as could be riding around in a ring as Pip practiced her moves, often drawing a crowd, because she did a few death-defiers and liked to show off her bare legs.

After Cullen cut her face so badly and we'd all scattered to the winds, she'd wandered without much purpose save keeping that horse alive. I did not ask details about this period of her life. From what she'd let on, it was a dark time. But she had her little baby Olive and Big Henry and I believed that gave her some meaning.

Then she sent Olive to the nuns for safekeeping and Big Henry caught his leg in a hole and that was that.

She didn't talk about him now. That's how I know where it hurt her, in the deepest part of her heart.

Every horse she'd stolen since then had been nothing but a means to an end, each dropped in a stall or a pasture as she traded for another.

Now she had Satan the vicious trickster, who, frankly, I would trade off for a chipmunk.

She didn't like him and he didn't much like her, and both seemed to be biding their time and looking out for better days. Still, he listened to her.

I never knew one that didn't.

❦

The fire had dwindled to an orange glow.

"You think you'll ever get a horse again like Big Henry?" I asked.

"You think you'll ever see your kids again?"

"I think I will."

She got up and wiped off her trousers. "You keep that dream going, Ruby."

Then she squeezed my shoulder and headed to sleep.

I threw another patty on the fire then dropped my head to my hands. God only knew what John and Emma thought of me now. Rose had no doubt fed them a load of lies, saying the Ruby Calhoun in the newspaper was not the Aunt Ruby who lived so far out of town and had such wretched ways it would be impossible to visit. I didn't know if John thought of me at all, being as he was a baby when Rose took him in. Emma, however, might question the stories Rose told. She'd been a toddler before Frank made me give her up. 'Women and children are bad luck on boats and around a gambler,' he'd said. 'It's simply until the luck turns and we can do right by our children,' he also said. I believed him. I loved him.

Until I didn't.

By then, Rose had her claws in the kids and they called her mama.

I thought Emma might put two and two together, even if the news of my criminal ways was buried in the middle pages of the *Kansas City Star*. 'She's an avid reader,' Rose often boasted when I gave her money for the kids' upkeep.

I realized I might have wanted to see my kids, but I doubted they wanted to see me.

Rose had made me both invisible and a monster. And with my current outlaw situation, I had to agree with the latter.

A spark popped and seared the skin on my hand. I flinched, then flicked it off and blew on the tiny burn.

I looked over at Satan. He swung his head toward me. I kept my voice to a whisper. "You know what I'm going to do when we get to Mexico, horse? I'm going to lead an honest life. Maybe first I'll put my feet in the ocean, but after that, I'll show Rose she's wrong. That's what I'm going to do, horse."

❧

I WOKE TO A COLD BEDROLL. PIP WAS ALREADY OUT BY THE FIRE, stirring a can of something in the ashes.

"Peaches," she said. "I thought if I warmed them up they'd remind us of peach pie."

"How long you been up?"

"Long enough. Take a look at this."

I stumbled over, rubbing my hip where a rock had taken umbrage during the night. Pip had laid out the newspaper clippings, each held down by a rock. "Well, hell, you put together at least half a newspaper here."

"*Springfield Herald*. Last Friday."

"Mm-hm." The squares of paper held much of the same thing that could be found in any paper anywhere: The Cattle and Horse Growers were set for a convention in Denver. A Margaret Winstead died on Prosperity Lane, luckily in her sleep. *Go to Denney's for your shoes. Extra Quality. Low Prices.* A Mr. Haney was arranging to build a barn. A boy was tortured by eczema.

Pip picked up a particular square and handed it to me.

Take care of your possessions and lock your doors. The Quinn-Calhoun gang has been spotted on the Kansas border. Contact Paco Jones at El Otero Hotel, La Junta if sighted. Reward is generous.

"The *Quinn-Calhoun gang?*" I looked at Pip. "Why do you always get top billing?"

"Never mind about that."

"Wait a minute. The El Otero. That's where Dooley—there's two Pinkertons?"

"Could be. Keep reading."

"Oh, there's a sale on shirtwaists—"

"Not there. Here." She poked the middle column.

I scanned along the column of the comings and goings of such and such person to such and such town. Then I found it.

ARMED AND DANGEROUS - WANTED in all localities of Kansas and spotted in Colorado and Nebraska. Wanted for multiple robberies, attempted murders, and horse theft. Ruby Calhoun is petite and sharp-tongued, and Penelope Quinn is noted for her disfigured face. A third party is traveling with the women; name unknown but young and pretty. Do not approach but contact local law enforcement or telegraph Sheriff John Ward, Morris County, KS. Hefty reward.

"You're still good looking, Pip, don't let that hurt your feelings."

Pip folded the paper and put it in her back pocket. "Go take care of your business then we'll eat." She gestured past the rocks to a couple scraggly bushes.

I scratched up some of the less interesting squares of local news and went over to where she pointed.

A lizard darted past my feet and disappeared in a crevice. It missed its tail and I wondered what out here had bitten it off. Which made me step up the pace of my morning routine.

Water burbled down the slope, slipping up and over a few tumbled rocks. I washed my hands and face and sent a quick prayer no cow had died upstream before I took a bracing gulp.

The peaches were gone in no time. Pip wasn't much for morning conversation, preferring a few grunts and the rest of the time spent coddling the horse. I cleaned up our camp, rolling the bedroll and taking an inventory of the few items she'd brought from the previous hideout. Which didn't amount to much. Two canvas bags with canned goods from the mercantile. Two canteens already filled. Her leather satchel held three boxes of bullets, a toothbrush and tin of tooth powder, a jar of liniment, and a few loose lemon drops.

I dug further down. My fingers caught on the worn case that held the photograph of Pip's daughter Olive. I pulled it out, snapped it open and stared. I closed one eye, then the other, thinking that this time the image of the little babe surrounded by dried flowers and bits and baubles would look alive. But she still looked dead as a door nail, so I closed it and pushed it back to the satchel. "Remind me never to hire that photographer," I called.

Pip looked up from picking one of Satan's rear hooves. "What?"

"Nothing." I slung the satchel over my shoulder, lugged up the bedroll and totes, and clanged over to the two of them.

Pip gave Satan a pat on the haunch, tucked the pick to the saddlebag, and took the bags and canteens from me. "We're walking today. He's got a sore wither."

"We're walking?"

"That's what I said." She twisted the handles to the saddle horn, pulled her Colt from her belt to check it was loaded, and slung the strap of the rifle to her shoulder. "We'll take the farm road north."

"How far?"

"Until we run into something."

"I don't find that a confidence booster."

"The road has to go somewhere, doesn't it? Who knows? La Junta might be only an hour or so away."

"Or not."

"Whether it is or isn't, we've still got to travel that way." She looked up at the sky. "We'd better get on before the heat."

I sighed, for there wasn't much to do but the doing, and glared at Satan as I passed by. He glared back and snuck a bite that missed my tit by mere inches. "You are a barbaric creature."

❧

THE ROAD NORTH WAS STRAIGHT AND WELL-RUTTED FROM THE passage of wagons, but we spied only one. It was split in pieces, gray and wind-lonesome. Far out on the parched land, a couple pronghorn antelopes lifted their heads and watched us.

The sun seared as it rose high in the sky. Satan, who had been afforded an entire canteen of water, drooped his head and shuffled forward. Pip and I trudged along, taking tiny sips from the other canteen.

Just six weeks ago, I had been ensconced in the lap of luxury, my only decisions involving what cigar brand to discount and when I'd turn in young Willie Bledsoe for desecrating my wooden Indian. Olaf promised to take care of it, but Willie had a wily streak and Olaf wasn't the fastest at the racetrack. I wished I could write Olaf and ask how the statue was and my business, too, but the one time I tried, Pip ripped the paper in half and ate it.

Martha Ruth had witnessed Pip's chew and swallow of my missive. "That's excellent roughage," she'd said. "My sister Eudaly had a blockage the night before her secretarial course exam and chewing paper cleared the whole thing up."

Pip had smacked her chest as she struggled to swallow. "Give me that beer."

I did not. "It's against federal law to destroy U.S. Mail."

"Eudaly was third in her class." Martha Ruth reached for another bottle we'd kept cold in the pond we'd rested at and handed it to Pip. "We were over the sun and moon proud of her. Being she was the first in our family to graduate from anything. 'Course, I got that ribbon for my goat Sadie at the county fair, but it wasn't the same, except my ribbon was prettier than that piece of paper she got. She was real jealous of that. Then she got ringworm—"

"The goat?" I asked.

"No, Eudaly. That sure deflated her. She took up moping and that seemed to restore her. She's working at the dairy now."

"Still moping?" I asked.

"She says it's what comforts."

Pip had stared at her and we all finished off the beer and watched the sun set.

It was a long time until sunset in the here and now. "You think Martha Ruth is all right?"

"She knows how to take care of herself."

"It's hard to do if you're chained up and being grilled over the location of your gang."

There was no reassuring answer to that. Instead, Pip picked up the pace, and I suppose that was answer enough.

The back of my neck itched and I knew I'd have a nasty burn if I kept it open to the winds. I unbraided my hair and let it fall down my back.

"I wish we'd picked up my hat," I said.

Pip eyed me, then took hers off and gave it to me. She unbraided her own hair and it fell in all its magnificence down the middle of her back. She fluffed it to get a little fan of breeze and we trudged on.

To the west, a shallow gully cut the ground and, beyond it, a long ridge of squat trees took shape and beckoned with shade. We stopped and Pip peered over to consider it. Then she looked east and considered that. "Cattle," she said. "There'll be a waterhole."

I pointed the other way. "Trees. There'll be shade."

Which left us with a quandary, so we continued down the damn hot rutted road.

Something shiny gleamed in one of the tracks. Pip scooped it up, but it was just a shard of a blue bottle so she tossed it back. I caught the shine of another piece and toed it loose with my boot. "It's an arrowhead."

I held it up, admiring the light reflecting off all the facets of the black stone. The tip had broken off, no doubt lodged in a pronghorn or person. Or it'd been churned up by a tiller when the homesteaders came and kicked out the Indians who roamed around and called this home. I stuck it in my trouser pocket and poked around for more.

Pip showed me a cracked leather boy's shoe and a rusty hammer head. I caught sight of a hank of gingham stuck in the crack of an old board. But no more arrowheads showed themselves. Just beyond the detritus, the grasses dipped and rose, the mark of an old trail grown in. Pip bent down and lifted a post. A sign, cut like an arrow, hung from it. She turned it right ways. *La Junta.*

"That could be pointing any which way."

"It's pointing down here."

"If you turn yourself forty-five degrees it will be pointing back there."

"But it's not. It's pointing that way. I'm following the sign."

"I do not find this a good measure of your wherewithal, Pip."

She shrugged her rifle to her other shoulder and strode into the grass, giving the reins a small shake for Satan to follow. "You go that way, then, and I'll go this."

"I believe you are suffering the onset of heat stroke." I stood my ground. "This is a real road that will take us somewhere, Pip."

"Enjoy it."

"I have your hat."

She waved but did not turn around.

"You know, you don't rescue someone then abandon them on some deserted byway. Pip. You have all the food."

She twisted off a bag, dropped it, and kept walking.

"I swear to God almighty and the boat he rode in on, you are the most impossible woman I have ever met." I high stepped over the grasses, the satchel banging my behind, and hopped away from a prickly barrel cactus ready to ensnare me with its spikes. The bag lay in a heap. I grabbed a tin that had gotten loose. Fancy oysters. Fancy horrible disgusting slimy oysters. I slung it her direction. "You're going to let me starve, aren't you?"

Pip dropped to her haunches. She let go Satan's reins and he skittered around.

"Pip?"

She raised her arm and pointed straight to the ground.
So I dropped, too.
Something, or someone, was in the gully.

CHAPTER 5

THE DINOSAUR HUNTER—PIP GAINS A BEAU

I crawled forward until my shoulder touched Pip's, then the two of us shimmied to the edge, pushing aside the brittle grass to get a clear view of what lay below. A makeshift raft floated in a waterhole, its corner bumping against sandstone outcrops, and on the raft lay a man, spread-eagled to the sun and naked as his first day in the world.

"What the hell," Pip muttered.

"He is quite a fine looker. In all measures."

Pip did not find this amusing and had already drawn her Colt.

"That's a very unfair fight, you know."

"Shush."

Two horses, a sorrel with a wide white blaze and a stumpy Appaloosa, grazed along the slope of junipers. Lower down, a saddle and pack sat next to a pile of folded clothes and a pair of knee-high laced hunting boots.

"What should we do?"

Pip chewed her bottom lip in thought. "I do not know."

"I don't see a gun belt."

"There's a rifle against that rock."

"That's the neck of a guitar."

"Well," she said.

The raft bobbed and bumped the side of the water hole, wobbling enough the man stirred. His horses both lifted their heads. Then their ears pricked and they stared over at us. Or Satan specifically, who'd dropped his ears flat and dug a hoof to the ground, sending stone tumbling over the edge and into the water.

The man splashed around in a circle before scrambling up the other bank. He ducked behind the saddle and peered over our way. "I'm a peaceful man," he called. "I wish no one harm and expect none returned."

"We would appreciate the same," I answered.

Pip gave me a glare that meant to shut up and let her deal with this. "I'm going to stand up, sir. You put your hands to your head. I will shoot if you so much as move in any other way, do you understand?"

He nodded and complied, both hands resting on top of his blond hair.

"You get Satan," she said to me.

We made our way down, slipping in the loose rock and then crossing a dry wash.

The closer we got, the more the man trembled. I could tell he was anxious to cover his nether parts, as he kept shifting a hand from his head and forcing it back to the crown.

"You should let him get dressed, Pip. He's going to get a terrible sunburn, and you know how that feels."

"Why don't I help him get dressed, Ruby, then saddle his horse for him, strap the pack on the other, and let him go on home?"

"That would be the Christian—"

"Why don't I give him ten dollars on top of it?"

"We don't have—"

She gave a huff. "Wait here." She holstered the pistol and trudged over, lifting up his saddle and swinging it away.

He flinched and squeezed up tighter.

She turned to dig through the saddle packs, tossing out a couple books and hanging on to a bottle and a hunk of cheese.

She set those aside and unstrapped the packs, pulling out a tarp.

"There's just a tent there," he said.

"And this." She dug out a rifle.

"There's coyote around."

"Nothing else I'll find?"

"Nothing else. Can I please have my clothes?"

She slung them one by one his direction, then picked up the boots and set them by his side.

He dressed faster than a hen running from the ax, keeping his eye on her and every so often sneaking a glance at me, and hopped around as he pulled on his boots. His suspenders flapped around his jodhpurs.

Which looked about as ridiculous a thing as I'd ever seen. The sides bloomed out and pinched in at the knees. He tucked in his shirt and buckled a wide brown belt high on his waist.

"What are the suspenders for?" I asked.

"What?"

"You got a belt so why do you need suspenders?"

"Well, there's buttons for them."

"I think you're overdoing it. It would be like me wearing one corset and then another over the top."

He stared at me and so did Pip, so I closed my mouth and took Satan down to get a drink.

Pip sauntered around him, looking him up and down. She gave a tsk and then pointed up at the horses. "Which one do you like best?"

"I like them both."

"Why are you out here in the middle of nowhere?"

"Why are you?" His clothing made him confident and fractious. He puffed his chest and stuck out his chin.

"We're going somewhere that's none of your mind." Pip lifted her chin as if daring the man to retort, or perhaps hoping he'd read her mind and tell us the lefts and rights we'd need to take to get to our destination. "What do I call you?"

"Jack Roberts. Ranch owner and dinosaur hunter."

"I didn't know there were any of those still around."

"You would be surprised at the amount of bones and other artifacts one can find."

"That explains the pants and Teddy Roosevelt boots," I said. Satan and I walked over to join the two. I looped the reins around a tree limb then took off my hat and fanned myself. "May I ask the contents of that bottle?"

Pip had left it and the cheese in the shade of the saddle.

"That's a beer."

"I think I'd like a sip. Would you be so kind, Mr. Roberts, to share a sip with me and my friend?"

Jack put his hands to his hips. "No. I shall not share a sip. That's my beer, and this is my watering hole and all I wanted was a relaxing afternoon."

Pip wandered up the hill to the horses. She rubbed the Appaloosa's nose and muzzle, then lifted its lip to consider its teeth. "Give her the beer, Mr. Roberts."

"I will not. You two hooligans have shattered my peace and quiet and I don't get much of it. That is my beer, and I will drink it, and you two will return to wherever you came from." He paced about and snatched the bottle up. "And get your hands off my horse."

"I'll take her," Pip said.

"I'm not selling her."

"I'm not buying."

"You realize horse thieves are hanged around here?"

"We are aware of that."

I darted in front of Roberts to block him from rushing up and tackling Pip. We did a little dance around, and I touched his arm to stop us from getting dizzy. "We are not horse thieves, Mr. Roberts. I know you think that on account of my friend's curt behavior, but she gets funny in the sun, and if we leave it too long, she'll think she's Billy the Kid. You don't want that to happen."

He considered what I said, then spun around and trudged up the hill. "Miss Who Ever You Are, I do not like being snuck up on."

"You don't know—" I clamped my mouth shut. There was no need calling attention to our criminal infamy.

Pip ignored us and moved on to running her hands over the Appaloosa's legs. She lifted a front foot, dug a stone out of the hoof and threw it aside. "This how you treat all your horses?"

"I treat my horses fine."

She wiped her hands and stood. "What's her name?"

"Bessie."

"I need a horse. I would like this one." She untied the halter lead from a branch and started back down the hill.

"You can't steal my horse."

"I'm not stealing your horse."

"It sure looks like you are." He followed behind her, all sputters and small-grade profanities, then cut in front of her. "I could overwhelm you right now, you know."

"But you won't because you're a peaceful man. As you said."

"I am a peaceful man."

"Then you will peacefully let me borrow your horse."

"If you're going to steal one, take Blaze."

"I don't want that one. He's got a flawed confirmation."

His face went a deep shade of vermillion. "No, he doesn't."

"Look at him."

"He's a little square in the rump, I give you that."

"Just a little?"

"I won't have you discussing Blaze so cruelly."

"Please let me pass."

"I think not, madam." Roberts set his legs and grabbed Bessie's lead.

He tugged one way and Pip tugged the other, their hands inching closer with each yank.

"It's my horse."

"Not anymore."

"You are squandering my good will."

"Go catch a dinosaur, you cur."

"Where'd you get two different eye colors?"

"My mama. What's it matter?"

"I can't figure out where to look." Then, being toe to toe, he stepped on her foot.

Pip let go of the lead. "Damn it to hell." She hobbled around and hopped. "I think you broke three toes."

"I am so sorry about that, that wasn't my intention." He reached forward, his horse ignored now, and slipped his arm under hers.

"Do not touch me, you fool."

"We need to get your boot off. It'll swell otherwise."

Pip stuck her hand to his chest to hold him away and limped down to the camp. "You go get that horse, Ruby. I have to check my foot."

Roberts followed behind her, coming at a fast pace. He swooped her up in his arms, strode past me and set her on a flat rock. In the shade. He pointed a finger at her to stay put, then kneeled down and cupped the heel of her boot.

It was the hair flop on his forehead that did Pip in. Or maybe it was the dimple as he smiled up at her. Then again, it could have been the supreme gentleness of his handling of her boot, then her ankle, then her toes.

Any which way, it made my stomach clench. I'd seen that expression too many a time on her—a doughy, dewy, cross-eyed sort of nonsense we had no time for.

"Does this one hurt?" He brushed a finger to her big toe as if it were a soft kitten.

"It's all right."

He wiggled the next. "And this?"

"A tiny bit." She took in a breath and let it out in a small chirp.

I thought it high time to remind her of her luck in the Department of Men. "Cullen Wilder."

"What are you talking about?"

"Giving you a reminder of your tastes."

Her eyes fluttered and grew out of focus as she stared over Jack's head at me. "That's a lifetime ago."

"I believe it was five weeks and six days."

Jack crouched over his pack and drew out a hank of cotton. He waved it at me. "You wouldn't mind walking down and getting this wet, would you? We need to wrap this, give it a chance to heal."

"What's wrong with her toes?"

"They're bruised up." He gave her a long face. "Again I apologize. We cannot have you injured, not if—"

"It's accepted," she said.

"Fine." I stomped over and took the rag. "We're taking one of those horses as payment for you assaulting her. When we get to La Junta, Mr. Roberts, I'm going to get a lawyer and sue you for assault."

"Unsaddle Satan, would you, dear Loretta?" Pip's voice dripped sweet as honey. "You'd be ever so helpful to do so."

I narrowed my eyes at her. "Of course, sister Caligula."

"I'll do it." Jack stood and patted my shoulder as he passed me. "You can sue me, but you're the one trespassing." He smiled, showed off the gap between his front teeth. He then rubbed Satan's neck before moving to loosen the cinch.

"You be careful. He bites."

"Nah, he's a good fella. Look at him nibble my hand."

❧

Next thing I knew, we were lounging around a campfire, all the guns piled on the far side of the water hole in some parlay for peace. Two cans of beets, one of peaches, another no name beef and a tin of boiled okra cooked in the flames. Jack shared around some jerky and slices of apple as an appetizer.

He sat on his haunches, stirring each tin with a long stick. Pip crossed her legs and rested her chin in her palm, watching him as if he were the second coming of Christ. Neither of them asked for the beer, so I hunkered down by a log and drank it myself.

We shared Jack's tin plate and ate each course as it came. He'd seasoned the meat with some plant that looked like rosemary, and I could not complain as to the taste.

Afterwards, we—or rather I—rinsed out the cans and put them back in a bag, as they made useful tools for boiling suspicious water.

"Well, then." I clapped my hands together. "We had best move on before that sun sets. If you could point the way, we'd be ever obliged. I won't even sue you."

"You can't leave now," he said. "You've got to cross the canyon before you get to a road. It's pitch dark at night. We will all stay here, since we've become friends, and I will escort you myself in the morning. I'll even have Carnelia scramble up a big flapjack breakfast at the lodge."

"Your wife?" Pip asked.

"My cook."

Her eyebrow snuck up at the information.

"Flapjacks?" I asked.

"Yes, ma'am."

"At your ranch?"

"Vista Verde. It's a small concern I take care of, bringing in adventurers and...adventurous tourists looking for a taste of the Old West. Four bedrooms and a communal dining hall."

"Bedrooms. With beds. And pillows." I sighed.

He gave a chuckle and scooted sly as a fox toward Pip. "Each bedroom has a plethora of them."

I never understood the chemical that caused men and women to lose all common sense. It seemed to infect each person quick as snake venom. I myself had been besmirched by it, having in my youth fallen for a gambler with a pretty face and sweet-talking tongue. It didn't matter he left me more than once and shipped my kids to my sister's. I hung around, begging for another dose of that venom.

Pip, whose own proclivities for men who took advantage was a whole set of degrees worse than mine, should have learned her lesson with Cullen. She had wanted to kill him just a few weeks ago, which I first resisted then wholeheartedly looked forward to, being as he was looking to kill us, too. Her pig-headed obsession with him got us into this mess in the first place.

Lord forbid she remember that now.

The dinosaur hunter had taken up his guitar. He strummed and picked a few notes. "Got a song you'd like to hear?"

"Oh, you choose," Pip murmured. "I don't know that many."

To which my stomach flopped. "I'm going to bed."

Jack had set up the tent, and I did not refuse his offer to stay in it. I stomped over, flinging myself inside and onto Pip's bedroll.

Jack sang *Git Along Little Dogie* in a silky baritone. Pip joined him on the chorus and it was so pretty it burned my chest and made my teeth hurt.

"Cullen Wilder," I called out.

They moved on to *I Just Can't Make My Eyes Behave*, so I thumped the satchel into shape and squeezed my eyes tight.

❧

TOO SOON, IT WAS MORNING. AND IT WAS STILL ONLY ME IN THE tent.

"I'm going to kill you, Pip Quinn."

I sat up and crawled out. The fire burned hot, and a coffee kettle nestled in the ashes. All three of the horses shared flakes of hay that had been scattered outside the camp.

"Good morning." Jack sat against his saddle, oiling a bridle. He had that smug smile that gave away the goings on of the evening prior.

"Where's my friend?"

He pointed to the water hole. Pip glided along, tits to the wind along with the rest of her. She waved at me, then rolled over and side-stroked in a manner both lazy and provocative.

"You need to get out of that pond, Caligula. We have things to do."

She ignored me and ducked her head under water.

I turned to Jack. "What madness have you fouled her with?"

He laid out the bridle and took up a snaffle, rubbing the metal clean. "You and your clothes could use a long dunk in the water, too."

"That's rude."

"You two are on the run." He gave me a quick glance then returned to cleaning a set of reins. "She didn't tell me that. I guessed that myself."

"Intrepid of you."

"I don't need to know what you did or who you're running from. I just know two women shouldn't be out here in the canyons. So, we're going back to Vista Verde and figure this out."

"What sort of lodge did you say have out here in the middle of nowhere?"

"It's a tourist lodge."

"Oh, I understand. Neither of us is interested in that sort of business."

"What sort is that?"

"Don't make me spell it out. It's too early in the morning to discuss that."

"I run a stage down from Vogel Canyon to the Purgatory River, show people the dinosaur footprints."

"Dinosaur footprints?"

"There's at least a thousand, some big as a retriever dog."

"People come to see that?"

"Sure they do. And petroglyphs."

"What are those?"

"Paintings along the canyon walls, who knows from who. These canyons are old as the stars. Before me, before settlers, before the Mexicans and Cheyenne and Arapahoe and Comanche there lived many generations of other tribes." His eyes went all hazy. "I'd like to show it to you."

"How come you're being so nice to us? We were going to steal your horse."

"And now you're not." His smile grew, making those dimples irresistible even to me, who saw how he'd practiced their use to perfection.

A splash of water sounded behind us. Pip hopped up on a ledge and twisted her hair, squeezing the water out. "Take off your clothes and jump in."

"Me or him?"

"You. I can smell you from here."

"It's too early. I'd prefer to have a smoke first."

"Suit yourself." She tilted her head. "The least you can do is bring me a coffee."

"I'm happy to do that." Jack stood.

"You sit. You need your rest, Mr. Roberts."

"Fine." He sat down in a snit. "You take her the coffee."

I grabbed the handle with the rag left out for the purpose and poured the coffee to the tin cup. An eggshell floated on top, so I fished it out and tossed it.

Pip watched me as I neared, a strange half-lit smile on her face.

"I don't need you to tell me what happened last night."

She took the cup from me, blew on the top and took a sip. "Sit."

"I don't want to. I am ready to depart. Lest you have forgotten Martha Ruth needs our assistance. I have not."

"Get off your high horse and sit your ass down."

"Fine." I lumped on down next to her and she put her arm around my shoulders. "The water is pretty, isn't it?"

"I do not care about the water."

"Look anyway." She took another sip of the tar and grimaced. "There are visitors at his lodge right now. He says they're from Chicago."

"So what?"

"Visitors with trunks of clothes and cash is my guess. They're waiting for some friends to join them."

"And again, so what?"

"He said he didn't know how he'd have kept the place open, but then this group appeared from the heavens. So. You eat flapjacks, I wander around looking around his struggling ranchero and stumble into some of those trunks and loads of Chicago dollar bills. The horses will get a rest. Then we'll be on our way."

"No, Pip. He's being kind to us."

"You want new togs?"

"Yes."

"You want your own horse?"

"Of course."

"We need money to keep moving, Ruby."

"It would be helpful."

"Then we're robbing the guests. And maybe him. I'll let you know."

"Well, figure it out before he asks you to marry him."

"All we did was talk," Pip said. She tossed the coffee out to the dirt and sent Jack a dazzle of a smile. "I'll be dressed in a flash, Mr. Roberts. Those flapjacks are calling, yes, sir, they are."

CHAPTER 6

Pip and I had little time to discuss our new plans. Jack was like a nervous Nellie getting the camp closed up. We each took a horse, me being given Bessie as she was the sweetest natured. He had also given me his saddle. Jack rode Blaze bareback, a hand to his hip and his wide-brimmed scout hat flashing in the early morning sunlight. Pip and I followed behind him, working our way through the narrow canyons, up one mesa then down again then up to another.

"This is aggravating," I muttered.

How I wished for a streetcar. It came upon me in a great wave of melancholy how much I missed Kansas City, and the screech of the car's wheels as it passed my cigar shop and Olaf's haberdashery, and Lady Anne's before careening around the corner to the market. Two transfers could take me all the way to my sister Rose's and, if I timed it right, the journey was under an hour. Thirty-eight minutes, in fact, and I had timed that twice with my pocket watch to verify. I missed how the first car rolled by before a cock had crowed and remembered how much I'd like to stomp about and swear at the damn thing for waking me up. Looking back, I acknowledged its greatness for getting from one place to another with such efficiency. It was, in my mind, near as perfect a vehicle as one could ask for. Kansas City was near perfect, too.

Unlike here.

"I hope Mexico City has streetcars."

"I'm sure it does," Pip said.

"And running water."

"Definitely."

"And a menu or two in English until I can get a handle on the language."

"We can take classes."

"Maybe we can stop outlawing." I glanced at Pip.

She frowned. "Did you really call me Caligula earlier? What she-devil would call their child something like that?"

"It's the first thing that came to my mind."

Jack stopped at the turn into another canyon and looked back at us with surprise. "Come along, slow pokes."

We pushed the horses to a trot to catch up. A river lazed and peeked out at us from a snaking valley.

"The Purgatoire," he said. "Also known as The River of Lost Souls. You see right there?" He pointed at a stretch of mudflats, water pooling in various divots. "Looks like an elephant track, doesn't it?"

Pip squinted and pulled her mouth down in contemplation. "It certainly does."

"Being," I said, "as you've seen an elephant track before."

"I've seen an elephant."

"When?"

"Spokane Zoo. I've seen an elephant. I've actually seen two."

"Brontosaurus," Jack said. "Being chased by something with a three-pronged claw." He urged Blaze forward, keeping to a path that ran tight with the canyon walls.

I caught sight of drawings on the rock faces: mazes and wandering rivers, animals, geometric designs, *John Hardy Been Here 1877*, *X Marks the Spot*.

"Tell us about the three-pronged claw, Mr. Roberts." Pip took advantage of the wider path at the bottom and moved up to Jack's side. She gave him her undivided attention, even batting her eyes some. Her hat sat at a flirtatious angle that showed off her cheek bones and she wasn't at all shy about the jagged scar across her face that glowed bright white now on her sun-darkened skin.

Bessie hurried to catch up, her trot as bone breaking as Theodore's had been. I held onto the saddle horn and tiptoed in the stirrups to avoid bruising and a possible tailbone fracture. She shoved her head between Blaze's and Satan's rumps and was satisfied once we were crammed like a sardine between them.

Jack's face fell at the intrusion, but Pip set it right by kneeing Satan ahead and around to take up his other side.

"You were saying?"

"Tyrannosaurus, also known as the Man Eater, stood thirty-five feet tall with a great mouth of sharp teeth and a never-ending appetite for Bronties. Who are my speciality as an amateur paleontologist. There's nothing that excites as much as seeing a dinosaur skeleton come to life. Or finding tracks such as we have here. I can show you a melee set in stone, about an hour away, where I believe a terrible attack occurred—"

"Is this on the way to the flapjack breakfast?" I asked. Jack's lecture had taken on a tone that it might go on for a few dozen hours and I had in my stomach but a cup of sludge coffee.

A plume of smoke curled from behind the hills opposite.

"Ah," Jack said. "Home."

⁂

Home was more than four bedrooms with fancy pillows. We passed two corrals with at least twenty horses, then a pitch-roof barn with a copper weathervane. A yellow mud wagon, its canvas roof and window flaps stretched over the wooden struts, was housed outside.

"I'm a little bit short on help now. I left the guests with the cook in charge. I hope no one has succumbed to food poisoning."

"Have they before?" I asked.

"Of course not."

The lodge itself was long and low, wrapped with a screened-in porch and pretty flowers hanging in baskets.

A high-pitched "There he is!" came from inside. The screen door slapped open and a wisp of a woman in frothy, frilly white skirts bounded down the stairs. "My God. You—"

A man in waxed mustache and the finest of linen sat up from a lounger. He stared at me, his thick eyebrows pulling together. "What the bloody hell, people? I was taking a nap."

Jack touched the brim of his hat and hopped down from the saddle. The dimple worked double time. "Mrs. Armstrong—"

"Marjorie, please."

"Marjorie, then."

She wove her hands together and held them near her heart. "Is that...they look like...It's uncanny."

Pip hung behind and kept her horse and herself turned from the strangers. Satan did what he wanted and pranced forward. Pip clenched her jaw and struggled to rein him in. But he kept clopping around us and snorting like he had a head cold.

Mrs. Armstrong's hands crawled from her chest to her throat. "Oh my." Her gaze locked on Pip. "I'm not afraid of you."

"I haven't done a thing to make you so." Pip smiled so her mouth pulled up at a terrible angle.

"Let me introduce a few guests," Jack said. "Mr. And Mrs. Horace and Marjorie Armstrong, I give you—"

"Loretta Maldive." I leaned over and held out my hand. "Mr. Roberts here caught up with my sister Caligula and I on a brentasauri hunt."

Marjorie's eyes blinked fast. "Who names their daughter—"

"Mother had a cruel sense of humor. It was related to the twelve-hour labor and—"

"No." Mr. Armstrong snapped a pipe to his mouth. "She looks nothing like her."

"Like who?" I asked.

"But it is her," Jack said. "This is Ruby—"

"What'd you just—"

"Damn impossible, pain in my derriere, son of a cow's teat horse." Pip jumped off Satan and dropped the reins to the ground. She stomped back down corral way, kicking the dirt as she went.

Another man had come out on the porch. He was sandy-haired, lanky, and tall. His shirtsleeves were rolled up his ropy arms, the collar of the shirt open on account of the heat. His Levi Straus jeans were cuffed up, showing off scratched and dented ranch boots. "Ruby Calhoun. Finally."

"Who are you?"

"Dooley Corcoran."

My breath caught tight in my throat.

He stuck his thumbs to his belt and took his time coming down the stairs. "You were right, Jack. That old sign of yours was a stroke of genius."

I shot a look at Jack. "You tricked us."

"Only a little—to get you going the right direction. You would have ended up in Lamar taking that road you were on." Jack's cheeks blossomed with shame. "I've got bills, you know."

I took a quick glance over my shoulder in Pip's direction. She was sulking near the first corral.

Satan sulked where she'd left him.

"What have you done with Martha Ruth?"

"She's all right," Corcoran drawled.

"She's not part and parcel of any of this."

"Is Martha Ruth another of them? Who's she playing?" Horace asked.

I gritted my teeth. "You betrayed our trust, Jack."

"I know it." He crushed the crown of his hat on his head and gave a longing look Pip's direction. "Don't I know it."

Dooley took a long step to grab for Bessie's bridle. "Let's all calm down and settle the horses in the barn."

"Are you a Pinkerton?"

"No, I'm—look, just calm—"

"No, sir, I will not do such a thing." I rolled the reins around my hand and worked to back Bessie up. "I would have liked those flapjacks, Mr. Roberts." Then I wheeled round and gave Bessie a good kick. We sped past Satan. "You need to come, too, you damn horse."

Which Satan did, giving a buck before lunging past us. I put my head down and drove forward.

Pip stared at me as I flew by.

"Pinkerton! Get on your horse!"

I prayed she'd have the wherewithal to see we were in mortal danger.

Bessie galloped now, no longer on a path but over rough ground and brush. Then Pip and Satan were there next to us, her yelling something at me and pointing behind us.

"What?"

"Turn around. The road's the other way."

"What?" A fleck of Bessie's sweat caught in my eye. I rubbed at it and searched for Pip.

She split off and headed straight back to the lodge, slowing only to lift the latch on the corral gates. The horses spilled out, heading every which way. Everyone raced around like chickens, trying to fence in the horses who had escaped the corrals. Jack ran in circles, flapping his arms to keep the herd from trampling the Armstrongs.

"Oh hell." I gave Bessie her head and said a prayer we'd get our way through. As we passed the barn, I caught sight of Dooley throwing a saddle on a chestnut and white pinto. He yelled something that sounded like "I'll hang you on Tuesday," but I didn't stop to ask if that was the actual verbiage. "Double hell."

There was nothing then to do but hang on tight and pray again.

"Excuse me." I pushed a gray mare's neck to get her to move the confused horses, then smacked a sorrel on the rump, which gave Bessie and me just enough space to shoot through.

All I heard then was Bessie's hooves on the ground. The dirt road was hard-packed and wide. It lurched up out of the valley and onto barren high plains. Pip was far ahead.

Dooley gained ground behind me. My stomach twisted for I knew he would catch up and that would be that. Bessie huffed and snorted, giving all her heart, but I could feel her flagging.

"Oh, horse, I do need you to give your all."

Pip drew ever further away.

The thump of hooves grew louder. This was it. I was going to jail.

I slowed Bessie and let out a big breath, ready to give up. At least one of us would still be free.

Bessie lowered her head and breathed hard, her ribs heaving in and out.

Dooley pulled up by my side. "What'd you go and do that for?"

I shook my head. Watched Pip in the distance. "You may have caught me, but you sure as hell will not catch her."

Except Satan stopped. Then Pip circled him to face us. She did not move but stood her ground, like she was daring this Corcoran Pinkerton fella to chase her.

"Seems like I will catch her." He dusted his reins to the pinto's shoulder and took off.

Satan lunged forward. Pip pulled her rifle from the scabbard and held it up.

It was like watching two locomotives on the same track, neither about to stop and each headed for disaster.

They closed in on each other. Right as Dooley passed, Pip swung the rifle out and caught the barrel flat on his chest. He toppled off, landing flat on his back.

Pip made large circle, catching up the pinto's reins and loping over to the man.

He sat up, resting his elbows on his knees.

Pip handed me the reins when Bessie and I approached. She had tied her own to the saddle horn, which gave her both hands to now hold the gun on Dooley. "Did John Ward send you?"

Dooley shook his head. "No, ma'am, I—"

"Don't talk."

"You did just ask him a question, Pip."

"You be quiet, too."

"Fine."

"Put your hands up." Pip nudged the gun forward.

Dooley peered up at her. "I'd appreciate it if you lowered that."

"I said to put your hands up."

"No, ma'am, I will not."

Her mouth went tight. "Tell me where our friend is."

"Put the gun away."

"Tell me where—"

"She is not in any harm." He touched his chest and grimaced. "You didn't have to swing that at me."

"I want an answer."

"Give me my horse and I'll take you right to her."

"You mean," I said, "you'll take us right to the same jail you got her in."

Pip sneered down at him. "How dumb do you think we are?"

"That's going to bruise," I added.

He smacked a hand to the ground. "I am not here to arrest you."

"Never mind all this," Pip said. "You're wasting my time."

"I'm from Silver Star—"

"Give me your gun."

"I don't have one." He stood up and pulled out the sides of his vest. "As you can see, I am unarmed. Besides, you're worth a thousand times more alive than dead. At least, Paco says so."

"Paco?"

"I don't see it." He stared out at the land and sighed. "I should have stayed a cowboy."

"You keep away from us. You understand?" Pip holstered the rifle. "Come on, Ruby."

"We're leaving now, Mr. Corcoran," I said. "With your horse. What's his name?"

"Napoleon."

"He's a fine looking horse. Fast, too. Thank you. Are we going the correct direction—"

"Ruby," Pip barked.

Corcoran fisted his hands to his hips. "You can't get away with all this."

"Well, sir," I said, "we're going to try."

At the outskirts of La Junta, we rested the horses in the shade of an abandoned barn. We searched around the building and rotten foundation of a farmhouse, desperate for some water for the horses.

"We can always give them some peach juice," I said.

"Roberts nicked my can opener." Pip brushed aside some bushes, then moved on to another clump near the corner of the old house.

"That was uncalled for." I toed away a brick, jumping back in case the underside was laden with spiders. "I was certain you had besotted him. I was certain of that, Pip."

"I don't like being played a fool."

"At least you just talked and didn't get entangled up in intimate emotions."

She made a noise in her throat and stepped onto the exposed floor of what must have been a kitchen.

"What does that mean?"

"What does what mean?"

"That noise. 'Mmmmmm.' That."

"It doesn't mean anything." She bent a young tree trunk and held it down with her boot. "Come stand on this."

I trod with care on the loose planks, then stood as requested. The hand pump sat behind it.

Pip pulled and pushed on the handle. "We did not get entangled."

"You talked."

"Yes."

"About what?"

"Things."

"Pip."

"Do you mind? I would like to get water before our horses collapse."

"It was the dimple, wasn't it?"

"Stay out of business that isn't your business. You can do that, can't you?" She clenched her jaw and put more back into her efforts.

The pump belched rocks and sand, then with a wheeze came the water. Pip took off her hat, filled it, and hopped off the floor to the ground. "It wasn't the dimple."

The tree snapped upright when I took my foot off. "What was it then?"

"It was nothing."

"Well, maybe it was something."

She scoffed and held the hat out to Bessie, who nickered in thanks, then gurgled and drank her fill. Pip turned around and started for the hand pump. "Who goes to a dude ranch?"

"People from the city, apparently. With a lot of money and no sense."

"Did you count the swaybacks? And there were at least three who'd been put away without a brushing. God knows how old the sweat stains were. Jack Roberts may have dimples and charm, but he doesn't treat his horses right."

"They seemed all right to me. But I am not an expert on horseflesh."

She dropped her hat under the pump. "Hold down that branch again."

We returned to give Satan a drink and waited while he hemmed and hawed over a possible monster jumping from the hat. His thirst did him in, though, and he slurped all the water up.

Napoleon nipped Pip's shoulder as we passed by to get his fill. She stopped and turned on her heel to stare at him. "Hello, Napoleon."

"That's a laugh of a name."

Pip handed me the hat and stepped up to the horse. Her eyes flitted across his body, then she ran a hand down his front legs and back.

The pinto watched her and did not mind her examination. When she was done, she rubbed his ears until he closed his eyes and pushed his face to her chest. "He'll do."

She took back the hat and strode to get more water.

"You think the next round could be for you and me?"

It had grown miserably hot, and thus we all crowded together in the shade of what was left of the barn. Pip chewed on a length of grass and stared down the road we came. There was nothing blocking us from spying Dooley Corcoran long before he'd reach us.

"He's either walking here," I said, "or walking back to the lodge to rope another ride."

"Then we might as well have a cigar. Jack didn't steal those."

"You'd think he would. He's got low enough morals."

"He said smoking was bad for your health."

"He's never had a Hidalgo."

Pip reached in the saddle pack and took up a cigar and match box. She scraped a match on the sole of her boot and lit the cigar.

The first drag made me dizzy as hell. I shook my head to clear it, then handed the smoke to her and leaned my head against the barn. "We need to come up with a plan, Pip."

She blew out a smoke ring and followed it with another. "Once it cools off, we'll see about traveling. We'll sneak into La Junta when it's dark."

"Then what?"

"I'll know when we get there."

"That is not a plan, Pip."

"It's the best I can give you right now. We sneak in, we have a glance around, we find the El Otero, and we get Martha Ruth."

"How are we going to sneak in with three horses? Are we going to hide them behind one of the two trees in this entire county?"

"We're on the outskirts of the outskirts right now. What do you suppose is on the inner outskirts?"

"I have no idea." I rolled a second drag of smoke around and released it.

"If it's like Kansas there'll be farms. There'll be more trees, and then houses."

"People."

"People."

"Telegraph lines."

"Tele*phone* lines."

"Pinkertons."

"Police." She waved away the cigar, took up her hat and fanned our faces. "Ice cream. I haven't had an ice cream since—"

A faint long whistle caught my breath. I jumped up and darted toward the sound. "Listen."

It came again. "That is the most beautiful sound I have ever heard in my life."

Pip smiled. "The train."

"Not just any train, Pip. That is the Atchison, Topeka and Santa Fe. Martha Ruth is right up the road."

CHAPTER 7

SHERIFF EGG—A DAMN DARK NIGHT

We skirted La Junta proper, looking for any place to stash the horses while we continued our quest for Martha Ruth. I suggested a livery, which Pip kiboshed as it would bring too much attention our way, particularly with a stolen horse. Or two. Or three.

Instead we stayed between the train tracks and willows that ran along the lazy Arkansas River. Pip held the horse's reins, and I hoped against hope the railman wouldn't come down the line swinging his light and catching us out.

By the trestle bridge, a couple shacks leaned against each other, propped up by a tall tree growing between them and vines hiding the whole of it from prying eyes. It made for good bunking, for the windows had been broken out and it was easy enough for us to crawl in and stash the saddles and gear. The bank below grew green grass, so we loosely tied the horses and left them to a meal and fresh water.

We snuck back up to the tracks, hoping to make out the lay of the La Junta land and find the El Otero Hotel that Garvin and Mabel mentioned however many days before.

"What day is it?" I asked.

"Why?"

"It bothers me that I do not know, that's why."

"It's the night before tomorrow."

"That is unhelpful."

Pip crouched by the side of a coal shed and peered down the railroad track. A large sandstone and clapboard building graced the opposite side of the rails, boasting slate roof awnings with a delight of wrought iron frames and brackets and inviting benches lining the exterior wall. Light poured on the station and tracks, coming from the first and second floor windows, the steepled third floor, and huge brass lamps hanging six or so feet out from the exterior walls.

Glorious, incandescent light.

Light that I wished to run to and bathe in, for it didn't come from the sun, moon, oil lantern, candle, or match, but the God-given luxury of electricity.

I hunched up next to Pip. "I bet there's running water. And steam heat."

Pip directed my attention to the signs swinging out from the awnings. "Depot. Fred Harvey House."

"I could not see those," I whispered. "My eyes are too dazzled by civilization."

"Would you prefer to go back with the horses?"

"I would not."

Being as there were no trains and the station master's office was shut, we crept between the coal shed and a building of unknown use and hustled over the tracks, taking refuge in the shadow of a small building that smelled of lye and soap.

Now we could clearly see the front of the depot-slash-hostelry and the two-story brick businesses that lined the street across from it. Billiards and dining halls and saloons. My mouth watered at the chance of a shot of rye.

A group of men and women strolled out from the central hotel entrance. The men wore their bowlers jaunty and their celluloid collars gleamed under the lamps. The women clustered together in white and pink frills, their hair styled in impossibly intricate designs topped with fancy straw hats. The men each took the hand of a woman and all hopped over the tracks, laughing and gabbing as they made the other walkway and floated into a corner saloon.

We dashed to the covered stoop of a secondhand furniture store. The sign for the business had been painted on the windows in a garish yellow. Even in the moonlight it would make a person squint.

I peered again at the block with the saloon. "There's three other liquor establishments. Maybe we could—"

"You think they'll let us in looking like this?"

"Well, no."

"That's right, no."

A string of young women strolled out of a door on the restaurant portion of the station, waving goodbyes to each other and going different directions.

"Those are the Harvey Girls, Pip. I'd bet my right thumb knuckle that's who they are."

"Is it a brothel?"

"Don't be dense, everyone knows the Harvey Girls are innocent doves."

"I don't."

"Why, they're the angels of the rail line, and if you get a chance to travel—"

Pip backhanded my arm and pointed to the third-floor balcony and the grand sign painted above the line of windows. "El Otero Hotel."

"We're here."

"What do you know?"

"Martha Ruth—"

"Is somewhere in there."

We had to get in, but our rumpled road clothes would get us kicked right on out. The bright-lit building stared at us and we stared back at it.

"You thinking what I'm thinking?" I asked.

"Probably not."

"Guess then."

"I'm not going to guess, Ruby."

"I bet you're thinking the same, so it wouldn't really be a guess, would it?"

Pip sat back on her haunches and stared at me. "We're going to bust the window out of a clothing store here in town to get some fancy duds, then when you find out Martha Ruth's room, we'll head up and get her. We smack Corcoran or whoever else is there with a spittoon. Then we go out the side door and back to the hideout."

"That is not what I was thinking."

"None of it?"

"No, Pip. Not one tiny iota."

"Huh."

"We are not going to utilize a spittoon in any way."

"Then what is your suggestion?"

"Tomorrow the trains will be arriving and departing, and it'll be a melee of passengers and porters and luggage. People checking into the hotel. People demanding lunch. Rooms getting changed up, fluffing of pillows and sheets and so forth. Every damn employee under the strain of too much to do." I peered back across at the hotel, wondering which room in the sprawling building contained our friend. "I can't walk in through the front door. But I can walk in the back."

"During the melee."

"Just so. Who has access to every room and is completely invisible to the guests?"

"The maids."

"Exactly. I am going to get a job tomorrow. I'll have the keys to the kingdom, then, won't I? So, in all the comings and goings, I'll find Martha Ruth and sneak her out through the crowds."

"That's not a very good plan."

"It's better than causing bodily harm with a spittoon."

"So you find her. Then what?"

"You have the horses ready. Then we go." I stepped away from the laundry. "Peaceful interventions are always for the best, Pip. You know that in your heart."

We sprinted back across the tracks and hooked around the building, following the clang of pots and pans. A door swung open at the end of the depot, letting out even more bangs.

Pip plastered herself against the wall, tucking herself in the station master's entry.

"Damn," Pip said.

I dropped behind the end of a bench and peeked over the wood-slat seat. A robust man in a tall chef's hat and white jacket had stepped out. He held a silver platter mounded with food stuffs. "Here, kitty bitty kitty." After a few kissy noises and no cat appearing, he set the platter to the ground and returned inside.

My stomach grumbled and moaned. "When did we last eat?"

A click and ratchet of metal that sounded very much like handcuffs stopped my tongue and caused me to twist around.

Pip had been apprehended.

I had nowhere to run. A man with a hat so tight his skin puckered out underneath it stood directly in front of me. His head was small, and his waist wide and made more so by the thick belt chock full of bullets and a heavy holster. He reminded me of an egg.

"I would not move." He pointed Pip's shiny Colt my direction, then stuffed it into the back of his gun belt. His no-lip mouth slid into a twisted kind of smile.

"The hell not." I lunged forward either to pull out his legs and send him toppling like Humpty Dumpty or bite him.

He was too fast. He scruffed me up by my collar and had the other cuff clamped tight on my wrist before I could decide my plan of attack.

"You move very fast for an egg," I said.

"Ruby..." Pip gave me the look I knew well.

"I have a right to know why you have detained us."

His little black eyes shimmered in the lamp light. "Because you are under arrest."

"For what?"

"I don't have to tell you for what as you know for what." He gave a sharp nod, grabbed the links between our handcuffs, and tugged us forward.

"We are employees of this fine hotel," I said.

Pip dug her boots in and yanked backwards, which spun him around, but just brought him face to face with her.

"You try that again, missy, I will put leg irons on you, do you understand me?"

I had never seen Pip go quite so pale. "Yes, sir."

"Glad we are understood."

I could not say what turns he took, nor what streets we crossed. It was all a mix of brick buildings and wood and adobe, and weeds stuck up between the cement slabs of road, and horse manure piled against curbs. Then there was a fancy bulk of a building and then there was a square stone one set all by itself in an empty lot and a brown mangy dog on the stoop wagging its tail.

Here it was, our defeat. I should not have been surprised at this outcome. The next steps in this ruinous situation flipped before my eyes. Jail. John Ward. Prison. I would not see my children ever again. The reality of this distressed me.

"You might as well shoot me here."

Sheriff Egg did not respond.

"If you shoot her, you might as well shoot me." Pip had her bullish face.

The dog trotted down the jail steps, wagging its stump of a tail and nosed the sheriff for a pet.

"Not now, dog."

The cur made a funny yip too high for its size, bolted back up the stairs and sat in front of the door.

"Damn dog." The sheriff unsnapped a ring of keys from his belt and, still holding on to us with one hand, opened the heavy wood door with the other.

"I am not going in your building." I stood my ground on the first step.

"You will go in the building."

"No. I refuse. I am refusing this untoward arrest. You have not even told us our charges. You have not even told us your name. For all I know you are pretending to be an officer of the law. For all I know that is a den of iniquity right inside that door. I have rights, you know. As a citizen."

He sighed and squinted down at Pip. "She always talk this much?"

"She has her moments."

"Don't agree with him."

"I'm not agreeing with him. I'm saying that sometimes you talk too much."

"Which is agreeing."

Mr. Egg tugged us inside the jail. It was a stark room with a desk that looked like it had seen better days and a few chairs thrown haphazardly around. On the far wall, there were three cells, each empty except for one that had a pile of hay in one corner and a bucket in the other.

He shoved us both into the cell and slammed the door shut. The sound echoed around the stone walls. I winced, feeling the reverberations through my bones.

"Well, now." He hooked his keys and put his thumbs in his belt. "Girls, girls, girls. You are in a load of trouble, aren't you?"

I shuffled around so Pip and I faced him, giving a small relief to my aching wrist which had been pulled to the moon and back on our trek to this godawful place.

"I'd like to know with what we are charged." Pip's breathing was shallow and fast.

"Humph." He turned, waddled across to his desk and before sitting, pulled Pip's Colt from his belt and unloaded it. "This is an excellent firearm." He held it up to the ceiling light, turning it around and over in admiration. "How much this set you back?"

He opened a file drawer, smacking the side when it stuck halfway, then dropped the six shooter and the bullets inside. The drawer took a few jiggles to get back shut, but once done, he plopped into his chair. The coils squealed as he leaned back and rocked, staring at us with his tiny weasel eyes. "Yep. A whole lot of trouble."

"You have not formally introduced yourself," I said.

My sister Rose would be beside herself at such a lack of social graces. "Ruby," she'd say, "introductions are the sign of good manners, and good manners are the sign of good breeding and good breeding is the sign of future success."

Since Rose and I had been born to an employee of a glue factory who took off with his younger cousin and a mother I called The Harpy on her sweet days and every other type of word on her bad days, I thought Rose's fine airs delusional. I tried to remind her of our putrid past, particularly as her airs and fantasies hardened into stone cold snobbery, but she ignored me. Maybe it was for the best, and she was right to make up a whole pretend childhood. After all, she was the one with the white picket fence and banker husband and my children, whom she raised as her own, and I was the one now under arrest and in chains.

The Egg sat up, his heavy boots thunking the floor, then set his elbows to the desk. "I am Sheriff Leo Tartt. That is with two T's. *Tartt*." He elongated those t's with a hiss of breath.

Pip lurched over to the bars, jerking me with her.

"You need to warn me before you do that again." My wrist was already all kinds of throb and turning purples and reds.

She gripped a bar with her free hand and glared at the sheriff. "You cannot hold us here without stating charges."

"That is correct. I cannot." He sniffed and grabbed up a folded newspaper from the mess of papers before him. "There are so many it will take until next Tuesday to complete the list."

The chair squeaked in agony as he stood and brought the paper over. "Attempted murder is one thing, but horse thieving? That's another thing altogether. Isn't it?"

He narrowed his eyes and snapped them between us. Then he slapped the newspaper against his thigh and chuckled. "As I said. World of trouble."

"You haven't said that before."

He frowned at me. "What?"

"That was the first time you—"

"Never contradict the law, Miss Calhoun." He slapped the paper to the bars. I flinched. Pip went red with frustration. "Now. Being as I was on my way home to the wife, I shall complete that journey. You both have a sweet nighty-night's rest." He sauntered across the room, picking up a chair and setting it just so in front of his desk. "If you feel a set of whiskers on your cheek or gnawing on your toes, it's not the dog. We've worked on the rat problem for years, but what can I say? They're fond of inmates. I think it's the sweat."

He opened the front door. The dog looked up at Sheriff Egg as if the man was King of the Universe. "Get away, dog." He pushed his leg to the cur's chest which only moved the beast an inch. "Damn..." He muttered, then patted the dog's head. "All right. Good boy."

The door thumped shut.

Then it reopened, and Egg popped his head around. "Forgot the light."

He twisted the switch then went out again, leaving us in pitch dark.

"Huh," Pip said.

"I hate prisons, Pip."

"I know it."

"There's rats."

"I know that, too."

"He's going to send a telegram to John Ward in the morning."

"Or he's going to call him."

My heart banged. "He has a telephone?"

"It was right by the door, didn't you see?"

"No, I did not. I think I need to sit." I stuck out my arm and waved around for the single hay bale bench but ended up poking Pip's stomach.

"Ow."

"Sorry."

"Let's face each other and sidestep. We're bound to run into it."

Once found, we sat back against the wall and crossed our legs so as not to tempt the rats to climb them. A rumble of thunder echoed, then rain thumped on the roof like three camels had been set loose from the fair.

"It's raining," I remarked. "And we are in the belly of the beast, Pip."

"There's no need for such black thoughts."

"I do not see much light."

"I don't see any at all," Pip said. "If you saw some, I'd be worried of your sanity."

The room thrummed as the rain intensified.

Pip shook the handcuffs, then set our hands to her knee. "If you think about it, there is a small light showing right now."

"What?"

"We'd be huddling in a leaky shack hoping the river doesn't rise and wash us out. Instead, here we are. It's warm in here. It's cozy. There's nothing until tomorrow morning to worry about."

"Who took Pip and who are you?"

She pulled in a breath and without any ado jumped right into a song.

After the ball is over
After the break of morn—

"There are fine acoustics in here, Ruby."

"We're going to sing?"

"Yes, we are."

So we did, and it comforted me because we did sing a pretty tune together.

After the dancers' leaving;
After the stars are gone;
Many a heart is aching
If you could read them all;
Many the hopes that have vanished
After the ball.

I thought we had finished and was ready to propose a rendition of *In the Vale of Chillhowee*, but Pip took in a long breath and started the song over.

After my life is over,
After the rope has swung—

"That is enough, Pip."

"Sorry."

We listened to the patter of rain.

"We need Martha Ruth," I said. "She'd sneak in here and we'd be out before The Egg got his round ass out of his chair."

"She was an excellent sneak."

"Is."

"She got caught, though, didn't she? If she's such a good sneak, she would have snuck." Pip uncrossed her leg. "Let's walk around a little. My foot's falling asleep."

We ended up stamping in place as the cell didn't allow both of us to have a walk around.

"Why is she not included in that wanted and dangerous nonsense?" Pip asked. "It's not like she's an angel. She stole that ham hock, remember that?"

"That was delicious."

"And these boots. She even knew the right size to steal from that mercantile in...Whereverwhatsit."

"I don't even remember that town."

"It had the red water tower with the cyclone painted on it?"

"That's right."

Pip froze. "Did you hear that?"

"What?"

"That scratching."

"Where's the bale?" My shin smacked into it, but I gave that no mind, being as an army of rats and vermin were bound our direction. "Get up. Get up."

We crawled on up and stood with our backs to the wall. There was definite scratching from a multitude of directions.

"Did you ever read about the little kids got their toes and fingers eaten—"

"I do not need to know that, Ruby."

"It was in New York City. Now that's a place with a rat problem."

"All their toes?"

"I think a nose was involved."

"That's over the top. You made that up."

"No, ma'am, I did not. Frank brought me the paper when we were still married and asked if we could put a few coins on it. He said there had to be more than one nose involved and he was going to bet on that and the chewing of ears."

"Did he win?"

"It was Frank, what do you think?"

A boom of thunder made me wince and sent the vermin scurrying back where they came from.

Pip sighed. "Thank the Lord."

"That's called a silver lining."

"You think it's our last?"

"My grandmother Ottoline says when the bad luck boulder starts rolling, it doesn't stop. Just takes out everything in its way. Crushes. Splats. Flattens. And ours started its tumble quite a while ago."

"That doesn't make me feel better," Pip said.

"Maybe we should go back to singing."

"Maybe we should."

CHAPTER 8

In the morning, The Egg uncorked his Stetson, placed it on a hat stand, and then drew up a window blind. "Good sleep, ladies?"

I blinked from the sudden bursts of light as he lifted all four blinds from the chicken-wired windows. "Could you please lower those?"

"It's a beautiful morning. We shall let the sunshine in."

"I need to pee," Pip said.

"There's a bucket in the corner." He had a too-pleased-with-himself grin on his face.

"My hand is numb, Sheriff Tartt." I lifted it and let it drop limply. Pip did the same. "If we get gangrene and our limbs fall off, that is on you."

He wobbled over. "Let me see."

We put our hands to the bars. He pinched the top of my hand.

"What the hell, that hurt."

Pip was fast; she got his thumb pulled back and used her free hand to twist his tie up. His face smushed against the iron, with one lip curled over and showing off his unnaturally small teeth.

"You're going to regret this."

"I said I had to pee."

"I thaid thereth a bucket." He whimpered as she pushed the thumb further.

"Please don't break his thumb, Pip."

"Get his keys."

But he used his other hand to grapple around and get them loose. He chortled and tossed them behind him.

"You let us out of here." Pip fumed and spit as she talked.

"No." Sheriff Egg fumed and spit back.

"Can I please have my arm back?" My hand flapped back and forth and smacked him in the forehead. "That was not on purpose."

"You two..." His face scrunched as Pip pushed his thumb further. "...are going to rot...in..." He started to mewl.

The telephone rang.

Tartt's eyes shifted, a ray of hope showing. "I need to get that."

"No."

"What if it's John Ward?" I asked. "Pip?"

"That's impossible."

"It could be Sheriff Ward," Tartt said.

"It could be a prank." I stared at the phone. It jangled again.

"Someone's going to come looking for me if I don't answer."

"I don't care." Pip frowned.

"What sort of call could it be?"

"Could be an accident or fire," he said. "Or a baby being born."

"You help with the babies?" I asked.

"I do. When the situation is dire."

"That could be a grievous call, then. Let go of his thumb, Pip. There could be a woman and child in mortal danger."

"*We* are in mortal danger, Ruby."

"Pip, please. Stop flapping my hand around and let go so he can take care of it."

"It'll look very good on your record, ladies, if you do."

The ring came again.

Pip let him go.

He shook out his thumb then held it to his chest as he dashed across to grab up the earpiece. He put his lips to the mouthpiece. "Sheriff Tartt. Uh-huh. No, Thelma, I did not forget my lunch. I told you before, I eat with the fire boys on Wednesdays, I do not understand how...uh-huh. Yes. I could skip it this time. No, I do not overindulge in—" He looked back at us. *The wife*, he mouthed. Then he realized who he was sharing this information with. "Now, listen here, Thelma, I am a busy man and have prisoners to deal with, do you understand me, woman? No? Well, I...never you mind, I'll be home for lunch."

He slammed the receiver into its cradle. It swung around so he put a hand on it to stop it, then pulled it out again. "I'm going to call John Ward."

I held my breath, watching in dread as he turned the crank.

His voice went sweet as burnt honey. "Why, hello, Miss Fletcher, could you connect me with a Kansas operator who can put me through to a Sheriff John Ward?"

He drummed his fingers against the wall as he waited. "Morris County. You get that pretty operator over in that county to...well, of course, she's pretty. She's a phone operator like you so she must...all right. You call me back, darling, when it's all connected. He's a famous lawman, it shouldn't be too difficult. A lickety and a split, that's right."

This time the earpiece was set down with gentleness. "Easy as can be, isn't it?" His grin came back as he sauntered a safe distance over. "You two are vixens of the most dangerous degree."

I sank back on the bale, pulling Pip down with me. There was nothing to do now but wait for Miss Fletcher to call back. And every county telephone operator between Morris County and this one, every party line subscriber listening in because they had nothing better to do, would know our grand escape had come to an end.

The pretty morning light took on a grim tone.

"What'll happen now?"

The Egg, who leaned on the wall by the phone, looked at me and tsked. "You will be transported back to the locality of your crimes."

"By him?"

"Maybe me."

"Thelma would let you leave more than half a day?" Pip asked.

He ignored her comment. "Could be he'll send out a Colorado marshal. Could be he'll come himself."

The grim light dimmed to a shade of bleak.

"I'm never going to see my children, Pip." I said it quiet enough, only for her to hear. "I'm sorry we didn't get to your Olive. I would have liked to meet her."

Her lips went taut and she gave a small shake of her head. "She wouldn't remember me."

"Course she would."

"She was a little baby, Ruby. She's probably a full-fledged nun by now."

"A six-year-old nun? They make habits that tiny?"

"They're very handy, those nuns."

"Still and all." I blew out a breath. "I'd put my arm around you in comfort, but it's physically impossible."

"I appreciate the thought."

"Hey, Mr. E—"

He lifted an eyebrow.

"Sorry. Mr. Sheriff, sir. I would like to write my children. Should you have pencil and paper. And a heart."

"You have children?"

"I do, sir. Two. Emma and John. Emma is very good on the piano and John is, well, John is John." I winced at my lack of knowledge as to my son's interests, then shoved that under a rock of anger at my sister for creating such a vacuum to begin with.

"Two kids." He shook his head. "You're on the road trying to kill people and you've got two kids."

"When you say it that way…"

"How about I write the letter for you?" he asked. 'Dear children. I am a demon.'"

"My sister has shared a similar sentiment."

"Well, introduce me to your sister, as I will give her a peck on the cheek and say she is damn right."

"Give her the damn pencil and paper," Pip said. "See how red she is. She's going to start crying and having hysterics and I am cuffed to her."

"You've got a kid, too, Pip. You need to write a letter."

"If you recall, she's a nun married to Jesus now and has forsworn the worldly life, which includes the mother who abandoned her to begin with."

"Then why are we trying to go get her?" Now I was mad. "We could have cut straight down through Texas instead of fiddling around and trying to get to New Mexico."

"Getting my daughter wasn't my idea. If you recall. I would have been fine cutting through Texas."

"That's a very large state to cut through." The sheriff pulled a chair over to the phone and sat down, crossing his arms over his belly. "Coming through New Mexico is a better idea. But you're not going to make it that far, so it's not one way or the other that matters."

"This is not your conversation." Pip glared at him.

"Every conversation in here is my conversation."

There was no answering that because it was true.

"I'd still like a piece of paper and a pencil," I said. I thought I should also write Olaf about the cigar store and officially turn it over to him, and make sure he'd been taking care of the wooden Indian out front. "Two pieces of paper, please."

"I'm not writing Olive," Pip muttered.

"I'm writing Olaf."

"Okay. Send him thanks for my hat. It's still my favorite."

"You never take that thing off."

"I'm not taking it off in here. There's probably rat droppings everywhere and those can stain."

"The phone's not ringing, Mr. Sheriff, sir, so can you please bring me the—"

The front door swung open. The sheriff jumped up and puffed himself up to look tough and brave. I did not deny this was a good idea, being as jails and unsavory types tended to mix.

A man stepped inside and peered around the room. He had a suave, Latin look, with deep brown eyes and a pencil mustache. His clothing was all black and very clean, including a black ranchero hat he did not remove, and shiny boots with a high enough heel to give him a little extra lift. He shifted his jacket to show the five pointed silver star on his belt.

"I've come for the prisoners."

The sheriff stuffed his thumbs in his belt. "You are?"

"You know who I am."

"No, sir, I do not know—"

"John Culpepper Ward. Now you know." The man thrust a packet of papers at the sheriff and sauntered past him and straight up to us. "I am the scourge of the criminals who mar the plains and mountains."

"There's mountains in Kansas?" Egg asked.

"Do not interrupt me, sir." He turned on one of his fancy heels and continued his tour of the jail's interior.

I leaned close to Pip. "I think he's wearing eyeliner," I whispered.

Which brought him swinging around to pin me with a definite kohl-lined stare. "Did you say something?"

"No, sir."

"Are you Sheriff Ward?" Pip's voice trembled, which did little to nothing for my confidence.

The man's smile widened. He tilted his head, then gave a bow. "At your service."

"I've never seen paperwork such as this." Sheriff Egg's face was half-buried in the sheafs.

"That's Kansas paperwork. We do not skimp on our words."

"It's all where-to and whatnots. Here in Colorado we say who we are and where we're taking them."

"I'm Sheriff John Ward and I'm taking these two ladies."

"Where?"

"Wherever I want."

"That is not an appropriate answer."

"Page thirty-five line twelve states I may do as I please. It says it in legalese but it says it."

Egg's tongue peeked out against his lip as he flipped through the paperwork. His nose wrinkled as he looked for the line that turned us over to God knows what.

Ward yanked the papers back. "I'll mail you a summary. For your simple Colorado mind. Now, open up the cell and let me get along with my duties."

Sheriff Tartt shouldered Ward aside and shoved the keys to the cell door.

"Uncuff them."

"You sure?"

"I have my own. But they are going to behave like the ladies they once were, are you not, ladies?"

"Yes, sir." We said it in unison.

"This is not standard procedure."

"Think of the commendation you'll receive. You, a sheriff of minor acclaim, will find yourself commended for your single-handed capture."

"I did do that, didn't I?"

"Your final act, which will push you into the history books, is to uncuff these malefactors."

Tartt nodded his head and hurried over to us, key in hand. He stopped and turned to Ward. "You may need my help with the transfer."

"I'll lean on your aid if needed."

"Just say the word. I am your man." Tartt unlocked the cuffs.

I rubbed my wrist. Pip shook out her hand. "My fingers have been asleep the last five minutes."

"Come along, ladies." Sheriff Ward gestured to the door. "I'll be following behind."

"What if we run?" Pip asked.

"I'm a superlative shot."

"Oh, hell," I mumbled.

"Hell, indeed, girls. Hell, indeed."

❧

I froze on the jailhouse steps. "You have got to be kidding me."

To my surprise, Jack Robert's bright yellow mud wagon idled right out front. Bessie and Napoleon pawed their mismatched hooves to the ground and swung their heads about dismay at being hooked up to the traces. Dooley Corcoran sat wide kneed on the driver's bench. He touched the brim of his bowler.

Ward prodded me in the back. "Keep moving."

I looked over my shoulder to see what Sheriff Egg thought of this all, but the jail door was shut tight. "What in the hell is going on?"

Ward wrapped his arms around both our waists and hurried us into the wagon. We all squatted as the cotton roof was low.

Ward reached for a rolled canvas siding, undid the leathers, let it drop, then reached across for another. "Pardon me."

The wagon lurched forward. I grabbed a support pole and Pip grabbed onto me.

He opened the lid of a basket, lifting out a pile of skirts and shirts and petticoats which he tossed toward us. "One set is small and one's a little larger. You can work it out. I swear on my honor, I will not peek."

He swept the hat off his head and held it over his face.

"I'm not wearing the coral." Pip made a face and shoved the dress at me.

"It's a good color on you."

"Not with this sunburn. It's going to make my scar stand out."

Ward riffled in the basket again and held out a veil. "You'll want this."

Pip took it. "I just wear it plain?"

"Hats are on the way."

We dressed. The wagon made a couple of turns, and I wished I could ask where we were headed. But I was afraid he'd say, 'You're headed to your certain death or, at the minimum, lifelong entombment in a prison cell.' I think Pip was worried the same way, so we changed as he'd asked.

The other skirt and shirtwaist were a light blue check that turned out to fit me fine. The coral was a bit much for Pip's complexion, but I settled the veil on her head and it draped prettily enough.

Two short whistles came from outside.

The wagon halted. A flap lifted and two hat boxes were tossed in. This was followed by the entry of a woman in a very intricate hat of feathers and birds and doodads. She took Ward's hand as she lit in, then lifted her own veil.

"You two smell like one hundred cows with a stomach ailment."

"Martha Ruth?" My throat went dry and tingly. I pointed at her then pointed at Pip.

Pip lunged over and wrapped Martha Ruth up in a hug hard enough to make the girl squeak.

"Make that one hundred and one."

Pip released her. "Has he hurt you?"

"He has been nothing but a gentleman."

"Nothing but," Ward said.

"Well, come on, put on these hats. Be careful, as the hat pins are extra long."

Pip held her Rough and Ready hat.

Martha Ruth sighed and put out her hand. "I'll take good care of it."

It was swapped for a fluffy thing of down and silk roses.

"I am not wearing this." Pip set her jaw firm.

"I'd suggest you do," Ward said. "For your own safety."

"You're very famous," Martha Ruth said.

"Infamous," Ward added. "Beautifully, perfectly, gloriously, notoriously infamous."

"One synonym would have done the trick," I muttered.

"One synonym isn't enough."

Then the wagon moved on with a jolt. Pip landed on a bench and I landed on my ass on the floor. Ward held one of the posts and stared at us with a cat-who'd-eaten-two-canaries-and-a-mole grin. The sway of the wagon hadn't affected Martha Ruth in the least. She sidled in next to Pip, her face clear of any worry that we had all been captured and she had abetted the law rather of us in the doing of it. She hummed and jangled a silver charm bracelet on her lace and silk clad wrist.

"If we are captured fugitives," I asked, "why are we all dressed in finery and you are wearing eye makeup, Mr. Ward?"

Ward unclipped the star from his belt and chucked it to an empty hat box. "That was theatrical subterfuge, Miss Calhoun. I am not John Ward. Allow me to introduce myself." He tried to straighten up but smacked his head on a beam so instead bent his neck at an uncomfortable angle. "I am Paco Jones, producer and director of Silver Star Motion Pictures. And I, ladies, am going to make you famous."

CHAPTER 9

We took a few more turns, then Paco and Martha Ruth rumbled and tumbled us out of the mud wagon and up the stairs of the El Otero Hotel, with many synonyms of doom proffered as to what might happen should we be recognized by the unwashed masses. Paco Jones-alias-John Ward peeled off toward the clerk at the front desk who presided over keys and such things.

"Come on, stinkies." Martha Ruth flounced up the stairs in front of us, blowing kisses and murmuring sweet nothings to everyone and no one in particular.

Pip hopped two steps to lean over Martha Ruth's shoulder. "You mind telling us what's going on?"

"You look terrible in coral." Martha Ruth scrunched her nose. "Maybe the pink veil was too much."

An elderly couple with matching burled wood canes stopped Martha Ruth on a second floor landing full to the brim with ferns.

"Thank you for the beautiful bouquet," the woman said in a trembly voice.

Martha Ruth put a palm to her chest and gave a pretty dip of her shoulder. "You are on your honeymoon and honeymoons deserve flowers."

"You are a bright light, my dear Miss Honeywell." The newly betrothed husband's cheeks pinked up.

"Adelaide." Martha Ruth batted her eyes. "Please call me by my first name. I do not stand on any ceremony."

The couple turned matching milky blue eyes to Pip and me, their expressions clear they were awaiting a formal introduction.

Martha Ruth took to her tiptoes to kiss the mister's cheek, then stooped to kiss the missus, and sashayed her way up the next flight of stairs. "Come along, dear hearts."

"Nice to not meet you," Pip said with a little bow. Then she picked up her skirts and bounded up.

"Happy nuptials," I added and went up, too.

On the third floor, Martha Ruth took a key from a dainty bead purse and with that we found ourselves facing a long carpeted hall with crystal and brass chandeliers and three doors to each side.

Martha Ruth ushered us in before locking up tight. She dropped the key to her beaded purse.

"This isn't a kidnapping ring, is it?" I stared at the lock on the door. "I've been recently released from such an experience. I do not think I'm emotionally stable enough to repeat it so soon."

"What's with this Adelaide name?" Pip asked.

"Mr. Jones told me it had a better ring than Martha Ruth Platt. It's more cosmopolitan."

"Why would you need that?"

"For the motion pictures. He says I have the face for film." She pushed up her chin with her index finger and turned her head to show one profile and then the other. "Ethereal, he says."

Pip pulled the pin from the crown of her hat and yanked it and the veil off. "You have a lot to explain."

A light kick came at the door. "Can you open this?"

"I'm sorry, Dooley." Martha Ruth went through the unlocking ritual again.

"Jesus, Mary, and Joseph." He held two valises, with Pip's hat balanced on top. "You three look like a tragic flower arrangement."

"I'm in checks," I said. "I've never seen checks in nature."

Pip swiped up her hat as he trundled past.

"One of you take Room Three E and the other Three F." He pointed to each then brushed his thumb along his chin and peered at Pip. "What'd you think of Napoleon?"

"He's a damn fine horse."

"You have a fine seat."

Martha Ruth bounced on her toes. "She was a trick rider. You should see the conjugations she makes."

"That right?"

"The Highland Twist, the Scissor and Hammer, the…oh what's the one where you stand on your head and—we should put those in one of the films, I bet that would bring in a crowd."

"What films?" Pip asked.

Martha Ruth batted her eyes. "The ones you'll star in. And you, too."

Dooley Corcoran had his eye on Pip. "You don't try those tricks on that hothead gelding of yours, do you?"

"Satan?" I laughed. "That would be courting suicide with the nuptials set."

"You call my horse Satan?" Pip asked me.

"You have any idea how often he's bit my—I thought that was his name."

"It's Horse."

"That's…" I shook my head. "Just Horse?"

"Horse works." Dooley ambled down the hall, stopped at a far door and considered Pip. "You look better in trousers."

He went in his room, and that was that.

"Don't mind Dooley," Martha Ruth said. "Well, come on. I got loads to tell you soon as you've scrubbed up. I can't wait to hear all about you trying to find me. And Theodore, of course. How's his hoof? I've been dreadful worried about that. Uncle LeRoy had a mule with a sore foot. You should have seen what came out of the abscess he found when he cut it open. Is he with you?"

Pip put on one of her dancehall faces, all cheer and brightness. "How's Theodore, Ruby?"

"Oh, he's a dream. Cleverest mule I have ever encountered in my life. Why, he is perfectly fine and dandy. But we can talk about him later."

"How about that bath?" Pip asked.

"You will not believe your rooms. You turn a tap and water comes out so hot, it's like the Devil's belly on a scorching day."

❧

DO NOT DENIGRATE THE MIRACLE OF SOAP. NOR HOT WATER THAT comes from a pretty chrome tap. Or a toilet with a pull chain. Towels. Tooth paste instead of powder. A lion claw tub with a brand new scrub brush hanging within reach.

I peeled off my clothes and dipped my toe into the bath water but it stung too much to leave it there. I rested my foot on the tub's edge and took in the damage. Blisters on blisters. I couldn't make out my little toe and reached to check if it was still there or had fallen off somewhere around the Kansas-Colorado border.

Then, because I could not resist any longer, I took a breath and stepped right in. A sponge and soap sat on a porcelain shelf above the tub. I made baby swipes and dabs at my feet, and choked up at the black grit that stained the water when I squeezed the sponge. Little by little, the grime gave way to skin. I rubbed and scrubbed, then drained the tub and refilled it. The water was so warm it felt like the finest silk and velvet. I could just stay here ogling the pristine white tiles and refreshing the heated water until the Lord chose to take me to Heaven.

I rested my head against the towel I had folded over the tub's lip, watching the clouds outside and listening to the rumble and whistle of the ATSF coming into the depot. It was like music to me.

All my pent-up tensions dissipated with a long sigh. I had only once had such luxury, and that was years before on a Mississippi riverboat. Frank was flush with cash and when he had such riches, he freely shared them around. Our suite ran from port to starboard and had its own promenade. The rooms were draped in satins and velvets, the carpets so thick and inviting we spent much time upon them, and the bed floated like a private island, with curtains you could tug all around for the utmost of privacy.

It wasn't until later that I realized the luxurious tapestries were padding to keep the noise in and the curious out. Frank didn't even tell me to be quiet when he hit me. He just did it. He'd made bad string of bets and blamed his luck on me. He dropped me at a wharf in Galena, Illinois, with a nickel to telegraph my sister to come get me.

I sat up in the tub, wrapped my arms to my knees and squeezed my eyes tight. There was no need for that memory at all. This was not the river, Frank was long gone, and I'd be damned if I'd let that old life soil a moment as grand as this.

"You ruin everything, Frank."

I had saved a pitcher of water for my hair and leaned out of the tub to pour it. Before I could lift the handle, I heard the bathroom door open.

"We need to discuss this situation." Pip closed the door with a soft snick. She wore a too short pair of cotton knickers and a man's tank top.

"Hello, Pip. Glad you enjoyed your luxurious bath and have chosen to come interrupt mine."

"What's with this Silver Star business and this Paco Jones?"

"He wants to make us famous."

"I don't want to be famous," she said.

"You're not doing a particularly good job of that."

"Says the pot."

"At least he's not John Ward. Can you imagine where we'd be if that really were him? Would you mind washing my hair?"

She grabbed the pitcher and poured the water.

"I'm offended at your lack of blisters," I said.

She rubbed the soap into a lather and massaged my scalp. "I have good boots. You should always have a good pair of boots. Haven't I said that in the past?"

"Mmm." It was all I could come up with.

"You got a dead newt and a tree growing in this nest."

"I thought I pruned that back." I wiped my nose and spat out a dribble of water. "To my way of thinking, if someone declares they can make you famous, they're spouting a load of flimflam and nonsense. It's akin to saying, 'I can make you rich but I need ahold of your life savings to do so.' Snake oil comes in many forms."

"Martha Ruth—pardon me, *Adelaide*—has bought a wagon of it." Pip twisted my hair into a quick braid. "You know what's in my room?"

"I have not been in there, so, no."

"Shoes." She handed me a towel and sat on a stool while I dried off. "Not just any shoes. Button-up shoes. With heels. Three pair in cream, black, and brown."

"That is not useful footwear."

"Go check your own wardrobe."

I traipsed into the elegant room and opened the walnut chifforobe that certainly did not come from a Sears Roebuck catalog. Sure enough, three sets of shoes. Hanging pretty as a picture above them, a dress with dainty yellow daisies embroidered all around and a straw hat. Another hanger held a lace shawl.

"What in the..."

Pip opened the top drawer. "Intimates."

Then she hauled open the next. "Stockings."

And the bottom drawer. "That's empty in my room, too. I just wanted to check."

She put her hands on her hips. "I think we are being seduced with fineries."

"They're very nice togs."

She bit her lower lip and let it go. "But we don't know their price."

A knock came at the door. "Hi-dee-ho." Martha Ruth knocked again. "You presentable?"

I could have been stark raving naked; Martha Ruth waltzed in anyway.

"Oh, excellent, you're both here." She flounced about the room so her skirts swept around at the hems. "I hope you like the pattern on that skirt. I spent hours figuring out what would look best on you. Pip, I know you are not a flowery sort of woman, though you could wear peonies and it would turn heads. I think the plaid I picked will be just right."

"The plaid is fine."

"I'm glad." Martha Ruth looked at the floor, then above Pip's head at some ghost of something in the corner. Her cheeks flushed. "You came to find me."

"We did." I buttoned one of the new petticoats and twisted it in place before dropping the daisy dress over my head. The hem came to my ankles. "This is the first time I've ever had something too short."

"That's all right, the maid will lengthen it. She's ever so helpful."

"There's a maid?" Pip asked.

"Only for this wing. Just for us. Well, Paco and Dooley, too. And I think the cream shoes would be awfully smart with that plaid."

"How do you know they'll fit?" she asked.

Martha Ruth's blush deepened. Her idolization of her idol knew no bounds. "I know."

"Well, I'll wear them because my boots need a good airing. And I want my clothes back, smelly or not."

"You used to be a doodad wearer, Pip."

"That was another life, Ruby."

Martha Ruth made a show of pulling a silver watch from her skirt pocket, letting the delicate chain swing. "Paco's waiting for us in his suite. You might want to get dressed, Pip."

"I don't trust this Paco."

"Well, you should. He's going to make us more famous than the dime novels."

Pip gave her a sharp look. "What dime novels?"

"Ooh, you'll love them. I'm already on Volume Five and—"

"Has he asked you to do something untoward?" I could not think why else she'd be dressed to the nines, being as she owned three ounces of nothing a week ago.

"No, ma'am, he has been nothing but a perfect gentleman. A rich perfect gentleman, yes. I say to him, 'Paco, I would like bonbons at midnight.' And they are delivered. He says I am worth every penny and more so and more so. He has even promised me an apartment, and my own maid and—"

"Oh, he's flimflam, all right. He's going to ask for something eventually and you're going to have to give it." Pip paced the room. "We need to find that spittoon I talked about."

"I'm not conking anybody. *I* already told you that."

Pip grabbed Martha Ruth by her elbows. "You are being had. I don't know what he wants with us, except maybe enough reward money to continue his hustle. I don't care to be here long enough to know what that is. So, as soon as I dress…in the plaid…we are leaving."

"Don't talk about Paco like that. It's hurtful." Martha Ruth pouted. "You need to apologize to him for such thoughts and thank me for keeping your sorry asses alive."

"Really?"

"Yes, ma'am, really." Martha Ruth flattened her hand with her palm up. "Number One, you are no longer imprisoned. The rat problem of that abode is well known." She curled her pinky to her palm and moved on to her ring finger. "Number Two, I took care of your horses, because you are terrible at hiding and I saw Satan from my bedroom window, and I said, 'Why that is my friend's horse and she must be in danger.'" Number Three came with the fold of her middle finger. "Three. I made sure Dooley did not kill you for stealing his Napoleon." She tapped the base of her index finger. "Four *A* would be getting up early to take coffee and two donuts in the dining hall and overhearing that Sheriff Blowhard boast that he caught two girly bandits the night before."

"Is Four B the tip of your finger?" I asked.

Her eyes flashed. "It is related, yes. Because instead of prison, you're going to be in a motion picture. After that picture, Paco is sending us first class to Tijuana, Mexico. Sleeper cars and all. Now get your ass dressed, come listen to what he has to say, and have some respect for your redeemer."

"Is there going to be food?" I asked.

"He's ordered roast beef sandwiches and lemon meringue pie from the Harvey House."

"Fine." Pip stalked back through an interior door to her adjoining room, shutting it with a bang.

Maybe it was all bunco and rook. But there were sandwiches, so I'd keep an open mind.

CHAPTER 10

BONBONS AND ROAST BEEF SANDWICHES—WE MAKE A DEAL—PIP
IS AWESTRUCK

"You star in my films. I pay you a fee that includes your lodging, food and other essentials. Then I take you safely to the Mexico border. Freedom, ladies. Isn't that what you long for?"

Paco Jones's room was three times bigger than Pip's and mine combined, with paned glass windows running the entire back wall. Four overstuffed chairs surrounded an overlarge table on which was the promised food stuffs. I stayed perched on the edge of my chair, for the bath and previous events at Sheriff Egg's had made me sleepy. I needed to keep my wits. Pip lounged in the chair next to me, and Martha Ruth 'Adelaide Honeywell' took another.

Paco peered at us, arms crossed over his chest. He rocked on his heels and brushed the corner of his mustache. He threw a smile and nod Martha Ruth's way, then snapped his gaze to Pip, who was about to take a bite of her sandwich. "How's the roast beef?"

"It's fine. Thank you." I could see her mind whirling at the offer presented.

"I like it with triple horseradish. Gets the heart racing." He watched her. She watched him.

"Are you going to eat it?"

Pip took a bite from the corner and chewed. Then she took a bigger hunk because they were very tasty sandwiches and we hadn't eaten in twenty-four hours or so. She swallowed the last bite down and set her plate back on the marble table by her chair. "So, you make money because you've got the real deal bandits in your films."

"Precisely."

"And how much money do we get?"

"Fifty a week. Each."

"Fifty..." I couldn't even get the rest of the Midas-sized amount out of my mouth.

Pip coughed.

"I don't want you choking. You can't choke now, I need you." He zigzagged around various chairs and potted ferns, stopping at a glass-fronted cabinet. "Sherry? Whiskey? Lemonade?"

"Oh." My ears perked up. "I'll take—"

"We'll both have lemonade." Pip cleared her throat. She narrowed her eyes at me.

"Adelaide, my star, what shall I get you?"

Martha Ruth did a funny twisty motion. "You know what I like best."

"And the best you shall have."

Bottles clinked and liquid gurgled and then Paco returned with a tray of two tall glasses of lemonade and a mountain of chocolate confections littered with powdered sugar. He set the tray down on the oval table between the chairs then jerked forward to pick up a full glass and swing it to Pip.

"For you."

She held it far out as it sloshed about.

He then handed me the disappointingly alcohol-free drink. "Thank you."

"Rum bonbons. For my Adelaide."

She clapped and made the sort of squeaky noise children do when they find candy in their stocking and not the expected pair of wool socks.

"Straight from a confectionary in Denver." He grabbed the swirled handle of a chair, lowered himself down and crossed one leg over the other. "Nothing is drugged."

I put down the glass I'd taken up.

"I'll prove it." He popped a bonbon in his mouth, chewed twice and swallowed. "Now, let's get down to business."

"You didn't drink the lemonade," Pip said.

He jumped up, zigged and zagged again though the forest, and darted back with the pitcher. "Proving my word again." He tipped the pitcher to his lips, took a large gulp, winced, and set it down. "Remind the staff to add more sugar, Adelaide."

Martha Ruth made a mewing noise around the chocolate she'd bitten into.

"Ladies. I am beyond flattered to have you sitting in this very room with me. It's a dream, really. No, more than that. You have been a quest, like the Holy Grail, and I am humbled to be in your presence."

"How did you find us?" Pip asked.

"How could I not? You two are in every newspaper between Kansas City and the Utah border. All those petty crimes you've been doing don't go unnoticed. Every little town has its own little paper. When you hit a town with a population of one hundred or less, you even make the front page. It's like the President coming through."

This made me pause. "So anyone could track us?"

"Only if they had enough money and wherewithal to have newspapers delivered daily. I have both."

"I get fifty and Ruby gets fifty?"

"That is correct, Miss Quinn."

"What about Martha Ruth?"

"The same. I will be playing the damsel in distress." Martha Ruth bounced on the edge of her chair. "Like the dime novels."

"Dime novels?"

"I'm called Lily Day in them, which is a pretty name, don't you think?"

"Lily Day?" Pip had a bemused expression. "Not Adelaide?"

"Oh, no. Adelaide is my screen persona. Paco says I will be luminous on camera and have the possibility of being lead actress in his production troupe. You're going to let me play Juliet in *Macbeth*, aren't you?"

"You know I am."

"Wait one minute," I said. "We chased a killer who was trying to kill us and ended up in a near gun fight," I said. "But you're not going to film that?"

Paco crossed his arms. "Well..."

"You might wish to film that as it will be evidence we did nothing wrong and we should be cleared of all these charges floating around."

"The kids'll like the bear fight better." Martha Ruth gave us a pitying shrug. "We really aren't that interesting on our own. Ruby, you can't aim worth beans. I think it will let down an audience to be expecting a terrible-but-justice-fulfilled vengeance and instead witness a small farmhouse window being shot out."

"The bear is more dramatic," Paco said. "Adelaide, go get the books."

"They have marvelous plots. Mr. O.H. Flint knows how to tell a good story." She darted into an adjoining room, which was either her bedroom or Paco's or both. Then she came back in. "I think Dooley has them."

"Why doesn't he have his own?"

"He loaned them to that fella he's getting horses from."

"Get them from Dooley, then."

"It's his nap time."

"Wake him up."

"All right." She toddled to the door to the hall. "He's very grumpy when—"

"Adelaide." Paco gave her a tight smile.

"Okay, but don't say I didn't warn you."

Outside, the train whistle blasted and the brakes screeched. Paco peered out at the depot below. He dug out his pocket watch from his vest and glanced at it.

"Forty-three minutes." He stuck the watch back. "It's a marvel. The train arrives, the passengers flow out. The Harvey Girls await them with open arms and a solid square lunch. And like that, an hour and twelve minutes later—and I have yet to see that waver—the passengers return to their train and away goes the Atchison, Topeka and Santa Fe."

"Are you an admirer of trains, Mr. Jones?"

"There's nothing finer than a Pullman car, Miss Calhoun, and a view of our country going by the window."

My heart softened. "I have a fondness for timetables, myself."

"Timetables." Paco perked up. "I do find them relaxing on tension-filled days. In fact..." He reached in the inner pocket of his jacket and pulled out the ATSF timetable. "You may have it."

"I could get one downstairs, you don't—"

"It would be my pleasure to gift this one to you."

"That is one of the kindest—"

Pip kicked my foot.

"It's a timetable, Pip." I said it singsong and shot Paco a smile of gratitude. "For which I am ever thankful."

Martha Ruth came back in, clutching a set of thin paperbacks to her chest. "Dooley says he's going to burn all your celluloid if he gets woken up again." She spread the books on the table.

The reading material, six volumes in all, was gaudy yellow and dog-eared, each hung together by two threads and a glob of glue. Every single one was printed with a lurid image of two half-dressed wild women on even wilder horses, guns held high and skirts higher than that.

Desperado Damsels emblazoned the cover.

Down near the bottom it read: *Follow the adventures of stone-hearted Pip Quinn and wily Ruby Calhoun and the Law that did them WRONG.*

Pip took a book and flipped through the pages. "Huh. I do kill a bear."

"With a slotted spoon and your bare hands," Martha Ruth said.

"After taking off with the Bank of Harneyville's loot," Paco added.

"Well, I never..." Pip wore a smug smile, as if her fictional self pleased her greatly.

"Turn the page. See that bear coat?" Paco touched the paper and the illustration of Pip with her scar and scowl, sporting a bearskin coat with two paws hanging from the belt.

"Give me that." I yanked the book away and thumbed through. "How come all I'm doing is drinking a soda at the fountain three pages back?"

"You just shot Garth Hamner, Texas Ranger," Martha Ruth said. "That was in Volume Four."

"Why would I do that?"

"To save me. Lily Day." She flipped to the first page.

Lily was a dead ringer for Martha Ruth, if you cleaned her up, gave her a fancy dress, and the profile of a Gibson Girl. In other words, Lily Day didn't look at all like Martha Ruth with her crooked smile and all the freckles she'd earned during our weeks on the run.

"So our real selves will be playing our make-believe selves?" I asked.

Paco spread his arms. "Think of the poster. *A Silver Star exclusive: Daring Outlaws Pip Quinn and Ruby Calhoun AS THEMSELVES.*"

"All we've got to do is act?" I asked.

"It's easy as pie," Paco said. "When I say 'be happy,' smile. When I say 'look fierce,' you look fierce. We'll cut it all together with dialogue cards. You don't even have to learn lines. *Banana orange strawberry* looks the same on film as *To be or not to be.*"

"We can do that, Pip."

"We know how to sing and dance, Ruby."

"It's just another of the performing arts. Very similar to mime."

Paco's eyes glimmered. "Remember *The Great Train Robbery?* You remember what that felt like to see?"

"I did adore that picture," I said.

"Oh, me, too." Martha Ruth nibbled a bonbon and her eyes went hazy. "You remember when the villain held up that pistol? I thought I might faint from the surprise. I thought it might shoot right through the screen. Minnie said I was being overdramatic and to stop screaming." She set the chocolate down on a plate. "I don't want to think about her."

I didn't want to think about Minnie DuBois, either. She'd been a horrible Madam who Martha Ruth did not deserve, and before that

Pip's dancehall partner and betrayer, taking all their earnings one night and skipping out on her without a la-di-dah goodbye.

"Well, I haven't seen it." Pip stood up and paced. "So stop talking about it. In addition, you can erase every mention of Minnie from future conversations."

"I'm going to make a better film. A series of masterpieces. *The Great Train Robbery* will be sent to the dust heap." Paco stood with his feet wide and fists on his hips. "I hear the money in the box. I hear the money overflowing the box. I hear the wagon taking it to the bank and the safe that has to hold it. I hear—"

Pip closed the book and slid it away. "Where are these motion things going to be shown when you're done with them?"

Paco took the chair next to her. "All over America. Every venue of entertainment that will let us in—saloons, churches, theaters of repute and otherwise, why I see this series illuminated on the wall of city halls and the townspeople sitting on the lawn to watch and cheer you both on. I can guarantee within a few years, palaces will be constructed to watch them. To watch you two. Every child will have Ruby Calhoun signed photographs and Pip Quinn miniature Colt pistols. Adelaide Honeywell bonnets. Every adult—"

"Have you made one of these moving pictures before?" Pip interrupted.

"I sat at the feet of the greatest of film visionaries and technicians. Why, Colonel William Selig himself calls me nephew, or did once at Christmas, and said to me, 'Son, I want you here at Polyscope.' Broncho Billy Anderson himself begged for me to join him in a new venture."

"I don't know who the hell you're talking about," Pip said.

"I know motion pictures. And I know how to make you both stars."

"But you personally haven't made a picture of your own."

His face colored up. "I have not."

"I see."

"I see you are not convinced. Fair enough. You don't know me, and I did rescue you in the guise of another. I want you to trust me."

"It's our lives you're talking about," Pip said. "You could be pouring snake oil down our throats."

"Think what we could do with that money, Pip. We could get Olive and have side-by-side mansions or a ranch, if that's what you want. You could have as many horses as you can count and then some. You could trick ride again, because why not?"

"One hundred and fifty dollars for the three of us *is* a lot of money..."

"I've contracted with O.H. Flint for the rights," Paco said. "The minute you say yes, we can get to the location and shoot the footage."

Pip leaned forward, elbows to her knees. "And safe passage to Mexico."

"As I said."

"No. You said to the border. I say safe passage *into* Mexico."

"Done."

"And new riding duds. I won't be able to do a thing in this skirt."

"As many as your heart desires."

Pip mulled it over. "I don't know, there's something..."

"Think of your legacy."

"Our what?"

Paco popped up and paced around us, flipping the back of his jacket as he strode. "That would be my first thought, were I in your shoes, and were I given such a generous offer. These books, and soon these films, make you heroines. Ill-used and unfairly charged. Why, in a few years, I think your public personas will allow you to be forgiven. Folk heroes as it may be. You'll be able to see your children again, Miss Calhoun."

Martha Ruth clapped. "There's really no downside to the whole venture. We'll all be rich."

"You'll be charged with aiding and abetting," Pip said.

"I'll take the risk." He held out his hand. "To our partnership?"

I put my hand in his before Pip could get in another negative word and shook. "You've got big paws."

"Boxing."

"Hence the nose."

"Hence the nose." He turned to Pip. "Partners?"

"I'll think about it."

My heart dropped. "Pip..."

Paco pressed his palms together. "What else can I give you?"

"Pip, really. This is not the time to be...."

"I said I needed to think about it." She stalked around the ferns to the liquor cabinet and picked up a whiskey bottle. "I'm going to go think about it."

◌⚜◌

THERE WASN'T MUCH TO DO WHEN PIP'S STUBBORN STREAK REARED itself. Beating on the door only made her throw things at it. Persuading her out of her fallacious thinking only made her find the twenty-eight ways she was right. If we had access to a horse, I'd tell her to go take a ride and come back clear-headed. But that was not an available option, being as she might run into Sheriff Egg on his walk about.

So I sat on the floor with my back to the door between our rooms and read the California Limited timetable, waiting for her to turn around and see this picture business was a good direction all around.

"Here is a very interesting thing, Pip." I could hear her in the other room pacing. "The Santa Fe splits down in Albuquerque. You can go southwest into Los Angeles or swing on up north to San Francisco, which I hear is a pretty city, except for the weather. Or...if you wish to turn down this offer of quite a lot of cash, you could take a spur straight south to El Paso. Head over the border there."

The pacing stopped. "Me?"

"You'll need to leave Horse, because I don't see how you'll get him on a boxcar."

"Me alone?"

"You may need to rob a bank or two just to make sure you have—"

Her door snapped open. I tumbled back and then righted myself, dusting my skirts as I stood.

"What the hell, Ruby?" She glared at me.

"I shook hands with him, Pip, and a handshake is a promise."

"You want to split up?"

"No, I don't want to split up. You're the blockhead with the closed mind. This is the one way we're going to get out of this town."

"We can't stay with him a week. We can't stay anywhere that long. It's too risky. We'll sneak out tonight. I can find the livery and—"

"That sheriff called John Ward, Pip."

"That doesn't mean he got through."

I held up the timetable. "If he did? He'll be here tomorrow at twelve thirty-two p.m."

She blanched and sunk down on the bed. "We're trusting a man we've only met this morning—"

"Martha Ruth trusts him and she's been eating bonbons for days with him. I'd expect her to tell us—"

"We don't have our clothes. I don't have my rifle. All the canned goods have been taken, and the horses, too. This movie producer has set it up so we have nothing but these dresses and what's left of the bottle of whiskey in my room." She bolted up and stomped around. "What did he mean by legacy?"

"He meant your daughter and my kids won't be embarrassed about their mothers."

"If they remember us at all." She slumped back on the mattress and looked around. "This wallpaper is awful."

"It is garish, isn't it?"

"These motion pictures. They seem like a passing fancy. Who wants to see mimes when you can go to a real live show with dancing and singing and such? I don't understand."

"This'll keep us from running for a little, Pip. I'm awful tired of running. He's making it so we have more money than I've ever seen and taking us to Mexico."

She nodded and considered the wallpaper some more. "I've never seen a motion picture.

"You've never—?"

"Never been in a place that had them."

"Then we're going to see one. Let me find out where they are." I opened the hall door. Paco and Martha Ruth took a step back from their spy positions.

He put his palms up. "I was passing by. Happened to hear your plight. I know just where to go."

It wasn't the threat of John Ward or the law bearing down. It wasn't Paco's promise of safe passage across the border and money for us to raise Pip's daughter, and not even a cabana on the beach that changed Pip's mind. It wasn't that she was as tired as me of looking over her shoulder and wondering if that view would be the last.

It was the flickers.

Paco snuck us up a set of alley steps behind the saloons and then down an inside wooden flight to a square room with empty benches. Up front, a white sheet hung on the wall. A violinist and an oboe player sat below it, both squinting at their music stands. A small oil lamp sat on the floor between them, giving off the weakest of light.

We slid onto the farthest back bench near the projector. The man running it gave a quick dip of his head when Paco put a few bills in his hand.

The film operator turned the crank on the projector. The film whirred and clicked, shining light through a haze of dust. The musicians took up playing.

Then the sheet filled with motion, with men in shiny top hats and women in the finest of hats and dresses that trailed behind them. A kid popped in front of the camera, his whole grin taking up the view. It cut to a street with buildings tall as a canyon, and we were on a trolley moving fast along the steel tracks.

A card cut in.

Lower Broadway, New York City

Pip grabbed my knee. She sat in awe through the reel of New York City highlights, pointing at the tugboats and schooners in New York Harbor, and men in another street scene buying oranges and melons and kids hopping in glee around a huge block of ice.

The main feature was a ten-minute comedy of errors, with an aging Cupid running around a painted canvas forest and causing all sorts of mischief. I missed most of it, instead watching the glow of light on

Pip's face and the wonder it held. I'd forgotten what her real smile looked like, but there it was when she turned to me at the picture's end.

"That's the most beautiful thing I have ever seen."

Paco leaned forward to smile at us. "Magic. You'll be part of it."

Pip's normal expression of dead seriousness returned. "Three days."

"I'm sorry?"

"You have three days. Any longer runs the risk of us getting caught."

Paco drummed his fingertips to his thigh. I wondered if he realized the actual danger presented. Pip was right; we had to stay on the move. Every minute remaining in on place was just another minute someone would recognize us. He glanced over at Dooley. "Is it possible?"

"We'll do their shots first. It's possible. Tight. But possible."

With a quick bow of his head and a satisfied grin, Paco held out his hand to Pip. "We have a deal."

Thus it was we became employees of Silver Star Productions.

CHAPTER 11

Necessities and Fluffles—A Timetable Mix-up—Dierdre
Diamonte

We were scheduled to depart the El Otero the following day for the location of the *Desperado Damsels* filming. Paco had said it was a remote location and very scenic. He also said we could blow up a cabin as in Volume Two and no one would mind because there wasn't anyone to witness it.

"You will need necessities," Paco remarked. "Adelaide will go to town for them, as she is the only non-wanted and unrecognizable figure among you."

I spent a bit of time chewing on a pencil and figuring out what was a necessity versus a fluffle, then decided whatever we didn't use in the wilderness could be taken to our new Mexican abode. Paco had already been generous with our new choices of attire, but there were other items that needed purchasing. So I added in two hats (one straw, one large-brimmed felt), two pairs of lace gloves, three extra sets of stockings, another pair of garters, rose verbena water with a spritzer, comb, mirror, brush, toothbrush, a trunk with shelves and silk lining, a good wool coat and also a light linen one, a cotton shift for sleeping, a dozen handkerchiefs, a waist purse, one pocket watch, two boxes of Dr. Worden's Female pills, female accoutrements, and a sewing kit.

Martha Ruth took the list from me, glanced down it, and then tore it in half. "I have enough time to do the top half or the other."

"I need it all."

She crushed the pieces of paper into her palms and held her fists out. "Tap the one you want."

"How about I help you? We'll be done in half the time. And wait until you see Pip's list." I gave a low whistle. "She's taking full advantage, I am sure."

"She asked for her clothes back washed, two pair of wool socks, a box of Peter Schuyler cheroots, leather oil, a combination cartridge-money belt and a pocketknife. Oh, and a can opener."

I stared at the door between our rooms and wondered how long ago the lover-of-doodads Pip had become a monk.

"The fact of the matter is, Martha Ruth, I would very much like to go see the town proper. Being as I have not seen one since, well, since a long time. And who would recognize me dressed to the flouncy nines? All these daisies do wonders to keep one's attention."

"Well..." Her eyes drifted.

"Wouldn't you like the company?"

"It has been a little tiring listening to Paco go on about camera angles and creating mood."

"Kind of like when Pip goes on about the correct way to clean a horse hoof."

"Kind of like that. But Paco, he's interesting. He sure has vision. But he doesn't like to shop." She looked down at her hands still stretched outright. "I guess we could both go. If anything happens—"

"I will say it's all my fault."

"We can get an ice cream. With fudge and strawberry jam."

My head swooned.

"It's very bandit-y of us, isn't it?"

"What is?"

"Hiding in plain sight." She took the halves of my list and gave them to me. "Let's go shop."

We made it to the second floor mezzanine. Down in the lobby, Sheriff Tartt paced back and forth, surveying the light crowd with his pokey little eyes. He said something to the clerk, then shook his head and pointed toward the tracks. Whatever the clerk said made him grab each side of his hat brim and screw it down tighter on his head.

"Oh, no," I whispered.

"He's mad."

"He's looking for us."

"He usually only comes for the seven o'clock breakfast."

The grand clock that hung between the double doors said 9:33 a.m. which was much too early for the train from Kansas and much too late for Tartt's donuts and coffee routine.

Which meant the real authentic Sheriff Ward had been contacted and would be arriving soon. There was no other reason for the Egg to be waiting around.

I grabbed Martha Ruth's elbow to keep her from continuing on. "Is there another train from Kansas except the twelve thirty-two?"

She sucked in her lips and shook her head. "I don't follow train timetables. There may be..."

Just then, Egg glanced up the staircase.

My heartbeat scattered around. "Hell and damnation."

His eyes narrowed down to slits. He stood straight and pulled up his gun belt, the universal sign of disaster for those in the crosshairs.

If I moved an inch, he'd peg that I was trying to make a getaway. It didn't matter if he recognized me or not. It would look like an equation to him: Lawman looks + Quarry moves = Quarry is guilty of Some Sort of Something.

A train whistle blew long and loud, reverberating in the lobby. The man behind the desk straightened his tie, set his hands on the countertop and peered across the room. The sheriff's attention ticked away, which gave me a split second to back out of view.

Martha Ruth raised a hand high. "Hi-dee-ho, Mr. Tartt." She fluttered her eyes and floated down the stairs, wrapped her arm under his, and steered him toward the Harvey House dining hall. "You are exactly the person I wish to see."

"That's so?"

"Of course, it's so…"

Through the doorway they went. The train wheels squealed as the train came in, and the floor rumbled and shook. A young man and woman raced along the hall, bags swinging, then bounded past me and down the steps.

"We have plenty of time, Ronald." The woman grabbed the railing to keep from tripping as her husband pulled her along. "It's just pulling in."

I stepped forward and leaned over the handrail. "Where's it coming from?"

She glanced back. "Kansas City."

"Kansas City? I thought that came in at lunch."

"That one heads south. This one goes east to Pueblo."

"Pueblo? This isn't the Atchinson—"

"This is the Missouri Pacific. To Pueblo and Denver."

I swallowed. "That's a different train altogether."

"Come along, love." The man's heels tapped on the tile, then hers did, too, and they were around the corner to the platform itself.

I lifted my skirts and dashed up the stairs. The door to our third-floor suite was locked tight. I hammered my fist to it. "Paco. Pip. Somebody."

The knob turned. Paco looked down at me bleary eyed and sans any clothing save his long johns and a pair of sheepskin slippers. "What time is it and why are you outside our safety zone?"

"There's two timetables, Paco." I pushed past him and rushed down the hall, swerving into his suite. "Where's Dooley?"

"He's out filming the train."

I darted across to the windows. The station was full of passengers getting on and off, hoses dragged to the engine tanks and spewing water around. A row of porters loaded trunks and suitcases to rolling carts, calling out to each other and shifting through the crush of people. Smack in the middle stood Dooley, turning the crank on a wood-box camera as passengers flowed around his tripod, some giving curious looks.

Paco peered over my shoulder. "What are we looking at?"

"That's the Missouri Pacific."

"Is it?"

"You gave me the timetable for the California Limited."

"Uh-huh."

"Sheriff Tartt called John Ward. In Kansas. Who may be right now getting off that train. Which also comes from Kansas City. So tell me how the hell we get out of here, because if we're going to go make movies, we need to go right now."

"That's not good."

"No, Paco, it is very very bad."

He pulled at his mustache and kept his eyes on Dooley below.

A flash of chartreuse skirts and bobbing feathered hat caught my eye. Martha Ruth sidled through the crowd and tapped Dooley's shoulder. He stopped turning the crank as she said something and pointed in five different directions. The last was up at us.

Dooley looked up. He lifted his hands in a shrug. Martha Ruth made a slashing move across her neck.

"Ward's coming." I could barely get the words past the gravel of fear. "We all need to pack, Paco. Right now."

"Excellent idea."

"And you need to get the horses and wagon."

"Uh-huh."

"And put on some trousers."

"Yes, yes."

I squeezed my hands to fists and shook them. "Then let's—"

He turned to me. "Those nerves are going to kill you one day."

"Well, you won't see that because I'm going to kill you first."

"Now, Miss Calhoun—"

"Don't Miss Calhoun me. We are in a possibly calamitous situation that may negatively affect our chances of fame, fortune, and freedom, do you understand that?"

"What's this Sheriff Ward like?"

"You don't want to know."

Paco sprinted to the door. "We'll leave within the hour. If you and Miss Quinn can pack up one trunk between you, I would be obliged. Room on the wagons will be tight. Tell her she's riding her horse."

⊛

"THIS IS DAY ONE. HE DOESN'T GET A FREE TRAVEL DAY." PIP'S voice came muffled from under the brass bed. "Where's my Bible?"

The trunk lay open near the wardrobe, the new clothes and shoes dumped in. I threw my original travel togs in, shoved it all together and smacked the lid down before buckling the leathers tight.

"You had it yesterday, it was in your pocket like it always is. Where'd you put it when the maid came for the laundry?"

"I thought I put it..." She crawled out from under the bed frame and sank back on her haunches. Our clothing had come back smelling of lye and lavender; I'd never seen someone switch as fast as Pip did from the plaid. Her trousers and shirt gleamed. She patted the empty vest pocket. "This is not a good sign."

"It's somewhere, Pip. It's got to be. Here—" I unbuckled her saddle bag to check again, but it was as empty as the last time I checked it.

Dooley had brought her saddle bag and bed roll, and added to it a pair of wooly chaps.

"Why didn't you know about that timetable?" Pip glared at me.

"You can't blame me for that. I didn't know it existed."

"But you know the Missouri Pacific line. I've heard you mumble it in your sleep."

"I only know it to the Kansas border, Pip. Why would I need to know it any further?"

"If this is what happens when I lose my Bible—"

"Please do not make the possession or not of your Good Book a magic talisman. I'll get you another."

She tensed her jaw and picked up the bed roll. A rifle butt slid from the end.

"Why'd Dooley—"

"My Marlin." Pip tugged it out, then unbuckled the bedroll and unfurled it to find a box of bullets and a note: *Just in case. Your Fellow Desperado, Martha Ruth.*

A quick rap on the door made her shove the rifle and bullets under the pillows.

"It is your intrepid producer, may I come in?"

I opened the door.

Paco stepped in. He wore a seersucker suit and a bowler and made a fuss of checking his pocket watch as if he wanted us to see there was no fast approaching calamity and thus calm us.

"Ladies." He clapped his hands and held them together. "Small hiccup in the travel plans. Nothing to worry too keenly about, but the roads out of town have been blockaded."

"They're looking for us," Pip said.

"That is the word on the street."

I leaned a hand to the trunk to keep upright. "Well, then, that's that. Yet again."

"How many roads lead out of here?" Pip asked.

"Too many," Paco said. "The ministers of the various churches have been deputized to stand guard, along with the owner of Venderman's Beer and the blacksmith."

"They'll be looking for you, too," Pip said. "For impersonation of an officer of the law."

"There is no way to connect that to me. My disguise was impeccable."

"We could hide in crates," I said. "You can mark them 'Film Equipment' or some such."

Paco removed his bowler and fanned his face. "They're opening everything."

With a squeal of wheels, Martha Ruth shoved a maid's laundry bin through the door. "Sheriff Ward is not only here, but he's checking every room of the hotel. So one of you get on in."

"What's after that?" Pip asked. "A coffin?"

"We'd thought about that," Martha Ruth said. "But the mortuary is the opposite direction of the livery. The laundry, however, gets us to the House of Mirrors and that gets us to the river."

Pip ran her thumb down her scar in thought. "That's a whorehouse, I assume?"

Paco's face went beet red. "I wouldn't know. Adelaide came up with the plan."

"Oh, you know where it is," Martha Ruth said. "It's two doors from the confectionary and up the side stairs. You remember, Paco, the door with the diamond mirror? That's in reference to the name of the place. You had dinner with Dierdre two nights ago." She looked at Pip and me. "That's the madam. Miss Diamonte."

"How do you know I had dinner—?" Paco asked.

"Well, I look around and am aware of such things."

"And then what?" I asked.

"Then *what* what?"

"After we're in the house of sin. How does that get us outside of town?"

"I don't know. We'll think of something." Martha Ruth's expression brightened. "So, who's first?"

Pip picked up the rifle, stuffed the bullets to her pocket, and grabbed up the chaps. "I'll go."

She clambered atop the trunk then swung a leg inside the bin. I yanked the sheets off the bed and stuffed them around her. "I can see the barrel—"

"Sorry." The gun disappeared. She reached out her hand. "Ruby?"

I took it. "It'll be all right, Pip. I'll be right behind you."

"Give me the damn saddle bag."

❧

I HAD NEVER BEEN HOLED UP IN THE INTERIOR OF A HOTEL LAUNDRY bin before, but it stunk exactly as I thought. Old socks, morning breath, and an overlay of lavender soap. But one sacrifices in the face of danger and thus I tucked up tight and didn't get too seasick as Martha Ruth, now dressed in a maid's uniform she plucked from somewhere, wheeled me to the other end of the third floor and around two corners. The bin rocked to a stop, then I, along with the sheets, was dumped down the laundry chute and landed on a huge pile of linens below.

A hand clamped on my wrist and tugged me from the mess. It was Dooley. He gave a nod, then lifted me around the waist and dropped me in another bin, this one with a lid that clamped shut. Then we were outside, bumping over the rough roadway. The sun hit the bin and heated it to a boiling point.

"This all better be worth it," I murmured.

We hit a pothole that slammed my head to the bin top then my rear end to the base.

The bin stopped rolling. Dooley lifted the lid a hair. "You all right?"

"I'm suffering a concussion and on the point of suffocating but continue on."

He pushed forward. The street sounds surged and then fell; the bin tilted on what was some sort of ramp and bumped against a wall.

Nothing happened then.

I knocked a knuckle to the top. "Dooley?" I pushed the lid up and peered out at an empty alley. "Dooley?"

"Second delivery!"

I twisted about to see a woman's waist and hips clothed in satiny reds and purples. "Hello." Her mouth widened in a red-lipped smile. Then she pushed the lid shut and I was stuck in the dark again with the smell of socks. She said a few curse words and tugged the bin to motion.

We bumped over what I guessed was a threshold and came to a halt. As a door thudded shut, I thought how nebulous trusting a madam of a whorehouse was.

I thought I had better damn well get paid for this day.

❦

IF THERE WAS A MIRROR IN THE HOUSE OF MIRRORS, I DID NOT witness it. I supposed they graced each of the warren of rooms that ran a floor above us. The woman who wheeled me in helped me out. I found myself in a small laundry room with shallow ceilings and tubs and wash racks and clotheslines all tumbled together. Pip waited near a narrow entrance across the way, her rifle held in a seemingly casual manner and those furry chaps and her saddle bag slung to a shoulder.

Another woman strode through the laundry and brushed past Pip. "I am only doing this because it's Paco."

She seemed out of place, dressed in a prim blue-and-white striped outfit with a plain navy-blue fitted jacket. Her hair was pinned under a straw hat small enough I would call it a "hint." The only vibrant colors on her were the very red of her lips and her sporty two-tone button-up shoes.

My own dress was now a slog of crushed daisies, which irked me, even though this was a small problem what with the larger one I needed to focus upon.

We followed her down a dim narrow walkway of dusty brick The noises emanating from above proved the house to be a busy establishment, even on a midmorning between the Missouri Pacific departure and the California Limited arrival.

"Where are we going?" I asked.

She didn't slow her clip, just glanced over her shoulder then returned to her on-a-mission pace. We turned a corner and made another quick right, passing two unmarked doors that I could guarantee had stairs leading up into the back of a barber shop or cigar store that the well-respected gents of town would use as subterfuge for their activities.

Pip was tensed up, her shoulders hunched and her eyes scanning every which way as we moved along.

I shook the nerves from my arms and tried to ignore her.

"Are you Dierdre Diamonte? The Madam?" I asked.

No answer was forthcoming, so I took it as a yes. My experience with madams had been limited to a total of two: China Mary, who scared the hell out of me, and Minnie DuBois, who irked the hell out of me. This woman had a high and mighty tone, so I was leaning toward the irksome. Yet, I would keep an open mind as she alone was keeping Pip and me from the clutches of Sheriff Ward and what I guessed was a humiliated Sheriff Tartt.

"This seems a long way to the river," Pip said.

"You're not going to the river."

Pip and I halted.

"Oh, hell, yes we are." I smacked Pip's arm because she was right next to me and I was too far away to smack the madam.

She peered at us. "No, you're not." She spun on her heel and continued on. "You can trust me or you cannot. That is your prerogative." Then she rounded another corner.

"Huh." Pip chewed on her lip.

"She's not a figment from your past, is she?"

"I do not know every madam in the west, Ruby."

"I wish you did, as it would help suggest a plan of action."

The sharp echo of the woman's heels grew loud as she returned. She clasped her hands before her like a schoolmarm at best and a librarian at worst and screwed her face into the same sort of castigating disapproval. "Did I not say?"

"We don't know where you're taking us," I said. "If the shoes were reversed—"

"You take us to the river or I'm going to shoot you dead."

The woman sighed. "Fine."

"Fine?" The barrel of Pip's rifle wavered. "Fine you're taking us or fine I can shoot you?"

"Neither of those options get you very far, do they? There is a manhunt underway, do you not think they're checking the river? If you shoot at me, you'll just add another murder to your record. Besides, you'll go deaf from the blast."

"We haven't murdered anybody," I said.

"You should read the newspaper. Cullen Wilder is dead."

All the air left my lungs. "No."

"How do we know you're not lying?" Pip trembled and could barely hold her aim.

"Why would I do that?"

"He's really dead?"

"Infection from a gunshot. So it says."

"Good." Pip's gun clattered to the ground. Then she swayed and dropped to a faint.

It was one thing to live one's day thinking it all a matter of people exaggerating things: Pip shot a wall and it was called attempted murder. Then she busted a farmer's nose and that was considered the same, though I'd venture it was healed up now and he had a good story to go with it.

My shooting at Cullen Wilder was not an exaggeration. I meant it. I meant him dead for what he'd done to Pip, oh, even before Burdick. Well before Burdick. That one shot was in revenge for how he beat Pip any chance he got, and how he'd taken that knife so coldly to her face and left her open to derision from anyone who saw it.

When I decided to pull the trigger, I meant it. I had guilt after, plenty of it. At the moment, I had none at all.

I did not care he was now dead. But I cared very much I had been charged with something I was clearly innocent of.

"I didn't kill him." I sank down next to Pip and wrapped my arms around my knees. "You need to believe me. My kids are going to—it says murder?" I pressed my hand to my mouth to hold in a sob.

"It implies it."

I perked up. "Well, that is entirely different from the actual 'M' word. Maybe I don't trust you after all."

"I have loaned most my money to Paco for this motion picture venture. Keeping you out of the law's way will make it back for me in spades. Do you know how expensive it is to replace all those mirrors?" She shifted her waist purse around and took out a small vial of smelling salts. "Tell him the interest has increased to twelve percent."

She swung the vial in front of Pip's nose, which did the trick of waking her up.

"He's really dead?"

"So it seems. I hope you're hungry. I always have a substantial lunch ordered in. We'll watch the chaos from my window."

CHAPTER 12

WE TAKE TO THE RIVER—OUR FIRST LEG OF FREEDOM

There was indeed chaos down on 2nd Street. Pip and I peeked out the thick curtains to see a jam of wagons and surreys all waiting to get out of town, and all the drivers and passengers milling between them and yelling at each other and whoever up ahead was stopping the show.

I spied Sheriff Egg parading around near a grocery, sticking a piece of paper with Pip's and my image right up in people's faces. Next door, the butcher stood out front in his bloody apron, arms crossed and shaking his head.

Dierdre had left us to her lodgings without an explanation as to where she was going, except to say she'd be back in an hour and there wasn't anything to steal so not to try it.

Pip dropped the curtain and considered me. "Should we trust her?"

"If something happens to us, then she'd lose the money she loaned Paco. I'd say we were valuable assets to her right now."

"Okay. Then let's eat something." Pip strode across thick oriental carpets and took a seat at a round table piled high with meats, fruits, and buttery biscuits.

Dierdre's lodgings were on the abundant side of opulence, with a mass of burgundy velvet curtains and tassels and plenty of mirrors, some dripping rows of pearls and others studded in glass and paste gems. Egyptian-styled pillows took up one corner. A long desk graced with crystal oil lamps sat along one wall. The other had a twin bed with even more pillows. A tiny tan dog of questionable background and marked underbite perched on top of those. He growled every time I looked his direction. Pip, of course, got a wag and a funny dog smile.

Pip filled a plate and slathered mustard on a hank of ham.

"How is it you can eat?"

"We didn't have breakfast. There's a parfait here with berries that you'd like."

I eyed the tall glass. "I am fond of raspberries."

"Come sit."

"It doesn't seem right." My stomach felt a touch churlish. I glanced at the dog, who growled, then paced around. "I need a cigar."

"You need to eat."

"This latest distressing news has dampened my appetite, and as per usual I wonder how you can find the capacity to eat—what the hell are you eating right now?"

Pip held her spoon up. A piece of green fruit swam in honey. "I think it's a fig."

"Your sweet tooth knows no bounds." I lifted the curtain to spy out again. The street looked much the same except for a kid hawking bottles of soda. "Are you all right with it?"

"Making motion pictures? Making money?"

"Cullen. Are you all right with that?"

"Of course, I'm all right. I don't have to worry about him finding us anymore." She scooped another fig from the tureen. She frowned at it, then dropped the fruit and her spoon to the dish. "Let's check that desk for cigars."

It was locked up same as it was when we'd tried the first time. We moved over to a peculiarly carved cabinet, thinking there might be both an aperitif and a cheroot of some sort, but it held teacups and saucers and tiny silver spoons.

The dog yipped, sharp ears quivering and eyes glued to the door. He was a ball of motion, flying off the bed as Dierdre came in. She bent down to pick him up and cuddled him as he licked her face. "Fabian, my little rat-a-tat, who loves you mostest?"

Then she set him down. "Enough."

Fabian sat and gave one pleading wag before hopping back on his throne of pillows.

She patted a handkerchief to her cheek then folded it back to her waist purse. "You leave tonight."

❧

DIERDRE, CHANGED NOW INTO FISHING VEST, TROUSERS, AND sturdy knee-high hunting boots, zigzagged us through buildings and piles of rubbish, not slowing her speed until we bolted through the cottonwoods, slid down the riverbank, and slogged through the mud toward a trestle bridge.

"Hey," I called to her.

"Hey what?"

"Hey, where the hell are we going?" My boot stuck in a glop of muck and I tumbled forward, slipping face first into the grunge.

Pip grabbed up my shirt along the shoulders and tugged.

"I can get up on my own."

She just kept pulling.

"We'll meet Paco at the river." Dierdre kept her voice low.

I heard the plop of my boot sticking tight in the goo. Lantern lights wavered beyond the treeline, taking a straight line like a search party would do.

"Holy Hell." I wrenched my foot free, pulled off the other boot, tossed it into the bushes, then followed Pip and Dierdre under the bridge. We sat half in the water and half squished behind clumps of river grass. The lantern lights swung out over the water, then arced against the iron bridge bed.

"Now I have no shoes. Explain to me what I should do now."

"Be quiet for once," Pip whispered.

Footsteps echoed on the bridge then went away, the search for us given up or moving to another location. I crawled to a ledge of dry earth along the abutment. Dierdre slogged in the water to peer out one direction then the other.

"It's all clear," she said. She let out a whistle, which was answered back from out in the river. A small boat slipped from behind the piles, oared by Paco in a poncho and slouched hat. The prow cut into the soft bank.

"In," he said.

Pip sloshed out and slung a leg over the edge, tipping the boat and causing Paco to grab onto her and drag her the rest of the way in. She made a motion for me to join her, so I picked up my skirts and squished through the mud.

I looked around for Dierdre, but she was nowhere at all.

"Get under the tarp," Paco whispered.

We squeezed ourselves near the prow and pulled the heavy canvas over. It smelled like fish and the base of the boat held water that smelled worse.

"There better not be minnows swimming around," I muttered.

"Better'n rats, ain't it?" Pip said.

"If I have three toes missing by the time we get out, it's your fault."

"Why is everything my fault?"

"Because it is."

The boat rocked as Paco poked the oar to the riverbed and pushed off.

We were on the Arkansas now, and by the sound of the oars and Paco huffing and puffing, heading upstream.

Pip gave a long sigh of relief. "We're off."

"Your rifle's hitting my shin."

"Sorry."

She maneuvered around, moving it out of the way, then sighed again.

"I will say, Pip, that honey has given you sweet breath."

I DO NOT KNOW HOW LONG WE TRAVELED. IT WAS MISERABLE LYING in an inch of water that was a degree or two above ice. Every so often, Paco gained enough breath to try for conversation, but it came out in strange half-sentences that got swallowed up in his fight against the flow. It generally seemed to be small talk about his little sister Imogen, boiled crawfish, his rowing team in college, or moving pictures replacing both theater and God.

I tried to respond with "Is that right?" and "Oh, my." But between Pip thwacking my arm and Paco saying "What?" I gave up. Then he gave up.

Finally, the boat bumped against a small pier. Paco lifted the tarp. "We'll need to add a river scene. I'll ask O.H. to put those in another volume," he said. "Marvelous. We'll add a few men shooting at you from the shore, and that will be..." He tossed a rope over to the dock, then leaned to tie it to a cleat. "My God, the stories!" He hopped out, leaving the boat to wobble.

"Could you please take my hand and assist me?" I asked.

Which he did.

Pip slung her saddle bag and chaps to a shoulder, waved him off, and climbed out herself. "There better not be any water in my rifle."

She tramped past both of us, then turned back at the dock's edge. "What next?"

Paco pulled the edges of his poncho and wiped the tops of his shoes on the back of his legs. "Always the question, isn't it?"

THE PATH FROM THE DOCK RAN ALONG THE RIVER AND WE WERE soon walking along sandy flat banks dotted with campfires. Two kids in rags poked sticks in the mud, looking for crawdads or worms. The older one lifted his stick like a spear and threw it at me. Pip snatched it up near my feet and, with a string of invectives, harpooned it back.

"You did mean for that to miss, didn't you?" I asked.

On we went. I didn't like the looks of anyone we passed, and they did not like the looks of me. Some gave nods to Paco and returned to turning food on makeshift spits. Others just spit. A few people had lean-tos and others had pieces of canvas on poles. One woman tossed a pot of liquid that splattered close to my bare feet. I did not wish to know the contents. The air was thick with smoke and burnt meat and the sludge smell of the river. The further we wove our way down the bank, the more I thought about the civilized company of Jack Roberts and Sheriff Egg. I even longed for the comfort of the jail cell. It felt mean here. It tasted mean.

"Are you sure this is the way to go?" I asked.

Paco threw me a weak smile. "Dierdre said..."

His words trailed off. It made me realize how I had grown used to men of the west, who sometimes could not be trusted and sometimes were to be feared, and yet had hardy natures and confidence in their way in the world. Paco had his own nature and it was called citified.

"Where did you say you were from?" I asked.

"Chicago."

Pip made a pfft noise.

"What does that mean?" He glared at her.

"Pfft means pfft," she said.

The brush and river gave way to a muddy bank scored along its ridge with a few adobe huts and a couple simple frame houses. Lamps brightened windows. At the last house, a man came out on his porch, curling his work worn hands over the railing. "¿A quién buscas?"

"We're taking a stroll, sir. A simple innocent walk under the moonlight, no need for concern." Paco picked up his pace. He ducked through a stand of trees, not once worrying if we were following him, though I now fretted about the old man stepping off his porch and tagging behind.

We came out from the stand near a wide circular corral with an open air shed. Kerosene lanterns hung from nails on the posts, giving it all a festive spirit. Two horses, one a chestnut and the other a bay pony, were harnessed up to an enclosed milk wagon that sported *Silver Star Productions* along its side. Just beyond, Dooley lounged against a buckboard wagon filled with trunks and suitcases. Bessie and Napoleon looked as mismatched and annoyed as they had before. At least the wagon wasn't the yellow monstrosity we'd been rescued in, as that would draw attention from three miles in all directions. Satan, bridled and saddled with the reins slung around a fence post, huffed and swung his rump around.

"Hi-dee-ho!" Martha Ruth, wedged between two trunks, raised her hand in greeting, then leaned over to poke Dooley in the shoulder. "You owe me two dollars."

I did not wish to know what the bet was for; I guessed it was whether we'd make it in one piece without drowning in the river or getting waylaid by John Ward and the newly deputized citizens of La Junta.

I also did not wish to know who bet which way.

Pip unhooked Satan's reins and without ado mounted up. She stuffed the rifle into its holster. "Wherever we're going, let's go."

WE RATTLED ALONG A BROAD ROAD FOR A WHILE, WITH LANTERNS swinging from the fronts of the vehicles and illuminating the way. The sway of the wagon lulled me and I dozed. When I opened my eyes again, we were surrounded by fields of wheat stubble from a recent harvest and the sun had peaked up. It warmed my left shoulder and far to the west turned the Rockies a line of gold and silver blue.

Our caravan rolled forward, with Dooley driving the buckboard and Paco steering his glorified milk truck. Pip rode Satan, looking much like an old cowhand in woolly chaps and her wide-brimmed hat. She didn't pay us much attention, letting Satan travel alongside the wagon while she read one of the *Desperado Damsel* novels.

"These are damn good," she said. "What the hell are you reading?"

"The timetables."

"Why?"

"Because someday I'd like to ride a Pullman with velvet seats to my destination instead of dragging my ass on dirt roads behind you."

"You'll be able to reserve an entire car soon."

"I may do that."

She legged Satan around to ride next to Paco's wagon, pointing at something in the book which made him laugh.

La Junta lay behind us, as did the law. The relief made me

lightheaded, for there was no more looking over my shoulder and instead a lot more looking ahead. John Ward would have to give up his search and turn his obsession to another poor criminal, because we would soon be well away from his clutches and out of the country for good. And not running. I could catch a breath. And after that, I could figure a way to write my kids and have somewhere they could write back.

"What does he look like?" I asked Martha Ruth.

She leaned around the cases. "Who?"

"John Ward. You saw him at the depot."

"You seen a weasel? We got a lot of them at the farm in Gravette. I had one as a pet that curled up in a little ball on my pillow. I called her Nina Rae. She smelled a little like mothballs. I don't know if he smells like Nina Rae but he sure looks like her."

"I never wish to see him."

"You won't. We're a long away from there." Martha Ruth stretched. "Some days are as perfect as perfect can be." She smiled at me. "We are all together and—"

"Cullen's dead."

That wiped her smile away. "Oh."

Dooley looked over his shoulder from his box seat but didn't say anything.

"Well." Martha Ruth worked her lips and frowned. "That's one less person to worry about. My Uncle Hiram always says it's best to get rid of the chaff before it chokes you."

"I have never heard that saying before."

"Uncle Hiram has a passel of them. 'You're only a spring chicken for a little then you're in the pot' and 'A full purse is better than a happy heart' and 'After victory, tighten your helmet chord.' I don't know what that last one means exactly. He said it was something you had to do after losing an argument with the wife, and it was also useful to lock yourself in the barn for a night or two."

"Uncle Hiram is a smart man," Dooley intoned, then he gave a *chook* for the horses to step it up.

"Oh, he is indeed. He doesn't like church, though, so we only talk to him once a year on his birthday."

There were things about Martha Ruth that made no sense. I wondered how she squared her Sunday school upbringing and encyclopedic, if superficial, memorization of the Bible with being a working girl in a run-down den of iniquity in a town in the middle of Kansas. Every time I thought to ask, my manners stopped me from doing so.

My sister Rose would say "That is stepping the line," and for once I agreed with her.

I assumed Martha Ruth would present the full story when she felt it appropriate and thus I did not pry.

"Parasol?" she queried.

The sun beat down on my shoulders and head. "I wouldn't mind."

She squinted at Dooley. "Your hat is already sweat through. Would you like a parasol?"

"I wouldn't mind a little shade, thank you, Adelaide."

She twisted around, climbed over a trunk and unclasped another, holding the lid up and riffling around the contents. "Pink or violet? There's a very nice mauve one with ruffles..."

I got on my knees to see. "How many parasols are in there?"

"Maybe ten? There's a scene in Volume Three where you and Pip keep switching them around and confusing a Ranger, who thinks he's caught you but then finds out he's looking at an old lady with wood teeth, which allows you to climb up the side of a bank building..."

"These trunks are all props and costumes?"

"Our own togs are mixed in, but being a traveling film company, all materials come along with us. The bear costume is somewhere around here..." She lifted and dropped the lock on one of the trunks. "Guns."

"Guns?"

"There's a whole arsenal."

"They shoot blanks," Dooley said.

Martha Ruth continued picking up parasols until she came up with three that pleased her greatly. "You take this yellow, Ruby, and Dooley, you don't mind the one with the peonies on it, do you? It's extra-jumbo for that one stunt."

"Thank you kindly." He took it, popped it open and twirled it, then held it in the crook of his arm.

"That's not very cowboyish," I said.

"Shooting a man dead isn't very womanish."

"I resent that."

The trunk dropped shut with a bang. "I've got the mauve, as I think it's an Adelaide film star color, don't you?"

She clambered back over, tugged down her skirts, and snapped open the parasol. She slowed enough to gaze back at Paco. The corners of her mouth curled up. "Another perfect thing on a perfect day. There's only one thing'll make it better."

"What's that?"

"Seeing Theodore. You have no idea how much I have missed that mule."

I swallowed and busied myself unbuttoning the top of my dress to get some air. "I don't know when we'll see him again. He's...oh, got to be miles south of here. I don't remember exactly where the ranch is. Pip has all that information. All I know is Theo is happy as a clam and spoiled rotten eating clover and laying on fresh beds of downy hay. I think they even have pillows."

"Now you're pulling my leg. The only ranch down there is the Vista Verde. Jack Robert's place. You were supposed to stay there but you decided to fly off the handle and lead poor Dooley on a goose chase."

"You know how long it took us to catch all those horses?" he said.

"Vista Verde?" My throat clogged up and I cleared it with a wheeze. "Where Jack Roberts...whose horse we stole?"

"You stole mine, too," Dooley said, "but I'm not going to hold it against you. I should, but I won't."

"Paco rented the whole ranch." Martha Ruth tapped the top of the suitcases. "For us."

"With the horses." My breath went odd.

"And we'll go get Theo."

"About that..." I cleared my throat again. "There's another ranch down there."

"There is?"

"Yes, ma'am. It's called Greener Pastures."

"Then we'll head on over during a filming break."

Pip loped up to my side of the wagon. She shook the rolled-up dime novel, then pressed it to her chest. "We're going to be folk heroes, Ruby. I don't just kill a bear. I save an entire town from Black Bart. Dogs and all."

"I don't help?"

"You have a thing or two you do."

"Lucky me."

"How's those shoes working out?"

I peered down at my white button-up boots. They weren't the best for traveling, but they were the first Martha Ruth found before we took off. I was grateful to Paco for getting them and grateful to the world for dry feet.

"I have no complaints."

"All right." She trotted up to Dooley. "I apologize for smacking you in the chest."

"Accepted."

"Have you read the books?"

"I have."

"You're wrangling?"

"No, ma'am. I'm your cameraman."

She gave him a long look. "Cameraman, huh? Where'd you learn to ride like that?"

"I was with Pawnee Bill's show. I rode in the Little Big Horn reenactment."

"How'd you end up with Paco?"

"A company came out to film us. We were in Joplin. Caused a whole ruckus and a cameraman got kicked in the head and quit on the spot. I asked how much they paid and it was more than Gordon Lillie did. So I took the job and pretended to know what I was doing."

"You left a Wild West show?" Martha Ruth whistled. "I don't think I'd ever leave something like that."

"It had its moments. Mostly it was trains and tent sleeping and tiredness."

"What makes your new line of work better?" Pip asked.

"Besides the money? Making the world beautiful. Or frightening. Making light and chemicals and a strip of celluloid transform into magic." He twisted to stare at us, his eyes fervent in the way of Carrie Nation devotees and a few snake handlers I'd met.

"But it's all make-believe," I said.

"Who doesn't need some of that?"

"It *is* magic. You make magic." Pip made a quick kissing noise and Satan loped ahead.

Martha Ruth frowned. "That was for the horse, right?"

CHAPTER 13

Vista Verde—We Meet the Troupe

We soon made the turn off to Vista Verde. The road descended in a long curve that hugged the shallow canyonlands. Pip let Satan pick a way along the rocky edge above us.

"That'll make a grand shot," Paco called out. "Dooley, remember that shot."

Dooley lifted his hand to acknowledge the directive and squinted up at Pip. "Can you get him to rear up?"

"I can get a horse to do anything." She touched the brim of her hat, then dug her knees and ankles in. Satan tucked up his haunches like he was listening to her, all aquiver.

Martha Ruth held on to the side of the wagon in wild expectation. Paco stopped behind and set the brake on his vehicle.

"You want him to spin left or right before he rears?"

Paco stood on the driver's seat, hands to his hips as he admired the show. "How about one way then the other?"

She gave a chook, and Satan turned on a dime one way then the other.

"You're too close to the edge, Pip." My warning came a second too late. A few rocks tumbled down, then Satan lost his footing, his back legs slipping in the loose dirt before the whole of him following with them. Pip kicked and prodded, but his front legs splayed out as they slid.

Dooley drew the brake and jumped out, lurching up the hill with arms spread wide as if that could stop a two thousand pound horse that liked to bite when things upset him. This surely did. I saw it in the whites of his eyes and how he pulled his lips back. Pip knew it, too, for she jumped off and let the horse finish his slide to the road.

Dooley circled back to catch him, while Paco stood watching it all, eyes round and mouth opening and closing.

"You can leave the damn horse to do whatever he damn well wants." Pip stomped the rest of the way down. "Switch him out with Napoleon."

"Your horse isn't built for teamwork." Dooley ran a hand along each of Satan's legs and gave small whispers to calm him.

"Is he all right?" Pip asked.

"Got his confidence knocked, is all."

"He's not my horse." The scar on her face glowed against the rest of her skin, which was a mottled temper-tantrum red. If there was one thing that turned her into a screaming child, it was being humiliated in front of a crowd.

She looked at me. "You saw what he did."

"Actually, if you'd paid attention—"

"Are you blaming me?"

"I'm saying that when you boast—"

Dooley yelped and dropped the reins. He twisted to look at his trousers. "He damn took a bite out of my pants. You damn—"

Satan bolted down the road, leaving a long trail of dust.

"Good riddance. Go join the mustangs, if they'll have you," Pip yelled. "Say hello to Theodore when you're there."

Martha Ruth's back stiffened. "What'd you say?"

Pip took off her hat and smacked it to the side of the wagon. "I said nothing."

"Where's my mule?"

I threw Pip a look and touched Martha Ruth's shoulder. "I told you, he's at Greener Pastures."

Martha Ruth flinched. "Don't you touch me. You told me a great big lie."

"Well...you have a sensitive nature and—"

"Where is he?" Her lower lip started to tremble.

"No one's lying," Pip said. "He ran away with the mustangs. Which means he may be at greener pastures. We had a funeral, just to be on the safe side."

"You killed my Theodore." Martha Ruth had gone greenish-gray and looked about to disintegrate.

"That was just a play-act funeral. Tell her, Pip. We were bored and...where are you going?"

Martha Ruth clambered over the wagon edge and jumped down. "Hand me my parasol."

I did.

She snapped it open. "I am not talking to either of you." She stomped over to the other wagon and pulled herself up to the seat. "You two have betrayed me greatly."

Cigar smoke tickled my nose. I traced the scent back to Paco, who puffed and watched us from the shade of a piñon tree.

"That's all you can do?" I asked.

"I find these situations best waited out."

Pip climbed up on a wagon wheel, slung her leg over and thumped down beside me. She crossed her arms tight over her chest and ground her teeth. Then she jumped up and twisted around, thumping the top of a trunk for good measure. "I had nothing to do with your mule defecting."

"You held a funeral."

"I read a passage from the Bible."

"That don't make it better."

Pip smacked the trunk again.

I maneuvered up to the driver's seat and hopped out. Dooley straightened up from his pretend job of checking the traces and leathers. He side-stepped to the front of the team and rubbed both horse's forelocks.

I joined Paco in the coolish shade. "They'll work it out."

"It would be better for the smooth running of the production if they did."

"I'm not familiar with that brand you're smoking."

He held his cigar out and studied the band. "Ponce de Leon."

I whistled. "Too rich for my customers. I tried to sell it but it ended up being a loss."

"You had a cigar store?"

"I certainly did. It's under the protection now of a friend. Until I can get back."

"But you're heading for Mexico."

"I know. I can pretend, though." I trudged back to the wagons. "Any chance we can get on the road before we die of old age and Pip's tantrums?"

❧

"WELCOME TO VISTA VERDE. I HAVE A HORSE OF YOURS." JACK Roberts stood near his barn, arms out in greeting and dimples flashing every which way. He hurried over to help Martha Ruth down from her perch, kissed the top of her hand, then darted across to hold a hand out to Pip.

She glared down at him. "You stole my can opener."

His dimples went even deeper. "I needed a memento."

"You also conned us into trusting you."

"I couldn't leave you out there in the hinterlands."

"You are a con artist and I am not talking to you."

"But that night..."

"Pffft." Pip dismounted Satan and handed the reins to Jack. "If you wish to live you take good care of my horse."

"He's in good hands." His expression was as serious as if he was at his mother's funeral. "I like them better than people."

"Me, too."

Paco beamed as he took in the whole of the ranch house and barn and the corrals. "It's exactly as you said, Dooley."

Dooley jumped down and gave me an assist.

"Are we filming everything here?" I asked.

"Remote enough no one can find us. Close enough we take the raw stock to the train and escort it to the laboratory in Los Angeles. My laboratory. I'm going to beat Selig and his Polyscope empire to the punch." He rubbed his hands together and watched Dooley as he strode to the Silver Star wagon and slung open the rear door.

Dooley was halfway to stepping inside when he twisted around. "Listen up, everyone. Celluloid is flammable. There will be no smoking anywhere near the camera, the film canisters, or this wagon. There will be no guns going off unless they have been written into the scene and loaded with blanks. A single spark can set this all ablaze. Last year at Easter, my friend Merle lost three fingers and the tip of his nose to an explosion of this exact film product."

"Which three fingers?" Martha Ruth asked.

He peered at her. "Index, middle, and ring. Right hand."

"Well, he's still got his thumb. That's a blessing in disguise."

"He lost half of it."

"That's unfortunate."

Paco raised his hands. "We all heard from our most esteemed production manager and cameraman. Now, ladies, let's meet the troupe."

He put out an elbow for Martha Ruth to take, which she did with a coy drop of her shoulder and a simper.

I kept myself from rolling my eyes at her behavior. Pip, however, did not.

"Is your stomach upset?" I asked Martha Ruth.

"No."

"I heard a strange noise. Did you hear that, Pip?"

"Sounded like a gas leak."

Martha Ruth shot a look over her shoulder. "That's just your own voice, Pip Quinn."

"I thought you weren't talking to me."

"Ladies..."

It was a beautiful place, now that I had a chance to see it without the worry of being turned in and all the chaos of thinking Dooley a Pinkerton. The barn was solid, with a pitched roof, big doors, and a hayloft above. Sycamores and some trees I could not determine shaded the corrals. Beyond that, a packed-earth drive led out to the canyonland.

"I contacted O.H. Flint yesterday. Via telegraph. I invited him to visit and meet you, should he be able to get a train in time. He'll be here day after tomorrow."

"Where's he from?"

"Kansas City. Your hometown if I am correct." Paco smiled down at me. "You won't kill him, will you?"

"None of us has killed anybody," Martha Ruth said. She twisted her parasol. "The papers get away with nonsense, such as blaming Ruby for Cullen Wilder's demise. No one takes six weeks to die from a gunshot. Particularly one that missed."

"Yes, well." Paco put a knuckle to his lips to squelch a small cough. "Horace Armstrong is our lead character actor. He and his wife, Marjorie, were long-time stars of the vaudeville circuit and old family friends. He will be playing our main villain and Marjorie will be playing various roles, such as Adelaide's mother."

"Does she look like me?" Martha Ruth asked. "My mother doesn't resemble me in the least which I do not understand as my sister could be a spit image."

"Marjorie's a beautiful woman," Paco said. "She glimmers, but you, my dear, shine."

Martha Ruth tittered and blushed. Pip gave me a look that showed the same concern I had: Martha Ruth had lost her mind and was being led on all sorts of side roads by a man with money. We would need to sort this out with her and remind her that her sheltered life on the Gravette farm and subsequent employment at Minnie's pleasure house left her without discernment. I decided the talking-to should come from Pip, as she would say it more plainly. I expected she'd say 'Martha Ruth, don't be a dope.'

I slowed a bit and tugged Pip's elbow to join me. "You thinking what I'm thinking?" I whispered.

"This time, I am."

We strode up to Paco's side, Pip with a fake 'I am terribly

interested in every word smile,' and me feeling that we had to get Martha Ruth's mind to rights and get her back on track.

"Jack has agreed to play Ranger Hart Hartley."

"Hart Hartley." I grimaced. "That's a terrible name."

"Doesn't matter. He dies in your arms in Volume Three, Miss Calhoun."

"You really should read the books," Pip said. "That one's a weeper. Except now I know it's Jack, I won't cry if I read it again."

Our feet crunched along the dry soil as we neared the lodge. A gnarled weeping willow grew perilously close to the veranda, its branches brushing the ground.

A long wet snore emanated from a man sprawled in a cane chair on the porch. He had a mustache of walrusian proportions and a stomach to match it.

Paco put an arm out to stop us on the stairs, then marched over to the man and kicked his shoe.

This caused a riot of snorting and arm-flailing, then the man's eyes rolled open. "Poppy."

He stood with the great enthusiasm of the very drunk, smacked his thigh, grabbed Paco by the arms and shook him. "My God, we thought you'd abandoned...my God, Poppy." His mouth and chin quivered. "But here you are arrived."

Paco twisted from the man's grip and smoothed his shirtsleeves. His face was a deep red.

"Poppy?" I asked.

"It's an old family moniker."

The man made a flowing gesture with his hand but thought better of bowing. "Allow me a proper introduction since our previous was cut short by flailing horses. Horace Armstrong. Thespian."

The screen door flew open but was then held from slamming by the willowy Mrs. Armstrong. She paused, hooded eyes looking down her aquiline nose at no one. I could not tell her age; her art with powder and rouge and lip stain had been perfected all her years on the stage. I assumed her to be at least in her motherly years, as those with the bloom of youth do not hide it.

She tilted her head. "Our celebrities have been corralled, Poppy."

Pip did her best to hold back a snort.

Paco sidled over to Marjorie, his arms outstretched in greeting. "Marjorie...you are as ravishing as I remember."

"And you're a good liar." But she pinked at the compliment.

"Miss Ruby Calhoun, Miss Adelaide Honeywell, and Miss Pip Quinn," Paco said, "I'd like you to meet two of the finest actors the Chicago stage has ever known: Horace and Marjorie Armstrong."

"Don't listen to Poppy. We're song-and-dance people. And trying this new-fangled business—"

"Because we need the job." Horace took a flask from the pocket of his seersucker jacket. "This calls for a toast."

Nobody took him up on it.

The screen door flapped open. A frazzled woman in an apron that looked as if it needed a cleaning last Wednesday stomped by us and out to the yard. Her legs bowed out and she weaved like she was on the deck of a ship. She stopped in front of a mass of prickly pear cactus and sliced off a chunk that thumped to the ground.

"Carnelia," Marjorie called out. "No more of that. Please no more of that."

The knife stopped, then Carnelia scooped the cacti into her apron with the back of the knife before weaving her drunken sailor way to the porch.

Paco held the door for her. "Cookie, I'd like you to meet..."

Cookie Carnelia kept walking.

"I brought you the soap you like. No? It's rose scented."

"Dinner's at six."

"Six? Excellent." Paco ran his thumb down his suspender and snapped it. "Dinner at six."

"Where's everyone else?" I asked.

"The rest of what?"

"The troupe?"

"This is it." He swept his arm around to take in each of us and then gestured toward the barn. "This is Silver Star Productions."

CHAPTER 14

"This doesn't look much different than one of my old Paradise costumes." I swiveled in front of the full-length mirror in our assigned bedroom, pinching the white silk fabric near the belt to neaten the soft pleats.

The dinner had been declared by Paco as a formal start-of-production affair. We'd cleaned up pretty as could be, picking out costumes from the trunks lined up in the great room, and twisting up each other's hair. I measured and pinned and sewed until the clothes fit moderately well and wouldn't fall off or split at a seam. It reminded me of all the nights in our tiny backstage dressing room, sharing powder and rouge and making certain our costumes did not unravel before they were supposed to. It reminded me of times we laughed or held our ears to keep out the screech of Darby Price's singing or blew spit wads at the back of Verna's head while she played the piano and waited for us to strut on stage.

Pip stood next to me in a pearl-tinted gown of sateen and tulle. She tugged the neckline and bent over to double-check her cleavage.

"You've still got the goods, Pip."

She made a small adjustment. "Just not the face."

We stared at each other's reflections. No amount of powder or kohl could hide the past weeks on the road. We'd both lost weight, and it showed at our waists and on our cheeks.

"I hope the lights are dim," I said.

"Maybe they'll turn them off." Pip turned away, her eyes averted from her own reflection.

"Jack and Dooley won't like that. Unless it gives one of them a chance to steal a kiss." I reached for a pair of gloves on the dresser.

"Dooley?"

"You know that trick riding you do has bewitching effects on the opposite sex."

Pip sat in the chair by the window. She picked at a tear in the rough tweed on its arm and stared out the window. "Where did all the money come from?"

"Paco's?"

"He throws it around like it's rice at a wedding. All these costumes. That camera. Renting out an entire ranch."

"As long as we get our share, it can come from the King of Timbuktu."

A small knock came at the door, then Martha Ruth entered. She nodded to me and then to Pip before crossing between us to the dresser and opening a drawer. She took out a silver bracelet, slipped it on, then left.

"She's really not going to talk to us, is she?" Pip stared at the now closed door.

"Theodore was in your charge."

"Not you, too."

"I'm just saying."

"Well, don't." She smacked her thighs and stood up. "Let's go pretend to be ladies for an evening."

"Pip."

"What?"

"You're beautiful."

She dipped her head. "You clean up okay yourself."

MAYBE WE HAD TOO MUCH TO DRINK AT THE DINNER THAT NIGHT. Paco had brought a good cadre of wine and Jack had a good cook who made arroz con pollo and something sweet with prickly pear. My stomach was full for the first time in ages, which made me prone to liking everyone sitting around the table.

Horace Armstrong had the look of an actor, his features more pronounced than the average man and thus optimal for the stage. He had the self-aggrandizement of an actor, too, spying himself surreptitiously in the mirror on the wall across, eyes catching on himself as he combed his walrus mustache and made funny faces.

Marjorie's dinner dress was of the thinnest of materials, with décolletage giving away more than her age allowed. Still, she had a jolly way about her, and laughed a lot. I figured the two were down on their luck, as the dress looked a lot like one from her vaudeville days.

Jack had dressed in dinner clothing with a high collar and satin vest. He sat across from Pip and assiduously stared any direction that did not involve her breasts. He squinted up at the flickering candles on the large wheel-shaped chandelier and stretched his neck to alleviate the pinch of his collar.

Dooley sat near the other end, where the candlelight didn't completely reach.

"Pip and I are also song and dance people," I said.

"Is that right?" Marjorie asked. "Where?"

"Oh, we were quite famous in our region before taking up what we do now. Pip had an act with a string of feathers that would bring the house down. You remember that one time, Pip, they were throwing silver dollars at your feet?"

"I would much like to see that," Jack said.

Pip slugged back the rest of her wine. "You won't be seeing that."

At the head of the table, Paco held up a wine bottle. He had oiled his hair with Brilliantine, and wore an even higher collar than Jack, though it did not seem to bother him. "Who wants a topper?"

I held my empty glass toward him. "It is very good wine."

"Drink up, then. Tomorrow we shall all be sober as monks."

I pressed my napkin to my lips, then set it down by my plate, careful to not run the cuff of my dress through the honey on my dessert plate. Martha Ruth poked her fork at the prickly pear and looked around to see if anyone else had determined it too foreign to eat.

"I'll take yours." Pip reached across me to take Martha Ruth's plate.

"You are a hearty eater, Miss Quinn." Horace tipped his glass to her. "But all artists need food."

Paco pushed his chair back and stood. "And wine."

Dooley, who wore a simple suit and tie, put a hand over his glass when Paco came around to his end of the table. "Long day tomorrow."

"Dooley, loosen up a little. We're going to be at your beck and call in less than twelve hours, let's celebrate while we can. In fact, now that your glasses are full, I'd like to make a toast." He shifted the edge of his coat to set a hand to his hip and lifted his own full glass perilously high. "We are like a band of brothers—"

"Henry Five." Horace peered around as if someone was going to challenge him. But no one did, so he humphed and crossed his arms to listen to Paco.

"Yes, *Henry the Fifth*. Shakespeare had his stage. We have light and shadow. Celluloid and chemicals."

"No smoking while we're on set."

"Thank you, Dooley. Rule number one repeated for the seventy-eighth time." He took a breath. "May I go on with my story?"

Horace nodded for Paco to continue.

"I come from a long line of adventurous businessmen. My great-grandfather sold wagon axles. He saw those pioneers going west and he moved the entire Jones line to Independence to serve them. Do you know how many prairie schooners schooned that prairie?"

None of us had an answer, so he went on. "After a few dozen years, my granddad grew tired of tornadoes so he moved the family to Peoria, bought up the furniture stores, and created a factory to stock them. My father—"

"Does this have a point?" Horace asked.

"Yes, it does. In eighteen seventy-four—"

"Perhaps you could move to this century, Poppy."

Paco dragged his teeth across his upper lip then took a deep breath. "Horace—"

"My wine is starting to evaporate."

"In eighteen seventy-four, my father fell in love with Juanita Morales, the local beauty. Not being handy at the lathe, he chose a business more suited to his nature. Through hard work, he became world renowned for his soap, which is carried along the entire Harvey House chain. Which you have recently enjoyed. Now, you have a personal connection to my father and my beautiful mother, whose face is stamped upon each bar."

Pip leaned back in her chair. "Must be odd to think about that when you bathe."

"I shall ignore that remark."

"How'd you get out of soap?"

"Boxing. But my father did not approve of the pugilistic sports, so I found myself given two choices: make a man of myself on my own or stay in the family business. That dragged my humors down and I wandered the street struggling with the decision. It began to snow."

Pip cut a laugh. "You forgot your coat and had to sell matchsticks, right?"

"That's rude," Martha Ruth addressed this to Dooley.

"I didn't say anything."

"Pass the comment to the woman on your right." She made a point of turning her back to Pip and giving all her attention to Paco. "As you were saying?"

"Right. Yes. I found myself at a little theater. In that plain little theater I found my calling. Which led to this moment. With all of you here. My artists. The sky's the limit after this. Wait until we get to Los Angeles."

Marjorie shuddered. Then her mouth drooped at the corners as if the very words 'Los Angeles' carried rabies.

"Is it that bad?" I asked.

"Avocados and fruit flies." She shuddered again.

"No theater." Horace shivered. "No culture."

"But plenty of money to be made," Paco said. "This is the next big thing. It makes Barnum and his side shows as miniscule as fleas on a burro. You can afford to found a theater of your own. Do that *Lear* you talk about."

"Ad infinitum," Marjorie muttered.

"It's a dream, darling."

"How does the 'Armstrong Theater' sound?" Paco asked.

"Well..." Horace looked at his wife.

"Have I let you down before? Didn't I get you these contracts when Selig wanted to hire that two-bit Ames and Haskell? Just because they pulled in a vaudeville crowd—"

"Their dog pulled in the crowd." Marjorie shuddered again.

"We're with you for these films only, Poppy."

"Can you not call me—"

"We're Chicago people, we're only doing this for—"

"May I make this damn toast?"

The chair squeaked as Horace sat back. "No one's stopping you."

"Hold up your God-forsaken glasses. Let's toast to the *Desperado Damsels* and all our success."

The wine was imbibed by all save Dooley.

"My lips are numb," Martha Ruth said. "And my cheeks."

Jack stood and started to sing.

Beautiful Dreamer, wake unto me,
Starlight and dewdrops are waiting for thee;
Sounds of the rude world heard in the day,
Lull'd by the moonlight have all passed away!

"That song's going to put me to sleep." Pip drained her wine. Her face was flushed from the drink, which made her scar gleam white. She tapped out a beat on the table. "Who knows *Bill Bailey*?"

"Who knows it?" Horace clapped his hands. "Who made it the most popular hit in Chicago in nineteen-ought-two? The Armstrongs, that's who. Come on, my wife, let's liven the party."

We moved to the great room. Jack was as talented on the upright piano as he was at singing, and we all sang one song after another. Marjorie showed us a new-fangled dance called the Turkey Trot, which wasn't much different from a four-step except we flapped our elbows up and down.

Horace spun me around for no reason and I ended up in front of Dooley.

"You don't dance, Dooley?"

He shrugged. "I dance."

I swayed forward, as the wine and spinning had taken hold of my balance and stopped myself with a hand to his chest. "Then I wish you to dance with me. You can tell me all about your camera."

His face brightened up. "All right then. May I have this dance?"

"Yes, sir, you may."

He had a light touch, nothing like the men at the Paradise who groped about when China Mary wasn't watching, and sometimes when she was.

Martha Ruth and Paco squawked on by us. Horace spun Pip and then Marjorie. The three of them stumbled over to the piano and stood behind Jack as he played a ragtime. Marjorie slung an arm over Pip's and her husband's shoulders, all having become the best of friends two dances and three wines ago.

Somehow a beer got passed around and then another.

Marjorie tapped Horace on the head, made a broad face and raised her voice like she was on the stage. "My friend has just been elected mayor."

"Honestly?" he asked.

"What does *that* matter?"

They both clapped once and did a quick step-ball-change.

"Doctor," she asked. "How is my health?"

He put his ear to her chest. "You'll live to be sixty."

"I am sixty!"

"See? What'd I tell you?"

Paco staggered across the room, putting his hand to the stone mantel to steady himself. He took out his pocket watch and flicked it open. "Tomorrow is today, ladies and gentlemen. Hoorah. One more song. Hell, two more. Adelaide and I need a dance."

Pip slipped by me, tugging me by the wrist as she passed. "Come on."

I followed Pip from the great room and into the hall, slowing at the kitchen. The oil lamps had been extinguished, so we trailed our hands along a center table and made it to the door and outside.

"It's pitch black out here."

"You'll get used to it. Just close your eyes a bit."

I did. Laughs and singing came muffled through the door. "Can we please go back inside?"

"In a minute." She touched my elbow and moved us to the yard. It was still dark as get out but I'd acclimated to it and made out a well and a chicken coop. Further out was a small cottage, which I guessed was Carnelia's. Pip gestured to keep moving, then lifted her skirts and crept around the side of the lodge.

"What are we doing?"

"Mapping the lay of the land." She reached for a window, tried to jiggle it up, then gave up and moved around a thorny half-dead rose bush to the next window. "This is our room."

"Good for it."

"Let's see who's left theirs open and maybe been dumb enough to leave things around."

"Like what?"

"Money. Jewelry."

"Let's not steal from them," I said. "I like them."

"And I'm just looking." She took a few steps back and peered into the dark. "Huh."

"Huh, what?"

"That."

Jack strode across the yard toward the barn, the lamp he held lit low. He looked over his shoulder toward the lodge. "That wasn't the agreement."

Paco jogged out to the yard and tromped next to him. "You've got to be reasonable—"

"It's not enough."

"Come on, Jack. You shook on the deal."

"But I don't like it. I have a note being called in."

"That is not my concern..."

The two made the barn and went inside. Jack slid the door shut.

"What's that about?" I asked.

Pip shook her head. Her eyes darted around the property. "We should be moving on, Ruby. This is—"

"We'll be gone in three days. Hell, maybe we're making more than Jack and that's got him stirred up."

"Maybe."

The evening fell in on itself like a balloon out of all its air. "I wish you hadn't dragged me out here. I just want to go in and dance a Virginia Reel and have fun. You ruin fun."

"We can't let our guard down. Any one of these people could take it into their heads to go back to La Junta and turn us in. You know that as well as me."

"Then why'd we agree to come, if it's so risky?"

Pip fisted her hands to her hips. "What drew you to Frank? When you first met?"

"When he wasn't the Damn Bastard?"

"Yeah. Then."

A warmth flooded me. No matter what Frank had done, those first few months still enchanted. "He was a charmer. Always looking out for me. Flowers and candies. He had all these plans. He wanted his own riverboat. 'Ruby, I'm going to have the best gambling boat in the whole of the Americas, the best known...'" It was as if I could hear the slap of the paddlewheel to the Mississippi and churn of the water. "...the most magical...'" I slumped against the wall. "Hell and damn."

"All those promises. Broken." Splotches of color darkened her chest and neck. "I wasn't any better with Cullen."

"You think Paco—"

"I think we need our money up front."

LATER, PIP SAT ON HER BED, KNEES BENT UP AND ARMS CRADLED around them. She watched Martha Ruth sleep on the cot squeezed between our two beds.

"That girl does not know how to hold her liquor."

"At least she's in here and not with Paco." I shook out Pip's skirt, folded it over a hanger, and put it away with the rest of our dinner clothes in the wardrobe.

"She's the only one the police don't know about."

"Papers say we're travelling with someone else."

"But they don't know who it is. We should let her go, Ruby."

I sat on the edge of my bed. "That doesn't feel right. She gave up Minnie's for us."

"She gave up Minnie's because Minnie is cruel. You were kind to her. If she stays with us, somewhere along the way she'll be identified. And her poster will be hanging next to ours."

My stomach soured. "I don't want to talk about that. I'm too tired."

"Open the window, would you?"

I kneeled on my bed and reached for the sash. "It's stuck."

The mattress sunk as Pip crawled over to join me. We jimmied the window until it was halfway open, then turned and sat with our backs against the wall and let the cool air roll over us.

"I was thinking in Mexico we could make a stage show. 'Valentina and Glorietta.'"

"Who's who?" she asked.

"I'm fond of Valentina."

"Then that shall be your name."

"We can use them as aliases, if we need to," I said. "We should figure one for Martha Ruth."

"She doesn't need one. First chance we get, we're going to send her home."

CHAPTER 15

A drawer squealed open and then slammed shut, rudely awakening me. Martha Ruth turned from the dresser, clothes rolled in her arms.

I sat up. Pip's empty bed was made, as if she hadn't even slept in it, its quilt laden now with a neat row of pretty shoes. "It's barely sunrise. What are you doing?"

"I heard what you all said last night." Martha Ruth dropped the garments and whatnots to a blanket she'd spread on her narrow bed, then took up two corners of it and made a tight knot.

My stomach lurched. "That was just Pip talking, you know how she gets."

She tied the other two corners. "Be that as it may."

"Look at me. Come on. You think we'd abandon you?"

One of her shoulders lifted and dropped.

"Pip was being silly."

"It don't matter." She stuffed the shoes into the opening between the knots and hefted the ersatz rucksack to her shoulder. "I'm going with Paco, anyway. You don't have to worry anymore." She looked quick at me and then away, finding something interesting on the rag rug. "Yes, ma'am, I am. He appreciates me."

"He sees a meal ticket in you."

She stuck her chin out. "That's the last I'm talking about this."

"Martha Ruth, you cannot—He's too old for you."

"He's thirty-seven. My mind's made up."

"Well, unmake it. We need you."

"No, you don't."

I shoved the covers down with my feet and scrambled up. "Why would we risk hide and hair to find you? Answer me that before you walk away and find yourself in a whole other mess of trouble."

She rubbed the back of her arm to her eyes. "You just wanted your nine dollars."

"What nine dollars?"

"The nine you loaned me at Minnie's."

"I gave you that to go home to Gravette and—what happened to that, anyway?"

"Minnie found it."

"You didn't hide it?"

"I hide things very well. She just knew where to look." She trudged to the door and turned the handle. "You tell me where you're going to be in Mexico when the two of you have your act. I'll send it on."

I let out a breath. "We can make it a trio."

She pitched her chin high. "Goodbye."

"I don't trust Paco—"

"Well, I do." She strode out and stumbled into Pip.

"Where are you going?"

"Far away."

"She's going across the hall," I said.

"Let me pass." Martha Ruth ducked around Pip, dropping her sack to the floor and dragging it. "Have a good life."

"What is that about?" Pip asked.

"Martha Ruth heard us."

"Well, better she knows—"

"She's taking up with Paco."

"What do you want me to say? She has a chance if she goes with him." She stared in the mirror and picked and pulled at the shirt. "It's her life to choose; you can't mope about it."

"Sometimes you're very cold, Pip."

I sank back to the edge of the bed, both in dread of Martha Ruth's future and Pip's new 'ready to film' look. Pancake makeup was layered heavy enough to her face to mask her scar. Her lips and eyes could have been traded for a china doll's, if you painted said features in chalk and greasepaint. "You look like a cadaver."

"Apparently, mortuary paint looks good on film." She pulled at her quite lacy and very low-cut blouse. "I'm supposed to ride in this?"

"I take it from your makeup Paco didn't agree to pay us up front."

She turned from the mirror. "He said we were in no position to negotiate."

I squeezed my hands to fists and stood. "Well, he can have a piece of my mind. We're the main attraction. He doesn't have one damn thing he can do if we choose to walk away from this production altogether."

"Except send us to prison."

My skin flushed with the threat of that.

Dooley stopped at the doorway, pencil tucked behind an ear and leather folder clasped to his chest. He blinked down at me. "Why aren't you in makeup?"

"Why should I be?"

"I put a schedule under your door. We're starting in ten minutes. Never mind. Go see Marjorie in the great room." He spun on a heel and hurried away.

Pip gave a weak smile. "No work, no pay."

❦

"YOU WANT ME TO WHAT?" I SQUINTED AT PACO FROM THE POSITION he'd maneuvered me into. We were on hour one-hundred-and-eighteen of Day One production and I was truly beginning to lose patience. My body, clothed in some fluffy ruffly nonsense, both sweat and itched. My face, slathered in white ghoulish paste with lips coated in five layers of rouge, felt like a chunk of melting glue.

Martha Ruth perched next to me on a log that Dooley had dragged over from the wood stacked near the barn. Jack held her wrist, frozen in a position more akin to a rope pull competition against ten loggers.

She tipped her head one way then another and kept her ankles crossed just so.

"Is this the best angle, Paco?"

We all looked at him. He pinched the top of his nose and then made a valiant effort to smile. Sweat stained the underarms of his white shirt, which should have given him an idea of how I felt in so many layers, and how Jack felt in all wool trousers, vest, and jacket. My guess was the tin badge was hot enough to burn the hair right off his chest, which made me feel sorry for him.

"Paco?"

"Adelaide, my dear, sit any way you want."

There was an undertone there I did not like at all. But I did not like Paco at all right now.

"Let's try this again. Ruby, you pull one of Adelaide's arms and Jack pulls the other. He wants to abscond with her, you want to save her. After that, I give the signal for Pip—"

"I have been pulling." I moved to wipe my upper lip but thought better of it.

Dooley straightened up from the camera's viewfinder. "You've been pulling yourself right out of the frame."

"It allows me to get a moment of shade."

He shook his head. "Pull smaller."

"My shoulders hurt," Martha Ruth mewled.

"I think we should break for lunch." Jack took off his hat and fanned his face. "I'm going to faint."

"You do seem pitched," I said.

"It is not lunch," Paco said. "It is not even..." He took out his watch. "It's not even eleven a.m. And you all are already driving me mad. You take one arm, Ruby, and you take the other, Jack, and let us finish this shot."

"You heard him." Martha Ruth posed again. "Should I be looking to the left or to the right, Paco?"

He growled. I had not, until this moment, actually heard a man growl, but he did a good enough job that Martha Ruth got the point to turn her head whichever damn way she wanted.

"All right." Paco shoved the watch to his vest and stuck his arm out. "Ready."

We took up our positions.

"Set."

Dooley took up his.

"Action."

Paco dropped his arm like he was starting a horse race.

"No!" Martha Ruth pouted and batted her eyes toward the camera.

"Yes!" Jack made a pretend pull.

I tugged the other way. "Cherry pie and whiskey!"

Then Pip flew by on Napoleon, leaning over in a one-two hitch, shooting blanks at something behind her.

Dust flew everywhere, including up my nose. Jack coughed and wheezed. Martha Ruth spit a clump out.

We waited for it to settle back down. Paco had his hands laced on top of his head and looked like he was going to cry.

Pip circled Napoleon around. "That was the best one yet. Damn, Dooley, this is a fine horse. Did you see how he laid out flat?"

"Did I ask you to gallop across my scene at that exact wrong moment?" Paco now scratched the part along his crown and smiled up at her.

"You gave the signal."

"No."

"Yes. You told me that when you dropped your arm, that was my time to come at a gallop."

"You did give something that looked like a signal," I said.

"It wasn't *that* signal. That signal looks like this." He made a big pinwheel with his arm. "Not like this. See. This is a chop. This means start the damn scene. And this—" He demonstrated the wagon wheel move again. "—does not look the same."

"Well, from down that way the signal looks the same as the last one and the one before that, and my horse is getting tired. And we are rolling up fast on the end of the first day and you only get three." Pip shifted in the saddle and fluffed the chestnut hair on Napoleon's mane. "Look at that sweat on his neck."

Paco pursed his lips and squinted. "Get back to the corral and wait for the correct signal and—"

"I need to change the film," Dooley said.

"What?"

"Give me twenty minutes." He put a lid on the lens, another on the viewfinder and lugged the camera to this shoulder. He pushed the tripod legs together and walked off toward the lodge. A couple of chickens pecked across his path and fluttered their wings to get out of his way.

"Twenty minutes," Paco muttered. "What takes twenty minutes?"

"I'm going to untack Napoleon."

He whirled to Pip. "No. You are going to do the What's-It-What Dunk—"

"The One-Two Hitch," Martha Ruth said.

"I don't like this firearm," Pip said.

"It's a revolver."

"It's a fifty-cent Sears Roebuck cap gun. I use a Colt. A twenty-three dollars and fifty-cents Colt."

"With a pearl handle," I added.

"We do not use real guns on the set, Miss Quinn. You signed a waiver about that. The possession of a real gun is a dangerous situation that involves hiring a nurse to bind up anyone who gets hit by a stray bullet. As you might have noticed, we have no nurse. The firing of blanks gives the right smoky illusion."

"I am one hundred percent behind the no-weapons-on-set rule," I said. "Paco is right; it'll look just fine when all is said and done."

"I bet Horace and Marjorie have already eaten lunch." Jack had slumped down next to Martha Ruth. He gave her his hat and she flapped it in front of them.

"One more time through," Paco said. "One damn perfect time and I will call it lunchtime."

THE ENTIRE AFTERNOON WAS SPENT MAKING FACES IN FRONT OF THE camera. Then making a face and running out of the frame of the camera. Then running in front of the camera with parasols and making surprised then angry faces. Dooley and Horace lugged various painted stage flats around one being a rendering of the corral behind us which made no sense at all.

"It's about chasing the light," Dooley said. But he didn't explain much more than that.

"I cannot make one more face," Pip said. "It's going to fall off in one giant lump."

Horace, who had been watching us from a comfortable cane chair, ambled over. "You don't mind..." He raised an eyebrow to Paco.

"Be my guest."

Horace smiled and put a hand to each of our shoulders. "You are working far too hard."

"I don't want to work anymore at all." Pip dug her boot heel to the dirt. "This is the dumbest business I've ever encountered."

"My face is numb," I said.

"Stop acting. Just stare." Horace looked just beyond my shoulder. "Let all your muscles relax. Stare to the far distance. Like this."

"What expression does that mean?" I asked.

"Anything the audience wants it to be. Comedy or tragedy, it makes no difference," he said. "What matters is each audience member will see what they want. They're happy, and you will have saved much effort."

He patted our heads. "I little bird told me your young friend moved her belongings to Poppy's room. You might want to share that our producer has a wife named Tess and little girl who goes by Lisbeth."

Then he returned to his chair.

"You damn son-of-a..." Pip stomped over to Paco and slapped him.

He flattened his hand to his cheek. "What the hell was that for?"

"You know what that was for you two-timing, two-bit nothing."

"Miss Quinn, look at me." Dooley cranked the camera.

"What?"

He smiled. "That was a perfect shot."

"Did you just film that assault?" Paco fumed.

"Her expression...that's exactly what you were looking for."

The lines of Paco's throat tightened as he glared at Pip. "Go back over with your friend and get in place for the next shot."

"You're a son of a bitch."

His whole body tensed, ready to hit something and hit it hard. There wasn't even a small hint of the man with the easy smiles who showered presents and grand ideas. "You would be rotting in jail if it wasn't for me, so show some damn respect."

Horace leaned forward, his face gray with concern. "Poppy..."

"Don't call me that."

Dooley stepped from the camera. "I think we're all overtired, overwarm, and overwrought right now. We'll call it a day and start early tomorrow."

Paco ground his heel to the dirt and stormed towards the lodge.

⁂

CARNELIA LEFT COLD CUTS ON A SIDE TABLE FOR DINNER AND THE atmosphere was anything but the party sort from the night before. Horace and Marjorie took their scripts to the far end of the porch and walked through their blocking for their morning scenes. Dooley and Paco poured over scene cards they'd laid out on the dining room table. Martha Ruth followed Paco as he paced one end of the table to the other, clapping and oohing at whatever pronouncement he made.

Pip and I stood at the other end of the porch, watching them through the window.

"I thought he was going to hit you, Pip."

She crossed her arms tight and glowered. "I'd have hit right back."

"We going to need to tell her."

"If she ever leaves his side."

"He doesn't seem to mind it."

"She's going to be heartbroken."

"I think, Pip, it's you giving up on her that broke her heart. All she wanted to be was a bandit and have you tell her she was doing a good job."

"I'm not her mother." She gave me a long look. "And I'm not going to tell her about him. Not until we get our money."

A loud thud on the steps made us all jump. Jack stumbled on the landing, grabbing a porch column to keep from planting face first at Marjorie's feet.

"You, sir, are drunk." Marjorie flapped her scene pages and stepped away when he reached to hug her.

"You're a very beautiful woman." He made a sloppy wag of his finger at Horace. "And you are a lucky man to have her." He nearly bowled over, his legs twisting up like a pretzel.

Horace slid a chair his way. "You need to sit, son."

"I do not mind if I do." He stretched out his legs and tapped his fingers along the wide arms of the chair. He stared at Pip, closing one eye and then another. "You're pretty, too. I was promised a twenty percent bonus for you. Well, I haven't got it. And I bet you haven't seen a dime either, Mr. Horace Armstrong and wife. The bank's called in my mortgage, what is your sad tale?"

"Poppy is a good man." Marjorie's words were clipped. "We needed work and he got it for us. We've been friends of the family for years, I won't have—"

"Has he paid you?" Pip asked.

Horace blustered a bit. "Well..."

"What'd he promise you, Ruby? Absolute freedom. Which does not exist." Jack's mouth twisted. "We're all being had."

CHAPTER 16

"Absolutely, one-hundred-and-twenty-five-percent, *no.*" I looked up at the peak of the abandoned barn we'd trudged out to then back at Paco.

Marjorie stared up at the great height, holding the brim of her hat so it wouldn't flap about in the wind. "You should request injury pay."

"Paco, do you have any idea—"

He spread his palms. "It's one of the final scenes I need you for. It's the climax. And I want O.H. Flint..." He clapped his hands. "Today is to show off for Mr. Flint, who has brought us an incredible thrilling story that will make each of us fame and fortune. I want this rehearsal to go smoothly, and when he arrives, we will show him how show business is done."

"I am not hanging from the tippy-top peak of the roof." I shaded my eyes and looked up at the hayloft where Pip leaned against the wall looking bored. "Pip."

"What?"

"How many feet up is that?"

"It's not that far up. You'll have a rope. Just in case."

"Just in case what? I fall to my imminent death or the barn decides it's giving up and I crash down with it?"

"The roof looks solid enough. And there's a mattress under the hay."

I ran my eye down the very long drop to the pile of hay and Martha Ruth fluffing it up.

"Pip says this is not in any of the volumes as far. What will Mr. Flint think of that?" I asked.

"We're improving the story." Paco bestowed a wide smile.

"Sometimes you remind me of a gambler."

"I find gambling and art closely related." He made a ninety-degree turn from me. "Horace. You look like a fine Black Bart."

Horace was unrecognizable in his heavy beard and black clothing. He had brought a cane chair and sat cross-legged in it, one of the parasols resting on his shoulder. Marjorie daubed powder to his forehead.

"Get up and come over. And leave the parasol." Once Horace neared, Paco took him by the shoulders and maneuvered him around. "Point up like you're shooting."

"I don't think that angle works," I said. "Pip can duck back in the loft but my character is tits to the breeze when he shoots. No one's going to believe he's that bad an aim."

"They'll believe what I want them to believe," Paco said.

"I think we need a dog," Marjorie said.

"No dogs, Marjorie. No dogs. No kids. No cats. No rabbits." Paco ran his fingers through his hair. "God help me. Where the hell is Jack? He should have been back an hour ago."

Martha Ruth tapped her chin and looked deep in thought. "If Black Bart shoots at Pip, then runs in the barn to set a fire," she asked, "how's he going to get out?"

"He runs and jumps on his horse. Flees the scene of the crime."

"I don't know, Paco. Wouldn't he do better to smoke them out of the barn and turn them in? He's going to get in a heap of trouble—Lily Day would know he's done something nefarious when he kidnaps her."

"How would she know that?"

"He'll smell like smoke and have that gloom of guilt around him."

Paco gave her a sidelong glance. "Is there a scene where he kidnaps you?"

"Well, no. But it would logically come next," she said.

"The barn fire is replacing the scene where the two desperadoes climb a brick bank building and run across the roof lines. Because, Adelaide, we do not have a brick building out here at Vista Verde. We do not even have a brick, unless we want them to perch on the lodge fireplace."

"Well, O.H. is coming, so we can ask him his thoughts."

"Or we can rehearse the scene, make sure Ruby does not break her neck—"

"And we're back to my problem with this. I say again I am categorically not getting on that roof."

"I am categorically saying in return you will get on that roof or I will dock your pay for each hour you do not."

"You can't do that."

He jerked his chin up. "I can. I will."

"No."

His heel dug in the dirt as he turned away. "Dooley, go get the rope. Pip, let's set this up and try it out."

"I'm not going up there, Paco."

He looked up at the barn then snapped his gaze to me and lowered his voice when he spoke. "Ruby Calhoun, every single bit of my reputation and money is riding on this. So you get up on the tiptop of that roof or I will have Sheriff Tartt and every other goddamn officer of the law out here before you blink, you understand me?" He stared at me in flat-lipped silence.

"You dock my pay, I'll tell your precious Adelaide about your more precious wife."

"Do you think that scares me? It doesn't."

I scored my nails into my palms. "Well, I—"

"Get on the roof."

ONE THING ABOUT TIN ROOFS THAT NO ONE TELLS YOU IS THEIR infernal heat factor. Had I not had my rear end padded with a pillow, I feared my rump would end up charred and medium-well before Dooley even set up the shot.

"Hey, you okay up there?" It was Pip, calling up from the safe, comfortable, and shaded hayloft. "All I can see is your dangling feet."

"If I get lockjaw from this roof, it will be your responsibility to feed and clothe me."

"If you get lockjaw, you'll die."

I knew about lockjaw. Every single time Rose and I went in our yard, my mother made sure to warn us of the dangers of rusty nails. She pounded that in hard enough I couldn't walk anywhere without sweating and dreading a nail through the shoe.

It wasn't the nail that bothered me so much. It was the idea of being bed-bound and nursed by Rose. Even at the age of six, I knew my sister well enough and had enough experience with her superior pinched smile and pretend affection. With my luck, she'd add cyanide to my water, ooh and ah over the pretty blue, and watch me drink it.

"Did you know cyanide is blue?" I asked Pip.

"What?"

"Nothing. It's very high up here and I'm thirsty."

"Look around at the scenery. Tell me what you see."

I pulled in breath. "Well, Kansas is over to my right. And to my left, I spy a fisherman waving at me from his sailboat on the Pacific Ocean."

"You're a fool."

"That is a true statement. If I was not a fool, I would have locked my cigar store door when you showed your ugly face."

"You're rattled right now. I won't take offense."

"Pip?"

"Yeah?"

"Are you wearing a rope when you come up here to get me?"

"Of course not."

"Oh." This did not comfort me.

"Black Bart shoots at me, I shoot at Black Bart. You scream. I come up the ladder, untie your rope, and we slide down the roof together."

That comforted me even less.

"Get set and ready!" Paco had taken to rolling his script notes into a megaphone.

I squeezed my eyes shut and mewled.

"It'll be all right," Pip called up. "I always make it right, don't I?"

"Pip, you think we're being had?"

"If we are, we'll figure our way out."

"I don't know, Pip."

"Have I led you wrong?"

"I think that conversation is for another—"

"Ready," Paco barked. "Set. *Action.*"

⊗

THERE WAS TOO MUCH SMOKE. SMOKE FROM THE CAP GUNS. SMOKE billowing from the barrels in the main barn and up through the hayloft and drifting about on the roof. I grabbed up my skirt and held it over my nose and mouth.

Everyone was yelling and hacking below me.

My eyes burned and teared, making everything blur brown. I had one choice: get untied and get off the roof.

But the knot that held me by the waist was too tight. No matter how much I dug, it wouldn't let up.

"Someone—" My words ended up a wheeze.

My vision wafted in and out. Voices rose and fell.

"She's still on the roof!"

"Who's going—"

"Get a bucket!"

This was it. I would be remembered only as charcoal.

My kids would never know they were my kids and not Rose's, and that they mattered greatly to me. I would never see the inside of Calhoun's Cigars again, nor drink too much at Lady Ann's Emporium, nor curse Doctor Kate for refusing me her Speciality. I would never learn to ride a bicycle or use a telephone or see Olaf at his haberdashery and tell him again I would not marry him. I'd never know if Joe Parker, my stage robbing compadre, made it to Mexico.

I wouldn't get to Mexico.

It was time to make peace with it.

I coughed one more time, then shut my eyes.

"Goodbye, world."

I let go, sliding slow along the tin roof. My back thumped on every rivet. Soon it would be over.

Then I felt a jerk. The rope cut into my waist. I was stuck midway between the peak and the edge, my head lower than my body, which was a very uncomfortable position.

The smoke had thinned out, leaving pockets of blue sky and a cloud that threatened a thunderstorm.

A woman's face blocked it all. Two blue eyes and lips pursed like a judgmental fish stared down at me. Her blue percale dress flapped about like a flag.

"Rose?"

"Yes Ruby, this is your sister Rose."

"You are not real."

"We need to get you down." She twisted to gesture to someone else.

Pip came up behind her. "What are you doing, Ruby?"

"I'm meeting my maker, Pip. I didn't know he looked like Rose."

Pip untied the rope from the post then grabbed one of my arms. "Get your ass up."

Rose snapped a look at her.

"Sorry for the language. Ruby, dear friend, we need to remove your behind from this roofage." She took my other arm and tugged me upright. "Now put on your best polite smile and give your sister your hand."

"Why?"

"Because she's not just your sister. She's O.H. Flint."

I had no idea as to the population size of America, but my guess was it ran in the millions. Millions of varied people with all sorts of talents, including that of writing cheap dime novels. I might have passed a few on the Kansas City streets and would not have been surprised at all as to their occupation. But out of that giant maelstrom of humanity I would never ever have believed my sister one of them.

She had never read a book outside of school. The only reading materials I had seen in her doily-filled house consisted of *McCalls* and that was just to see the new dress patterns. I had seen her sneer at the Woolworth's bookrack. "Pulp and nonsense," she said. Her lips did a little dance of righteousness. The last time, that pas-des-lip move forced me to buy a copy of *Fred Fearnot and the Kentucky Moonshiners* for John and mail it to him anonymously. If he got it, I do not know; if she got it, I hoped it caused a two-day bout of dyspepsia.

A thunderstorm rolled in, thankfully stopping production and a redux of the roof fiasco. After Paco's effusive introductions of "Our Glorious Creator," Dooley loaded the camera gear to the milk wagon and waved everyone in.

Jack jogged over to the buggy he'd picked Rose up with, patting Bessie's neck on the way to take the driver's seat.

"No, sir, my sister and I will not need your assistance." Rose cut in front of him, climbed on up, and unhooked the reins. "Get in the buggy, Ruby."

Jack kept a hand to Bessie's snaffle. "Are you certain—"

"Mr. Roberts, I am deeply grateful for your assistance in bringing me here. But I am certain as Psalms on Sunday that I do not need your service now."

"She means get the hell out of the way."

Jack nodded at me with a shocked look, then handed me up to my seat as if I were made of china and he deeply regretted the hammer now holding the reins. Then he leaped into the film truck and Dooley swung the door shut.

A soft-sided valise took up the space behind our seats. "You didn't bring much."

"I am not here long."

The wagon rumbled ahead. Pip, who had ridden over on Napoleon, drew up next to me, and leaned down to peer at Rose.

"Are you going to say something?" I asked.

"No. Just looking." She urged Napoleon into a lope and caught up with the wagon.

"That's Pip."

Rose's cheeks colored up. "I am aware." She shook the reins. Bessie's ears laid back, but she moved forward. Reluctantly, but forward all the same. The wheels careened from rut to rut, as if the horse were choosing to cause annoyance and pain.

"She doesn't like you," I said.

"I've done nothing but give her carrots and sugar."

"Well, you've given her a bellyache, then. We'll get her situated with a flake of hay and plenty of water, she'll be all right."

She gave me a long glance. "If mother—"

"Don't 'if mother' me. Why the hell are you here?"

"I needed to see for myself."

"See what?"

Her chin cut upward. She snapped the reins.

The rain came, plonking on the buggy roof and along the mare's back and splattering the ground. I could tell Rose was nervous. Her lips pursed and then grimaced, and she dabbed the sweat at her upper lip with the knuckle of a kid glove. She was a sharp dresser on most occasions, and her traveling clothes were new and well-made, in what I assumed was the latest fashion a banker's wife would wear. In other words, a good percale with too many pipings and eyelets and frills to be of any use in a place as rugged as this. I peeked down at her shoes and was not surprised to see them soft-leathered and not at all made for wear beyond an oriental rug.

Her eyes grazed down my face and costume, settling on my hands. "You're not taking care of your skin."

I made fists and picked a callous on my index finger with my thumb. "Never mind that. Those characters you write are nothing like me and Pip."

"They're not supposed to be. People can read the newspapers if they want to know that."

"People shouldn't believe so much of what they read. Hell, half—"

"Ruby. Language."

I scraped my nails to my thigh. "Half of what's written about us is a lie."

"Which half, though?"

"Any half."

"Which 'any half' do you want John and Emma to know?"

My heart pitched. "Which parts did you tell them?"

"The half in the dime novels. I wrote them for the children so they can see you as the Ruby Calhoun in those. Not what the papers—you do realize what they're saying. Every single morning, I opened the newspaper and I thought, 'That can't be Ruby.' Then the evening edition held something worse. The *Star* is particularly vindictive. I wrote the editors. Not one of my letters was printed. Not one. I did receive a response eventually. It was a cease-and-desist."

"Those aren't very nice."

"You've experienced one?"

"I've known of people. Friends of friends. We can leave that there." I waved my hand to stave off any further questions.

"Charles has lost his position. 'Too much scandal for a bank man,' they said."

"You have plenty of money."

"Not anymore."

"He never liked banking anyway."

"We'll have to move from Kansas City."

"Does he know you're here?"

"He thinks I'm in Independence with our cousin Ida."

"We have a cousin Ida?"

"Second cousin three times removed. You wouldn't know her."

"So, you're out here researching new opportunities, and going back to surprise him with your findings? As you can see, this a bubbling metropolis with the best schools—"

"Stop it."

"Stop what?"

"Do you take nothing seriously?"

"I take a lot—"

"No, you don't," she said, teeth clenched. "You don't think things through. You don't see the consequences and chaos you leave behind you."

Nothing ever changed with her. All judgment. Everything judgment. "Why did you come here?"

"I wanted to know."

"Know what?"

"I needed to..."

The wagon took a turn off the narrow road. "You're upsetting Bessie."

"You're upsetting me."

"I'm upsetting *you?*"

"I have had to take care of your children, your store—"

"Olaf's taking care of the store; don't make that one of the burdens you love to moan about and throw at me."

"He did a fine job selling strips of the wallpaper to the tourists. Fifty cents a strip. And the photos. And pieces of that wooden Indian."

"I don't understand."

"He sold each cigar separately with a new wrapper: *Property of Ruby Calhoun, outlaw.*"

I jerked up in the seat, gripped the front rail, and turned on her. "He sold out my store?"

"I closed the whole operation before someone bought your slop bucket."

"You closed my store?"

"My God, Ruby, you owed eight months' back rent."

"That much?"

I dropped in my seat and stared out at the lumps of clouds and the gray and red rocks. "I don't have a store."

"Mr. Hagerstrom used the profits to pay part of your debt. I paid the rest with the profit for these books. As per usual, cleaning up after you. I'm tired of cleaning up after you."

My mouth went dry. I tried to swallow but it made it dryer still. "Is that why you're here? To tell me this horrible news? You could have kept it to yourself." I smacked the leather bench between us. "Have you been gloating over this moment? Thinking the whole way on the train how fun it was going to be to tell Ruby another one of her failures?"

"That's not—"

"Yes, it is."

"I didn't come here to castigate you, Ruby. I came to—"

I twisted and jerked the latch on the door, then kicked it open and clambered out. "Go home, Rose."

"Get back in the buggy. It's raining."

"I will not." I slammed the buggy door. "I love my kids and I loved that store. You took both of them."

CHAPTER 17

I don't know how long I stood there. Rose had long gone down the road and the rain had dried up, leaving the sun to heave its heat. I unbuttoned my shirtwaist, slung it to the dirt, and then untied my corset and slapped it to the ground, too. I put my hands to my waist and picked at a seam of my chemise.

"It's too hot," I muttered, then grabbed up both bits of clothing and trudged forward. The air shimmered and steamed around the rocks and bushes. A couple of cactuses stuck out between the grasses, so I kept my eyes down to avoid any such other surprises. My boots crunched on the dry roadbed. The buzz of cicadas sawed at my ears, then it stopped of a sudden, and a low rumble took its place. I shaded my eyes and peered down the way the sound came.

Far out, the valley darkened with dots of brown and red. The ground trembled as a herd of wild mustangs came into view. They galloped on the horizon line, shoulder to shoulder and haunch to haunch, necks stretched out and manes flying. Roans and bays. A couple pintos and a dapple gray. The earth churned around their hooves, swirling up so it seemed they ran on clouds.

"Would you look at that," I whispered.

I ran my eye from leader to lagger. Then I tensed. A single gray-brown mule straggled a length or two behind. He looked much like Theo, all barrel chested and big-eared—

My heart knocked against my throat. "Oh hell."

I lunged forward, running as fast as I could. "Theodore, you damn mule, you—"

My lungs burned, and the gulps of hot air didn't help at all. "Theo!"

He turned at the edge of the herd, slowing enough I thought he might, after all, have heard my call. Then the string of mustangs disappeared over the low mesa as if they'd jumped off the edge of the earth.

A horse punched across my vision, the rider laid low on the horse's neck, hat brim flipped up in the wind. The horse lunged to the top of the mesa, then stopped and stamped in place, tail high. Then the rider turned to zigzag back down to the canyon floor.

I heard the pound of hooves before I saw sight of them coming straight at me. I jumped out of the way just in time. Satan pounded down the narrow path, his hooves reaching out and clawing the earth. Pip bolted by, the reins wrapped around her hands and hanging on tight to a hank of his mane.

I hopped back to the path. "What the hell? Are you trying to kill me?"

She wheeled Satan around and trotted up. "We got trouble." She dug a torn square of newspaper from her saddle bag.

QUINN-CALHOUN GANG SPOTTED NEAR MAXEY – ATTEMPTED MURDER REPORTED

Mr. Garvin Pearse of Maxey, CO, has been grievously injured at the hands of the Quinn-Calhoun gang. His wife, Mrs. M. Pearse, tells the *La Junta Tribune* that the couple was ambushed while doing laundry, held at knife and gun point, then tied up and $7.95 cash taken. "That was the last of our money," Mrs. Pearse states. "I do not know how I shall pay his doctor bill." Mr. Pearse, who suffers from an undisclosed heart condition worsened by the vicious attack, is now bed-bound.

The Pearses lost their crops and livestock to the twelve-year drought. Mrs. Pearse refuses to leave her property and vows to die on the land they homesteaded in 1887. Any donation to assist the Garvin's plight can be sent to G. Garvin. Maxey. LA JUNTA-LAMAR-TIMPAS-THACHER RESIDENTS LOCK YOUR DOORS. 8pm curfew. All trains will be checked by local law enforcement. Colorado and Kansas marshals are on route to Maxey and Picketwire Canyon.

I crumpled the newspaper. "This is a load of lies."

"We need to go," Pip said.

"Where did you get this?"

"Jack brought the paper back. Your sister...well, let's say she had a fit when she read this."

"Everyone's seen it?"

"We got to go, Ruby. There'll be lawmen scrambling all around here." She reached her hand down. "Get on up. I didn't have time to get another horse, so—"

"My sister thinks I'm the devil."

"Be that as it may, you got to get up. Now." She kicked her boot out of stirrup so I could take it. I hopped around until I got a toehold then slung myself up behind her.

She dug her heels in tight and Satan bolted forward.

"Stop!" Coming fast behind, Martha Ruth waved and then slapped her reins to a dainty little buckskin's neck.

"Pip!" I squeezed her ribs to get her to pay some attention. "Pip, slow up."

"Whoa." Pip leaned back. Satan stopped on a dime and I nearly pitched off.

"Can you warn me of that next time?" I asked.

Martha Ruth pulled the pony beside us. She took in a gulp of air and then let out it. "Your sister. He followed her."

"Who followed her?" Pip asked.

"Boudreaux."

"Oh, God," she whispered.

My heart slammed against my chest. Barnabé Boudreaux. Gambler, ex-Bible salesman, and Cullen Wilder's henchman. He'd tracked me and Pip and Verna Rolfe, all with the intent of getting us together so Cullen could take revenge for a slight we had not committed. When he got Verna and Pip locked in a basement, he thought it would be fun and games to shoot through the floor at them.

"Oh, no." Martha Ruth paled. "That's the man I hit in the head. He's not going to forget—"

"Pip wanted to bury him alive."

"That was Verna, let's clear that up."

"That's not how I remember it, Pip."

"Well you should." She swallowed. "Are you sure it's him?"

"Big man," I asked, "with a twig broom mustache, wobbly-belly, and fancy duds?"

"That's him," I said.

Pip tapped my knee. "Get down for a minute. I need to think."

I slung my leg over Satan's rump and dismounted.

Pip hopped off and handed me the reins so she could pace. "We've gone soft." She worked her jaw side to side and clamped her gaze on Martha Ruth. "Did he see you?"

"No, I was in the bedroom changing and heard a man outside my window talking to Jack."

"Jack?" I twisted the reins up tight.

"And Paco. Paco was hopping mad and waving his arms like a windmill."

"What were they talking about?"

"Boudreaux said one was lying and the other was an idiot, and I do not know which was which, and then they moved. I knew I needed to get on out here to you. I was right behind you, Pip. I yelled for you."

"I didn't hear." She crossed her arms and peered down the path the direction of Vista Verde. Then she gave a sharp nod of her head. "We need to move on from here."

"What are you talking about? My sister is in danger. We can't just leave her there. We can't leave any of those people. You know what Boudreaux's like. There's no telling what he'll...I'm going to have to hand myself in to him and then he can get the reward and go on his way. I think that's the best plan. I think I'm going to do that."

Pip grabbed both my arms and shook. "Get yourself together."

"I am together."

"You're dressed in a chemise and your petticoat," Martha Ruth said. "Pip may be right—"

"He followed Rose, Pip." The sky above me blurred. "Why'd she come out here? Why'd she do something so stupid? This is all her fault."

"I think it's my fault." Martha Ruth chewed her lip.

"Why would you think that?" Pip asked.

"I don't know, it might be."

"I'm going back." I lifted my foot to a stirrup to mount up. Quick as a whip, Satan bared his teeth and had them an inch from my knee. "Can I take your horse, Martha Ruth?"

Pip frowned. "Who else came with Boudreaux?"

"There was another. He was going through the rooms looking for you two. That's when I climbed out the window." Martha Ruth lifted her hands and dropped them. "What are we going to do?"

Pip paced and stomped in a circle. She muttered a few curse words. "He have weapons?"

"Two. I don't know about his friend."

"We have none. Dammit. We're better off—"

"I'm going back." I grabbed the buckskin's saddle to haul myself up. "If you think I'm going to turn tail on those people, you are very wrong. I knew you were cold, Pip, but not this frigid. I am going back and I will tell Mr. Boudreaux—"

Pip yanked me away from the pony. "Did I say I was leaving?"

"You're not?"

"Of course not. Your sister is there. Let's find a place to sit tight until it's near dark. Then we head up to the ranch and get the lay of the situation."

"And then what?" Martha Ruth asked.

Pip swung herself up on Satan. "Then we've got people we need to save."

It had grown chill as we waited for dusk. My arms broke out in chicken skin and I shivered. It would have been worse had Martha Ruth not found the clothes I'd torn off in a pique earlier in the day. They stunk of smoke from the disastrous scene, but at least I had some protection from the brambles and cold.

"We'll never make it to the house without someone seeing us." Pip trudged from one end of the outcropping we'd tucked up in to the other. "Too much open space."

Martha Ruth knelt down, picked up a stone and drew a square in the dirt. "This is the house." She walked her knuckles at a diagonal from a corner and drew another square. "This is the barn." Again the knuckles walked. "There's a dry creek runs along behind with a lot of brush. You can crawl up along that."

Pip crouched down and pointed. "To here. There's a line of willows..." She made three Xs which Martha Ruth brushed away.

"That's not where those trees are at, Pip. They're here."

"All you had to do was move one of my Xs and we'd be in the same place."

"You need to learn some specificity."

"And you both need to hurry up." I paced in Pip's place. "Before my sister gets killed."

"She's not getting killed," Pip said.

"You don't know that."

Martha Ruth swung her gaze between us. "He didn't look too happy."

So Pip picked up two stones and drew a plan in the dirt.

Martha Ruth was to take care of the horses as three Savers of People-in-Danger might get confusing. I made sure to point out that, in the past, this had been the case. Then Pip got mad because she was the one mostly in charge of the over-complicated plans and also the ones that were conking-people-on-the-head plans.

"This needs to be simple. You need to sneak up as if you were invisible," Martha Ruth said. "The only way to get from that barn to that house is with the duck hunting suits."

"The..." I stopped pacing. "Excuse me?"

Pip sat back on her haunches. "Volume Two. Ruby, I cannot believe you did not read these."

Martha Ruth nodded. "That's right. Pip and Ruby creep all the way across a field and right under Black Bart's nose using those. My daddy has one from Sears Roebuck. It won't matter what crosses your path. Pheasants, turkeys, wild geese. They'll just la-di-dah on by, thinking, oh, that's just an old pile of hay. Why, those bad men might step right on top of you and not have a suspicion their quarry is under their feet."

"We're going to disguise ourselves as hay bales?" I asked.

"There's eyeholes."

"Martha Ruth," Pip said. "I could kiss you right now."

"I'M NOT GOING TO DRESS UP IN THAT GRASS SUIT THING." I MADE A half-circle around one of the offending objects. Pip dragged the other from the back of the Silver Star wagon and onto the barn floor. The suits —stalks of hay and grass and what not—boasted armholes and eye holes.

"Those look like a couple thatched houses missing their window glass," I said.

"Do you have a better idea?"

"I'm already all cut up from belly-crawling across that field. We might as well snake our way to the house."

Pip shoved me out of the barn.

"Here goes nothing." She sprinted across the field, the grass thingamajigs bumping along on the bushes and rocks.

THE DISGUISES TURNED OUT TO BE QUITE ROOMY, ENOUGH FOR ME to sit cross-legged with my elbows to my knees. I leaned over to peer through the eyeholes, which gave me a view of Pip's grass hut and nothing much else.

"Pip?"

"Shhh."

"What's going on?"

"They're looking around the barn."

"How can you know that?"

"I see the lamps."

"We're going to get caught, Pip."

"No, we're not."

"I got to get word to Rose I haven't run out on her."

Voices drifted out toward us. I could not make out any words.

I wrapped my arms tight around me and squeezed my eyes tight. Boudreaux, or one of his men, must have been watching Rose for weeks. Maybe he even had another follow the children or Charles. Rose wouldn't have known because she would not think through the probabilities of such things. She'd go about her day and wonder who the lurker on the corner was, but then decide it was one of the real estate agents who harassed the neighbors into splitting their lots for fairness's sake to incoming residents.

She would not think she had become part of the noose that would hang me or the grave he might make me dig for myself.

"Pip?" I pushed my forehead against the stalks that made up the helmet so it bumped hers.

"What do you want?"

"I need to know you're there."

"I'm here."

"Are we sleeping out here?"

"Would you be quiet?"

"There's coyotes and bobcats and such. I thought after they all went to bed we could share one of these together. There's quite a bit of room. I'll make sure you don't snore as that'll wake up the whole lodge."

WE HUNCHED IN OUR INDIVIDUAL DISGUISES-SLASH-HUNTING HUTS for what seemed an interminable number of hours. The crickets picked up their song, and the horses in the corrals blew out breaths. Both my feet fell asleep and when I shifted around to solve that, my rear end took up slumber.

I was growing restless. I shoved the hut with my hip until it was right close to Pip's and I could whisper and be heard. "Turn your hut around so I can at least see your eyes."

"If I do that, I can't be lookout."

"Is there anything to see?"

"It's too dark."

"Think they left?"

"Could be."

"It'd be nice if someone..." A waft of aggressively rancid smoke stopped my talk. It was from a cigar.

A pungent, potent, cheap-as-all-get-out cigar.

One I had smelled before.

It grew stronger, rolling around in the duck hut like a loose snake.

There came the crunch of a pair of footsteps on the dry grasses, coming from the left and lodge way. Those were followed by another set coming from the right and corral way.

"Ladies, ladies, you are around. I know it. Yessiree, I do."

My heart leapt to my throat. I slapped both hands over my mouth to keep a yelp of surprise from tumbling out.

It was Boudreaux.

"I ain't seen them anywhere." The other man made a sound like he was toeing the earth with his boot.

"Who's where?"

"Nichols' on the east ridge. I put Rodriguez at the main gate. He'll flank the west ridge."

"Uh-uh." Boudreaux puffed the cigar. "Uh-uh."

"They could be on their way to Trinidad by now, even over Raton Pass."

"Noooo." He elongated it and then chuckled. "They're here. I can smell it."

The grass crackled as the two moved off.

"Yessiree..."

MY GRANDMA OTTOLINE ONCE SAID THAT FEARS ARE WORSE THAN reality. They take on gargantuan features and are given names like "No Hope" or "It Was Her Fault, Not Mine." She liked to tell me this when I was about to get a whooping for some infraction that had disturbed my mother's equilibrium. I'd be hiding under the bed and Grandma'd be sitting up on it so all I saw were her wool stockings and scuffed heel lace-ups. I'd keep my ear on the click of her knitting needles, which she clacked louder in response to mother's mutterings and stomping around in the hall.

"You know what that girl did, Mama?" Mother loved to shout through doors.

"I suppose you're going to tell me."

"She ate half the cake batter."

"Did she?"

"Then she added water to what was left to make it look the right amount."

"Clever."

"That's not clever. That's the evil she gets from her daddy."

"What're you going to do about it, Mattie?"

"I'm going to tan her hide. I'm going to use that wooden spoon she ate everything off of."

"Damn child..." Grandma lunged up and yanked open the door. "You give me that spoon. I'll take care of the what-for."

"She in there?"

"Leave it to me and go make another cake."

We both knew Mama had her ear planted tight to the door. Grandma would wait a beat or two, then get a huffy voice. "Ruby Red Shoes, lift up your skirt, drop your knickers and get your what-for."

She smacked the inside of her hand.

"Ow!" I said it as many times as required.

Grandma would then pull open the door, hand out the spoon, and say, "Justice has been served."

With that, she'd get back to her knitting and I'd get a lemon candy.

"Fear is worse than the reality, Ruby Red Shoes. You remember that."

I tried many times because I loved my Grandma Ottoline fiercely and she had never led me wrong.

But she wasn't there for Frank, nor Cullen, both of whom made fear seem like a lollipop dream.

And she had never met Barnabé Boudreaux.

☙❦❧

ONCE EVERYTHING WENT BACK TO QUIET, AND ALL MY TOES FELL asleep, Pip rustled out of her hut and scratched at mine. "Lift up."

I half-stood so she could crawl under the edge and squeeze in.

"It's a little tight by the head." I twisted my shoulders to get a bit of room, and pulled my knees up to my chest. She did the same, so we faced each other.

"This is not good, Pip."

"I know."

"He's dangerous. There's no telling what he's going to do up at the house. How much are we worth, anyway?"

"Enough he can pay off all the men blocking our exits."

"I don't want to be caught in a duck hut." My shoulder knocked against hers.

"We need guns," she said. "We don't have any guns."

"Pip stop breathing like that, you're going to use up all the oxygen."

"We were so close, Ruby. One payday away and—" She dropped her head to her knees.

"You're not crying, are you?"

"I'm tired, Ruby. So damn tired." Her back shook as she cried.

I rubbed it, said a few 'There, there's' and spied out the armhole situated by my right knee. There was nothing but low moonlight and dark. Not even a shift of breeze through the willows and brush.

"Pip, I'm going to tell you something important, so you listen. While this situation appears dire, we cannot let our fears and exhaustion beat us down. We need to buck up. I need you to have a clear head for that, so wipe your nose. On your sleeve and not mine, please."

She let out one last sob, then covered her face with both hands and took in deep long breaths.

"Are you feeling better now? A good cry is a cleanser."

"You're telling *me* to buck up?"

"I've always relied on you, Pip. You've always been the one ahead of the fears. That did cause a few encounters to go a little haywire, but still and all—"

"Ruby, we are squeezed together inside of the equivalent of a hay bale with four to five guns ready to shoot if we make one wrong move."

I straightened up and backhanded her thigh. "Have any of the papers ever said 'Dead or Alive'?"

"I don't think—"

"They have not. No one gets a reward unless we're turned in alive. We can make any wrong move we want, at least in the near future." My head buzzed with a golden noise. "Tonight this is the Calhoun-Quinn Gang. I'll be first on the bill for once."

"What are you talking about?"

"Get on up. We're going to turn ourselves in."

CHAPTER 18

I Come Face to Face with My Enemy—A Deal is Struck

Two things occurred to me after we shoved out of our hidey hole and started to stride confidently across the field:

One—this idea was not well thought through.

Two—I had no time to drag up more details save getting Boudreaux's focus on his greed and not his gun.

For I had no confidence in the 'Keep Them Alive If You Want Your Reward' article dissemination I had sold Pip on. I hoped she believed it and I hoped it was true. We were valuable commodities at this point; enough I hoped for Boudreaux to take us and leave the rest of the troupe alone.

"In for a nickel, in for a dollar, right?" I glanced around. Pip wasn't standing next to me. I crouched down to see if she'd had second thoughts and taken up residence in a grass suit again, then crawled along the line of willows hoping to hear her footsteps or see her creeping along. When the tree line ended, I stood tight in their shadow and stared back toward the duck blinds, wondering if she'd chickened out or decided one of us heading for a prison cell was enough.

A hand came around my wrist and tugged me through branches and brush.

"What—"

The other hand clamped over my mouth.

I kicked and dug my heels to the ground, but the man's arms were strong like lead, and he had a good foot of height on me and at least double the weight. He smelled like dirt and old sweat and cologne, which made me want to wretch.

"It'd be easier if you stop fighting." He hauled me around in a semi-circle. My skirt caught on a prickly pear, jerking us back. His grip loosed as he stumbled, giving me a split second to bite into his palm. "You little—Jesus, you need to let—"

I bit harder.

Then all I felt was a sear of pain as he twisted my arm around my back and bent it further than it was meant to go.

"You going to let go?"

I did.

"Will you be quiet if I remove my hand?"

I nodded, for I was running out of breath.

"I always knew you were a sensible woman."

I fell to my knees and made a fuss pulling in air so I could scan around for Pip.

Boudreaux brushed dirt from the sleeves of his checked jacket and tugged the cuffs of his shirt. He looked the same, with his broom-size mustache and mean mouth. He held his palm up and considered it, tilting his head and blowing a breath through his lips. "I hope you don't have rabies."

I wiped at my nose and clambered upright. "That was uncalled for."

"Maybe so, maybe so." He hooked his thumbs to his belt, making sure I saw the two pistols he wore. "One can't be too careful, especially with your reputation."

"I was coming up to the house to have a friendly conversation with you."

"Were you?"

"Yes, sir, I was."

"Just you?"

"Who else but me? You see anyone else around this netherlands?"

His eyes narrowed and he looked at the grass suits. Now that I was on this side of them and a few dozen feet away, I saw how they glistened in the moonlight. The phrase "sitting ducks" was appropriate for the two monstrosities.

"Those are excellent blinds, should you be in a swamp in Alabama. I haven't seen many cattails around here." He sucked saliva through his teeth. "If I were a betting man, which I am, there's fifty-fifty odds your compadre is tucked up in one of those."

"I told you, it's just me."

"How's about a little wager?" He took a pistol from his belt, pointed it at the left lump of grass and cocked. "If she's inside there, I win. And if she's not, I shoot that hat of hers laying on the ground just over yonder and then try the other."

My heart knocked hard against my chest. I rubbed my upper lip and chin, my hand coming away slick with sweat. "Don't you want to know what I was coming to talk to you about?"

"Don't you want to know how I found you?"

"You followed my sister, who is not savvy on heathen ways." I planted my hands to my hips and lifted my chin. "Did you kill Cullen?"

"Now, why would I do that?"

"How come you're not under lock and key, seeing as how you tried to murder us back in Kansas?"

"You have the situation reversed. I was a poor victim to your abominable temper. I got a chunk of hair missing because of you. You know how bad a scalp sunburns?"

"Maybe it was you who took care of Cullen. My guess is he didn't pay you."

"You have a suspicious mind. Now, which should I shoot? Left duck blind, or right?"

"I don't care. You shoot either. I'm hungry and I'm going to go eat." I crossed directly in front of the path of his weapon, tramped over to the damn dumb suits, and swiped up Pip's hat. I sent a single prayer. Then I kicked both the grass atrocities over. "No one here. I guess I win."

My knees at this point knocked hard enough under my skirts I'd have bruises until the next century.

Boudreaux stuffed the pistol back to its holster. "I knew that."

"What'd Carnelia make for supper?" I asked.

"Pulled pork and some cactus thing."

"She is fond of that cactus." In for a nickel, in for a dollar. "Well, come on. I'm ready to go, so you can call off your search dogs."

He took a match from his vest pocket and stuck it between his teeth. "There's vanilla cake, too. Strawberry filling."

"I like a good apricot upside-down cake. Soon as we get to civilization and you collect your fee—"

"You're not worth enough on your own." He stepped close, gripped my elbow, and sauntered toward the ranch house. "I have men to pay. Travel expenses and so forth and on and on." He jiggled my arm. "What's the name of your third associate?"

My stomach dropped. "I don't know who you mean."

"Yes, you do. The pretty one gets mentioned nearly every paper I read. So you are telling me a lie right now. Yessiree, you are."

"You know you can't trust what you read." My elbow tickled where he held it. I flinched. So he dug his fingers in tight.

"There's nowhere to run, Ruby Calhoun. If there's someone you need to warn."

"There's no one I need to warn. They both abandoned me here."

"Why would they do that?"

"They just did." My throat went dry. "They just...did."

"That's too bad." He stuck out his bottom lip and gave a mocking doleful look. Then he sucked it back and smiled. "I was going to let your sister go. I think I'll keep her for ransom."

I bit my lip hard so as not to cry out.

"People pay a lot for mothers."

"And everyone else?"

"Why they're not valuable at all."

A WHIP-THIN MAN, WHO I GUESSED WAS THE ONE TALKING TO Boudreaux earlier, kept the film troupe and my sister under his thumb. It wasn't because he was a threatening sort. He was only a couple inches taller than me and a couple inches leaner around the hips. It wasn't his frightening scowl; that looked about as out of place as a frown on a teddy bear.

It was the two guns he held.

They did have rather long barrels, so I could understand the cringing and shaking going on, at least by Horace who took refuge behind his wife and Rose who looked about ready to disintegrate. Dooley was grayish. Paco sweat like a waterfall, his handkerchief sopping enough it needed a wring out. Marjorie had a stoic look she'd no doubt practiced in the mirror for when she played some queen.

Jack was not among the captives.

Boudreaux gestured to the porch steps. "You first."

"Such a gentleman." But the good manners were more likely meant to block me should I choose to run.

My feet, to be honest, wished I would.

"I thought there was cake." My voice took on an unnatural pitch.

The young Praetorian squinted at me. One of his eyes took on a twitch, so he stopped. "I ate it."

"Who are you?"

"I'm Will."

"Will. Hello, Will."

His trousers hung dangerously on his hips, and if I were him I'd be thinking they needed a good pull up.

"There's a pair of suspenders in one of the costume trunks which might be of use." I swung a look to the frightened mass I considered my friends and pursed my lips. There had to be a way out of this where no one got hurt and my sister got home free. "Could you ask your monkey to drop his guns?"

"Hey, don't call me that."

Boudreaux gave him a nod.

I relaxed an inch as I heard metal slide into the holster. Then I raised my arms and dropped them. "Mr. Boudreaux has come to collect me for his reward and take my sister for ransom because my desperado friends left me high and dry. Then he's going to shoot all of you, or Will here might. We only returned so I could pack."

Rose let out a strange wheeze.

"Mr. Boudreaux, my sister has asthmatic attacks. Would you mind if she went inside to lie down?"

He ambled over to her and leaned in close. She arched back until her head bumped Dooley's chest. "You seemed fine on the train out here."

"It's called sudden onset." I mimed a cough, hoping she'd catch on to the act.

"I'm going to be sick," she said, not at all taking up my cue.

"Get back, Mr. Boudreaux, there's an explosiveness—"

A loud thud came from the other corner. Horace had fainted. Paco shouldered past Marjorie to attend him. "I think he needs water."

A low moan rolled across the wood floor.

"Does he have asthma, too?"

"Gout," I said.

Dooley jerked forward.

"No." Boudreaux's pistol was pulled, cocked, and pressed to Dooley's chest.

Will aimed his, too.

I clenched my jaw and scraped my teeth. This was the moment Pip normally crashed through on her horse and shot off her guns and caused general fear and ruckus. But there was just everyone breathing in various states of panic and a cricket singing away under the boards.

"Have you ever seen a moving picture?" Paco blurted.

Boudreaux, pistol still at Dooley's chest, glanced at Paco. "I saw one with a maid—"

"Not that kind."

"Then, no, I cannot say I am a connoisseur of such art."

"Not art. Business. An expensive business that requires much capital that comes from...Can I put down my hands?"

Boudreaux nodded.

Paco took out a handkerchief, wiped his brow and stuffed the wet cloth to his trouser pocket. "This film, if you let us finish it, is going to make its investors very very rich."

"What is 'very very rich?'"

"You'll never have to work, or whatever you do, again. Should you choose to invest."

"Give me numbers."

Paco shoved his hands to his pockets and rocked on his heels. He narrowed his eyes and considered Boudreaux. "Twenty percent of net profits for the first year—"

"I sold Bibles for a higher commission than that."

"Twenty-five—"

"Fifty."

Paco started to laugh but it came out a wheeze. "Fifty percent then five percent net on future—"

"Fifty."

"Fifty percent installments all predicated on distribution agreements with various entities, a majority stake in Silver Star Productions. All in all we're looking at hundred thousand, maybe one-oh-three minus production costs."

I might have believed Paco's flim-flam, if Dooley's mouth wasn't hanging so far open I could see his tonsils.

Boudreaux pocketed his gun. His faced screwed up into nugget of greed as he worked the high maths. "All right."

Paco moved to clap Boudreaux's back but thought better of it. "We'll need to draw up an agreement."

"Draw it up."

"It needs to be legally written. We could get that done in a heartbeat if we weren't out in the middle of nowhere. How about in the morning we head to La Junta and put ink to the deal and—"

"That's right up the road, Mr. Boudreaux," I said. "You can get all your business done at once and let these people go on with their lives."

"I'll take your payroll box, too."

Paco swallowed. "It's not here."

"Were you not going to pay these people their wages?" Boudreaux did his saliva thing.

"Of course, I...it's not here."

"So, where is it?"

"La Junta."

"La Junta."

"Listen, I have three thousand dollars I can request, in La Junta. It'll take a telegram. But we have to finish the film. No product from me, no money for you. And you need to promise everyone else goes free."

"Why would I do that?"

"One hundred thousand future dollars is why." He stuck out his hand.

Boudreaux sneered at Paco's hand like it was a dead trout. "What were you going to do with Miss Calhoun and Miss Quinn? Once you were done using them for your own profit?"

Paco lifted his chin. "Make them rich and get them to safety."

"And are you done using them?"

"We have a few more scenes left, isn't that right, Dooley?"

Dooley cleared his throat and took a notebook from the chest pocket on his shirt. "Let's see, there's…We have the bear attack, posse in the chaparral, um…then the final um…" He flipped the page, ripping one and trying to catch it as it fluttered down.

Boudreaux pinched it up and handed it to Dooley. "How long will that take?"

"Weather holds up, two or three days."

Boudreaux took a cigar case from his vest pocket "You have tomorrow."

A shot rang out along a ridge. It was answered by one on the opposite side.

His mouth curled into a smile. "If Pip Quinn's up there, my men will find her. Dead or alive. Makes no difference to me."

CHAPTER 19

A Glimmer of Hope and then None

Will was rough with Rose and me, dragging us to the bedroom and shoving us in with a boot in the back. I did not know how he treated the other four, but I feared it the same.

Rose's legs gave out. She crumpled to the floor and buried her face in her hands.

"Don't be a baby." Will stepped over her and ripped open her satchel, flinging out clothing and then gripping her purse. "This the only money you have?"

She trembled all over and shrunk back against the wall.

"Leave her alone. She's nothing to do with any of this."

"You got money?" His eyes, full of a desperate greed, caught on me.

"Are you collecting that money for your boss or are you keeping this theft to yourself?"

"I asked if you had money."

"I have not a penny to my name. But feel free to toss everything else around. I'll just peek my head out to keep Boudreaux appraised of your activity." Now I stepped over Rose and put my hand to the doorframe.

"I'm leaving." He stuffed bills and coins to a pocket on his denim shirt and chucked the empty purse to Rose's lap.

I shoved his bony chest. "That was uncalled for."

"Shut up." He shouldered past me to the hall, then spun so he was nose to nose with me. "Shut the door. And keep it shut."

"If it keeps your frog-toe breath from killing me, it'll be my pleasure." I reached to swing it shut. "You're going to need to move aside, Rose."

She mewled, but shifted herself so the door could be slammed and locked tight. It made a satisfying thomp, but I gave it a kick for good measure.

"Damnation to hell and back." I picked up Rose's scattered clothing and stuffed them to the satchel.

Rose took in shallow gasps of air. Her eyelids fluttered.

"Don't you faint on me. We got a situation and I need you to have a clear mind." I dropped to my knees to peer under Pip's bed, hoping against hope Pip's rifle was there. But there was just a pair of shoes knocked to their side. Nothing came from searching under the other two beds. I made a circle of the room. There weren't many hiding places. Just the shared dresser. The rifle was too big for the drawers.

I slapped my thigh. "How could you miss that man following you?"

Her lips trembled and she tried to answer. But nothing came out that made any sense so she gave up and lay flat out like a corpse, hands laid over her chest.

"It would be preferable to me if you didn't look quite so..."

She rolled her head toward me. "So, this is your life."

"In a nutshell."

"I made it worse. I didn't mean to."

I could say she indeed did, but that didn't solve a thing. "Let's not think about that now. Let's concentrate on the very next steps." I rubbed my forehead and took a few stomps one way and then the other. "We finish the film, Paco hands over the payroll in La Junta. You're free and Horace and Marjorie and Dooley and—"

"He's going to hold me hostage. You said so—"

"I won't let that happen."

"How will you stop it?"

"I'll figure it out."

She sat up, arms clutched around her knees, and stared a hole in the floor. Then she turned her head to consider me. "It's in the mattress."

"The rifle?"

"I have a derringer I keep tucked on my side of the bed. Charles would not approve, if he knew."

"You have a derringer?"

"Double-barreled."

I frowned and stared.

"Unloaded, of course. There are children in the house."

Which made the gun useless in case of an intrusion, but I did understand the point.

A ping sounded against the window glass.

"We're being shot at." Rose lurched to the side and rolled under the bed.

"Rose, if that were a bullet you would have been purchasing my gravestone." I shook my head, kneeled on my bed and peered into the dark. A hand floated in front of me, then Pip's head popped into view.

I pulled the window up a notch. "Where the hell you been?" I hissed.

"Give me the gun." The words weren't much louder than her breath. She glanced away, then back, and mimed shooting a rifle.

I twisted around to my belly and leaned over the edge of the bed. "Psst. Rose." I made the same gun action, pointed at the mattress then the dresser, then made the universal symbol for 'find the damn scissors in the etui in the top right drawer and cut the damn mattress open.'

I had never seen someone make as much haste to act on a command, but she had those scissors out and stabbed into the side of the mattress before I could turn back to Pip.

"You should have run, Pip."

She curled her fingers to the window frame. "We've got it all figured. Everything'll be fine and dandy by lunch time. Jack—"

"Jack?"

"He's helping. We're confronting Boudreaux with an element of surprise attached."

The bed dipped and springs creaked as Rose kneeled next to me. She slid the rifle through the gap in the window and followed that gift with the box of cartridges.

Pip dropped down from her tiptoes.

I pressed my cheek to the windowsill. "Pip."

"Yeah?"

"If I don't see you again, you've been a very nice friend."

"You'll see me. We got to get your sister back home so she can raise those brats of yours."

There was a rustle of bushes as she took off in the night.

Rose crossed her arms tight over her stomach. "They're not brats. And I want to see them again." Her chin trembled. "What are they going to do without a mother? And don't say that's you."

I could have let her have it for that. Instead, I coiled my anger in as I was too tired for a drag out fight and also on the edge of giddy, being as Pip and Jack had a plan. "Knowing Pip," I said instead, "we're going to be riding out in the morning. How long's it been since you've been on a horse?"

"A horse?"

"Yeah. With a saddle and—"

A sharp wrap on the door startled me. Dooley's voice came muffled through the wood. "Bear scene. Seven-thirty a.m. Marjorie's replacing Pip."

⚜

THE SUN ROSE, COLORING THE ROOM PEACH AND GOLD. I JERKED UP and slung my legs off the bed. "Rise and shine, sister. We're going to get saved today."

But Rose pulled the cover taut over her head. "Leave me be."

"Don't you want to see your stories filmed?"

"No."

I tugged at the sheet, but she clenched her fists and held tight. "Rose, you need to be ready for the saving."

"Come get me when it's done. I want to go home."

"Who doesn't," I muttered, then lifted the window frame so she'd at least have some fresh air. "I'd suggest being at least dressed and ready. Rose?"

"Mmmph."

"You're going to be back in Kansas City by tomorrow, all right?"

"And if not?"

"I'd suggest concentrating your attention on the other."

I dragged on my chemise and petticoats, then thought better of those and instead pulled on my old trousers, a blouse and my silly cream-colored boots. Then I rolled my hair up, popped Pip's hat on for good luck, and strolled down the hall to the dining room. "A happy good morning to you all on this most beautiful day."

Carnelia put tortillas and eggs and rancho beans on the table, but the only ones who had an appetite were Boudreaux and fuzzy-lip Will.

"I may need to steal your cook." Boudreaux wiped his lips with his napkin then tilted the egg bowl to his plate, shaking it to make sure he'd not missed a single bit.

Jack, in costume and caked in face paint, squinted out the dining room window towards the barn and corrals. "The horses are restless."

Paco walked over and peered out. "Storm?"

"I don't know. Something." He turned to Boudreaux. "Am I allowed to go see what's eating them?"

"Will'll go with you."

Will pulled at his belt and gave a serious nod. "I'm going with you." He yanked the screen door wide and gestured to Jack. "You first."

"Throw me a towel, Ruby."

I grabbed one from the makeup table and tossed it to Jack.

He stuffed it around his collar to keep it clean should his makeup run, gave a wink and flash of his dimple, then stepped outside.

"You're not in this scene?" Boudreaux tore a tortilla in two, chewed up half, then rolled the other and dipped it in the beans.

I shook my head. "Just watching."

"Where's your sister?"

He really was a pig of a man. He'd gone downhill since we'd first met on the streetcar a lifetime ago. I remembered him dapper in his gambler wear, with well-manicured nails and a shining pinky ring.

"What happened to your ring?" I asked.

"Never mind that. What happened to your sister?"

"She's poorly this morning."

"Missing her own artwork come to life?"

"Something like that."

"I might write a few of those. I was fond as a boy of *Deadwood Dick*. Perhaps I'll carry on the O.H. Flint line. Introduce a few different characters."

"She can write more herself."

"Maybe so, maybe not."

A door banged open in the hall. Marjorie swanned into the great room and over to the mirror. She didn't look at all like movie character Pip. Her skirt was badly hemmed and her lace-up shoes didn't have a bit of similarity to Pip's made-for-all-situations boots. The worst insult was the tiny spit of a hat she wore atop a bundle of curls. She swiped a jar of lip stain from the table and dabbed it on.

"I want to talk about my motivations, Poppy."

Paco blinked like he'd got a spit of lemon in his eyes. "You stand at the bottom of the hill, Marjorie. The bear attacks you from above. Claws out."

"So, fear. Mixed perhaps with a longing for the past."

"I think the motivation is 'Please don't let me die.'"

She rouged her cheeks. "That's very thin."

"I'm filming you from the back. Your back, bear's claws."

"We'll see." Her tiny smug smile dropped like lead when she caught sight of Boudreaux. "Mr. Boudreaux."

"Mrs. Understudy."

"You're mistaken," Paco said. "She's the star. No one knows where the real—she walked off the set, what, three days ago?"

Boudreaux squinted at me. "That's why you were calling and calling for her last night?"

"That's exactly right. I do say, Mr. Boudreaux, I think she's gone for good. Taken one of the horses and *poof*—off she has gone. We had a terrible falling out."

"*Poof.* Just like that." He stuck a toothpick to his teeth and began a thorough pick-and-clean. "Yessiree."

⁂

"NO GUNS ON THE SET." DOOLEY CROSSED HIS ARMS AND STEPPED away from the camera. He bumped into Will. "Excuse me."

"Sorry."

Boudreaux, who had squeezed into a wicker chair Will carried out, took his cigar from his lips and held it out. "Why?"

"It's the rule. No guns."

He pointed the cigar at the holster and sidearm Marjorie wore. "What about her?"

"That's not real," Dooley said.

"It looks real."

"It's not."

"I did want to ask about this." Marjorie patted the holster as if it were a sweet little puppy. "Would I not use this, Poppy? With a bear charging me? It would be tremendously exciting if—"

"Take it off," Paco said. "Give it to me."

She unbuckled the belt and held it out to Paco. "Artistically and realistically—"

"This is a bare hands and wooden spoon struggle."

"I don't feel it."

"Wooden spoon. Bare hands. Just as written in the books." He set the holster by the tripod. "Let's all recall the previous scene. Pip Quinn's come straight from the kitchen." Paco frowned and gazed around. "Do we have the spoon? Someone get Marjorie a spoon."

"I think our bear is going to faint." Marjorie hurried over to Horace, now suited up as the dangerous bear and sitting in the shade of a juniper tree looking for all the world about to list over from the weight of the headpiece. "I suggest we start filming."

She took a seat on the ground beside Horace who held a parasol over his head.

Jack's character was set to rescue "Pip" after her foray with the bear and stood in place, ready for the signal to run into the shot.

"What's the plan?" I whispered from just outside camera range.

Jack glanced at Boudreaux then straightened his bolo tie. "You'll see."

"I'd like to know."

"Just be ready."

Boudreaux poked the cigar Jack's way. "What about him? He's got a weapon."

"It's not live," Dooley said.

"Prove that it isn't."

"I'll prove it." Jack pointed the gun straight at his foot and pulled the trigger. "Nothing, see?"

Dooley went red. "That was a really stupid thing to do."

"Sorry."

"Everyone who has a real gun, walk it to that box forty-five feet that way."

Boudreaux slung an arm along the back of the chair and peered at Paco.

"I'd let you keep your sidearms, but insurance says no." Paco, whose white shirt was already wet with sweat, crinkled his lips in a pained smile. "You know it's impossible to fight with insurance companies. They do always win."

Boudreaux leaned over and twirled the tip of his smoke to the ground. Then he blew off the dirt and laid it delicately on the edge of the chair. He pulled out his pistol, raised it at Paco, then gave it to Will.

"Both guns," Dooley said.

Boudreaux handed the other gun to Will.

"What do I do with my own?" Will asked.

"Put it in the box, you imbecile."

"All right. No need for that."

He laid the weapons in the box, then stood next to it with his arms crossed.

"They don't have weapons," I whispered.

Jack's dimple danced. "And Dooley's got one at his feet."

Paco smacked one palm to the other. "Can we start this scene, people?"

"Places," Dooley called.

Marjorie took her mark to the left of the camera. Poor Horace lumbered up the hill, the umbrella above his head.

Dooley leaned into the camera's eyepiece. Then he straightened up, took his kerchief from his pocket to wipe the front lens and then mop his face. "I'm all right," he mumbled. "Absolutely fine." With a drawn-in breath, he bent again to the eyepiece, and took up the crank.

"Ready," Paco barked. "Set."

Horace waved the parasol around.

"It seems the bear," Marjorie said, "wishes to have an actorly conversation with the director."

"Jesus, Mary, and Joseph..." Paco trudged up the hill.

"Well, I need to know, too." Marjorie plodded behind.

"Stay here, Marjorie."

She gave Paco a long look then continued on.

"How many minutes is this scene to run? In the picture show?" Boudreaux asked Dooley.

"Ten to twenty seconds."

"And how long to film it?"

"Three lifetimes and ten hours."

Horace waved his claws about and poked Paco in the chest. Marjorie skipped down around some rocks. "They're having words. I guess the costume sits a little tight in places and he's working out how to..."

Her eyes caught on something behind us. Then her face went slack and her heel slid in loose stone and soil.

A cracking sound came from the barn, then the earth sprayed up by Boudreaux's feet. He hurtled from his chair and spun around.

"Raise your hands." Pip's voice echoed in the hayloft.

Will sprang for the gun box. He took out his weapons and aimed them at Pip. Jack grabbed the gun from the belt and holster Marjorie had set on the ground and held it up.

And aimed it at Paco.

Paco's face drained of color. "Jack—"

"We had an agreement. You shorted me." He shifted the barrel at Dooley. "You stay where you're at. You, too, Ruby."

Boudreaux smirked and stared up at the hayloft. "I do not think I will raise my hands, Miss Quinn."

"You do what I say or I'll shoot you in the heart."

"What do you want to wager that you won't do such a thing?"

"I don't bet."

"I suggest you come down like a commonsense sort of person." He put his hands in his pockets and ambled across the yard. "Come on down."

The barrel glinted as she raised it.

Everything went quiet.

The screen door slammed open on the porch. Rose stumbled down the steps, followed by another of Boudreaux's henchmen. He pushed his pistol in her back and goaded her forward.

"Rose..." I lunged forward, but Boudreaux caught me around the chest and pulled me tight to his girth. Pip's hat tumbled off my head and was crushed under his boot. Then he put the tip of a gun to my temple. "You shoot me, Miss Quinn, I shoot her. With her own gun. Rodriguez will then shoot the damn author. And Jack? Well, he's got an ax to grind, so there's no telling what he'll do."

"Jack," I kicked out at him. "You son of a—"

The cock of the hammer so close to my ear made my legs weak. "My patience stretches only so far."

Pip laid the gun down.

"Now raise your own hands. And I'd suggest not turning around too fast. Nichols has a happy trigger finger."

Pip threw me a small shake of the head. Then Nichols shoved her into the gloom.

Rose trembled and stared at me. "I'm sorry."

"The thespians can come down off the hill." Boudreaux raised his voice. Marjorie and Horace trudged down with their hands raised high.

Horace, now without the mask and claws, gripped Marjorie's hand. "Please don't let me leave this life in a bear costume."

"Jack..." Marjorie's face went three shades of pale.

"Money buys many things." Boudreaux said. "Desperate people are the easiest."

A scuffle broke out as Pip tried to kick her way out of Nichols' hold. He was a stumpy fella with a brush beard that took up all his face, save his nose and squirrelly eyes. His ten-gallon hat was more sweat than felt and had started to cave in at the crown. But he had her by the collar and twisted it up until she stopped fighting.

"Where's the pretty one?" Boudreaux asked her.

"She took off." Pip flattened her lips.

"Sad to lose friends." Boudreaux's chest and stomach rolled against my back as he laughed. "We'll leave her to the marshals. Yessiree."

Jack shifted his gun towards Dooley and pulled the trigger. The bang made me flinch.

Dooley dropped down, his hands covering his head. "Am I shot? Can someone look and—"

The camera wobbled next to him and burst into flame. Then it and the tripod hit the ground. Jack glared at the damage. "I hate movies."

"Oh God." Paco tore at his hair. "Do you have any idea what I paid for that? You've ruined me."

CHAPTER 20

Songs for Futile Circumstances—The Shadow of the Plains

First came all the film canisters. Tin after black tin lined along the porch rail. I had to give it to Dooley and Paco. They maintained a stoicism as they were commanded to set each up and kept their wincing to a minimum as Boudreaux's boys used them and the glass of the dining room and great room beyond as target practice.

Jack had been directed to load the wagon and harness the horses. The rest of us sat in the middle of the yard in the beating sun, hands tied behind our backs with wire. Horace, still in costume, sat with his head hung low. Sweat dripped from his forehead, staining his furry trousers.

"I knew this motion picture business was a bad idea," he muttered.

"What's he going to do with us?" Marjorie's skin was burnt a bright red. She leaned against Horace's shoulder. "Why couldn't you be like your father, Poppy, and stick to soap?"

Paco, his face frozen in a strange smile, gave her a look that would have withered my Grandma Ottoline.

Pip sat cross-legged to my left, and Rose to my right. She swayed like she was going to faint, then jerked herself forward and upright.

"Lean against me," I said.

She shook her head and wept.

"It's going to be all right."

Pip leaned forward. "Don't fret."

"No talking." Will kicked the dirt, then strutted in front of us.

The boys laughed on by, swinging their guns and making *bang bang* sounds. Will swaggered along with them.

"Your plan was terrible." I hissed at Pip through my teeth.

"It's not my fault Jack—"

"Where is Martha Ruth?"

"Out there. She doesn't know—"

"She'll be waiting."

"That's what I'm afraid of."

Will put his hands to his knees and narrowed his eyes at Pip. "Didn't I say not to talk?"

I heard the men *hawing* the horses and then the crack of a whip. One of the horses whinnied. "Damn devil horse."

"Leave him alone." Pip clenched her jaw.

"I should put it out of its misery." That came with another sound of the whip and the grunt of a horse hitting the fence.

"That's it." Pip unfolded her legs and stood.

"Sit down."

"You're not a horseman, are you?"

"I like 'em well enough. When they behave."

She was riled up. I gave him one more smart remark before she lit into him. Which would be worse for her than for him.

"Hey. You. Give me a hand." Will called over to Jack, who struggled to get Bessie settled in her traces and harnessed to the open air wagon. She reared, backing into the side of Napoleon beside her.

"Can't handle a mare?" Will smirked, then knocked the back of Pip's legs with his boot, forcing her to sit. "Now, you all stay where you are."

"Pip?" I asked.

"What?"

"This is really it, isn't it?"

"I think it is."

THE WAGON SEATS HAD BEEN PULLED OUT. PACO AND DOOLEY HAD been forced in first and now faced each other, backs hunched against the hard sides. One of Paco's eyes was swollen shut. He'd argued with Boudreaux about the ruined camera and didn't shut up about it. Will decked him and Jack took an ax to the thing.

"Get in." Jack's hands were rough as he yanked me forward to the wagon.

"I can't step up that high."

"Just get in." He hooked his arms underneath mine and swung me up and in. I landed hard on my rump. The binding cut into my wrists, but I bit my lip and didn't cry out. I scooched as best I could and sat across from Rose. "Don't you worry. Everything will be right as rain."

Jack reached for Pip.

"I can get myself up, you damn bastard."

No matter how hard she hopped she couldn't make it, so he grabbed her by the waist and thumped her in. She winced as she landed hard on her rump.

Marjorie did not ignore the help given. "Horace will need a step stool."

Jack eyed him, then went over to the barn and picked up a mounting block.

"Where's Adelaide?" Paco whispered.

"She's long gone," Pip answered. "And no concern of yours."

Once we were loaded, legs crisscrossed and wrists burning, Jack swung the back board shut and pushed a bolt through the cylinder. "Good luck."

Will climbed up to the spring seat and took the reins from the hitch. "What are the names of these beasts?"

"Bessie and Napoleon," Jack said. "Bessie's the—"

"I do not care who is who." He smirked down at us. "Settled in comfortably?"

"You're very young for such a mean streak," I said.

The wagon creaked and dipped as Boudreaux climbed up next to Will. "Move out."

Will released the brake lever and slapped the lines to the horses' backs.

The wagon lumbered up the slope and out of Vista Verde. Carnelia stood at the gate, a bright red scarf on her shoulders and skirt patterned in a geometric design of blues and yellows. She held up her hand as we approached, her wave a silent goodbye. I wondered if she had been paid off, too.

As the horses moved past, she darted forward and spit on the ground. Whether she meant the insult for Boudreaux or the rest of us, I could not say.

Boudreaux's other two men loped around the wagon, the butts of their rifles balanced on their thighs and trigger fingers at the ready. Rodriguez had a particular habit of laughing as he passed and giving us a clear view of his hoary never-cleaned teeth. He was hard on his horse's mouth, jerking the curb bit until his horse foamed at the mouth. If Pip had a weapon, the man would be dead and buried. It was Nichols who concerned me. He circled one way, then swung his mount around to circle the other, and each round he made the motion of pulling a trigger at one of our heads. "Bang."

Will pushed the horses faster. I worried about old Bessie up front, for the sun was as unforgiving as the land around us. Vista Verde, with its red-rocked canyon and cool shade of sycamores and willows, was nothing but a mirage. Here, from horizon to horizon, the flatlands stretched in sun-burnt grasses and emptiness.

This land would be the last I'd see before the cold bars of a cell and the colder eyes of a judge. So I did not hate it, but instead let the colors bloom. The sky was robin's egg blue and tipped in teal. The grasses glowed flax and mustard, butterscotch and fire. Far out west the thin line of the Rockies snaked in slate and pewter and ash. My chest filled with the damn full beauty of it and of the people in the wagon around me.

I pulled in a breath of air then coughed it out. "If you are going to partake of a cigar, Mr. Boudreaux, could it not be one of a better quality? You are ruining my final day of freedom."

He took a puff and twisted around to blow it directly at us, then turned back. "I am amazed you have survived to this day with a mouth like yours."

"I second that," Pip muttered.

"What are you going to do with us?" Rose sat upright, as if a rod had been glued to her back.

"That will be shared with you when I wish to share it."

My stomach did a twister. There was a fifty-fifty chance not one person in this wagon, save me, Pip, and Paco, would make it as far as La Junta. Boudreaux did not need witnesses.

"What are you plans for yourself, Mr. Boudreaux?" I asked. "After you drop Pip and me off with Sheriff Ward?"

"A bath and a shave."

"That's an excellent idea. You need to be presentable when you stop in at the House of Mirrors."

"Why would I stop in there?"

"To get the payroll and your cash. Dierdre—that's the proprietor of said house—is an avid investor in the Silver Star Film Company. Isn't that right, Paco? She'll be happy to give money to you."

Paco did a double take.

I frowned. "Of course, Sheriff Tartt might be there. He's no doubt burning up at Paco pretending to be John Ward, so you might hand him over, kill two birds with..." My breath ran out.

"You can pick up my silver Colt," Pip said. "It's worth twenty-three seventy-five. I'll let you sell it."

"Kind of you."

"Seems to me the House of Mirrors is your ticket," I said. "You take the money, leave everyone to the care of Diedre and Sheriff Tartt. You'll be an avenging hero. I bet they have a parade for you."

"I like parades."

"Or...now here's another option to consider...there's a possibility someone here might make a statement as to this kidnapping-extortion-possible murder plan of yours."

Pip shoved my ankle with her foot. "What the hell?" she mouthed.

"I'm giving him options, Pip. But I don't have to." I stared out past her, using Horace's long-stare-into-nothing trick.

Boudreaux glanced over his shoulder at me. "What other option?"

"You could pay all these people off."

"I don't owe them—"

"But they'll owe *you* loyalty. Look how easy Jack gave it to you."

"I'll think about it."

"You do that." I nodded then turned my head away to blow out a long breath.

The wind gusted. The smoke from Boudreaux's wretched cigar blew sideways, straight into Will's face. He coughed.

Pip jerked and dug her elbow into my ribs.

"Ow."

She bumped me again, her hip pushing against mine.

"I don't have any room to give it up for your fat behind."

She made a grimace and bugged her eyes. "My fingers are going to sleep. I need to move them around."

"Well, all right..."

She shifted again. Just enough for me to spy the wire clippers sticking out of the back pocket of her riding skirt.

"Jack?" I asked without moving my lips.

She gave a sly smile.

I shimmied until the cutters knocked one of my palms. But my hands were sweaty, and I could not fumble the tool loose. I shook my head.

Pip twisted the other direction and poked Paco's side. He glared, looked down at her hip, then his mustache widened with a grin. Both of them fumbled and knocked shoulders.

A loud snap froze them both in place.

"What was that?" Boudreaux glared over his shoulder.

"Just me starting the beat for a song to cheer us up," I said.

I stamped my boot heel to the wood. "You all know this one, so join on in." My voice gained a shrill edge so I took a calming breath and started to sing.

A sweet Tuxedo girl you see

A queen of swell society
Fond of fun as fond can be
When it's on the strict Q.T.

I cut a glance Marjorie's way and nudged her thigh. Then I shoved an elbow at Horace and bugged my own eyes out. "I need a good bass. Join in the chorus, will you?"

Ta-ra-ra Boom-de-re! Ta-ra-ra Boom-de-re!
Ta-ra-ra Boom-de-re! Ta-ra-ra Boom-de-re!

I warbled the next verse, an octave higher than I'd ever sung while Horace rumbled the low notes. Pip winced and picked up a harmony. Marjorie's voice could blast the back of any vaudeville theater she'd ever graced.

Paco blasted out a sequence of notes not at all part of the music, and as we cut the wires from our neighbor's wrists, the chorus grew loud enough to knock out the sun. Even Rose knew the nonsense words.

Ta-ra-ra Boom-de-re! Ta-ra-ra Boom-de-re!
Ta-ra-ra Boom-de-re! Ta-ra-ra Boom-de-re!

"Come on Mr. Boudreaux," I yelled above the fray. "Every man who's graced a dancehall and seen a pretty ankle knows this song."

The cutters made their rounds. Horace added in an *oompah* and scooted close to me. The hairy cuffs of his bear suit tickled my wrists as he cut the bindings.

Will looked back from the driver's seat. "Why are you all singing? What the hell do you have to sing about?"

"We sing for life, young man." Horace took a dramatically large breath and went in with gusto on the chorus.

Ta-ra-ra Boom-de-re! Ta-ra-ra Boom-de-re! Ta-ra-ra Boom-de-re!

We were free.

Or at least our wrists were. There was still the matter of the boys riding ahead and behind, of Boudreaux's pistols, and Will's, too.

Boudreaux smacked the seat. "Everyone stop with the *Ta-ra-rahing*."

"That felt wonderful," I said. "A rousing song does brighten the spirits."

"Speed the horses."

Will cracked the reins. The wagon jolted forward, catching a rut before righting itself.

The air snapped, arid as the desert, roused up for no reason and with no warning. It came from the east with a punch, stirring up dirt and stones that sprayed against the box boards and scraped my skin. I kept my head down, like the others, which saved my eyes from the worst of it.

Will's hat flew off. He pulled a bandanna up and hunched his head in his shoulders. Boudreaux smashed his cigar under his boot, then held the lapels of his coat over his own mouth and nose. His hair flipped all over, and he gave up smoothing it down.

"We need to cover the horse's eyes." Pip's voice swirled and whatever she said next was swallowed by the storm.

The riders floated in and out of view as the wind moaned and lashed around. The crack of Will's whip cut through as he urged the team to push faster. Napoleon stumbled.

"Stop the horses!" Pip shouted.

Rose ducked her head away from the flail of rocks and sand and, before I could stop her, lifted her hands to cover her eyes.

"They're loose!" Rodriguez pulled up alongside the wagon. He grabbed Rose's arm and yanked her halfway over the boards.

"Let go of her!" I clambered and grabbed at Rose's skirts. Pip put an arm around her legs.

"Now!" Paco bolted up and lunged for Will, kicking him hard in the ribs and grappling for the reins. Will tumbled to the ground. Dooley grabbed at Boudreaux and dragged him off the driver's seat, holding him down in the wagon while Horace yanked the pistols from Boudreaux's belt.

"Let go of my sister." My knees smacked the boards as I grabbed

Rose's waist. "She is the mother of my children and I will not let you hurt her."

The man pulled his reins tight to his chest. His horse revolted, rearing up and then dropping his head to gain freedom. He slammed his spurs into the horse's ribs and wasn't ready for the horse to lunge.

Still he held on to Rose, who flailed as she was pulled half out of the wagon. Paco hurled himself up and wrapped his arms to Rose, swinging her back into the wagon.

Rose lurched away from Horace and twisted a pistol from Paco's hand. She crawled over to Boudreaux, lifting the gun with shaking hands. "How dare you threaten my family."

"Rose," I said. "Give Paco the gun, you're going to shoot your own kneecap."

Pip climbed over us, yanked the whip from its holder and snapped it at Rodriguez. "Drop the reins, you son of a bitch."

Rodriguez put up his arms to avoid Pip's lashing, letting go of his rifle and then losing his seat. He toppled back and hit the ground.

"Dooley." Pip took up his horse's reins and circled. "Get the shotgun."

Dooley sprung out and reached for it.

"Give it to me."

She traded the whip for the gun, cocking it and setting her aim right at Rodriguez's head. But Nichols galloped in fast, his shotgun to one shoulder and beard flying out over the other and flicking the bottom brim of his ten-gallon.

"Pip, watch out." I gripped the edge of the wagon.

Nichols moved to her side, leaning in to take her gun. "Bang," he said. And laughed.

A shot came from another direction, startling the horses. Nichols swung his mount to look for its origin. Marjorie grabbed my sleeve, tugged me down, and pointed to Nichols' hat.

A bullet hole cut straight through the crown.

The wind gusted, creating swirls of brown like dervishes. Three specks grew from the horizon.

Satan galloped wildly, saddle stirrups flapping in the wake of the wind. Just behind him came that buckskin pony, fast as a flash.

The third made me look twice, and then again.

Not a horse at all, but an ungainly, too short, big-eared mule.

"Hoo wee!" Martha Ruth waved a rifle over her head. Then, as she heeled Theodore by, she took another shot at the hat.

"Shoot them!" Boudreaux barked.

There was gunfire and smoke as the men aimed at Martha Ruth. Booms came from shotgun shells and then the cracks of six-shooters when the first ran out of ammunition. I crouched down, covering my head. I couldn't watch. Marjorie hunkered beside me. She shook her head, for there were no words. Martha Ruth was outgunned. Pip and Dooley had no weapons at all.

Soon there was only the sound of clicks from Will's and Nichols' and Rodriguez's empty weapons.

Boudreaux bounded up, twisting his pistol from Rose's grip. He slammed an elbow to Horace's stomach, kicked Paco out of his path, and shot at Pip. She stuck her chin out, then made a show of great boredom and picked at her nails.

"Impossible." Boudreaux stared at a very alive Pip and then at his very empty gun.

Martha Ruth trotted up. No clothing ripped through from a rain of bullets, no blood. Not even a mark on her hat. "It's all right, everyone, you can get on up."

Dooley crawled from under the wagon bed, his mouth hung open in shock. He ran his hands along his chest and arms then stared at his palms. "I think I should be...What the hell just happened?"

"I put blanks in the guns. You all were indisposed and tied up and left the barn door wide open."

Paco's eyes shined. "My God, Adelaide, you are magnificent."

"Mr. Jones, I suggest you telegraph your wife and child and inform them of your safety." Martha Ruth rested her rifle across her lap and tipped her head. "And my name is Martha Ruth Platt. Though, if you wish, may now call me The Shadow of the Plains."

CHAPTER 21

GOODBYES ALL AROUND—A FALLING OUT

"Who's afraid now, boys?" Pip circled Satan around Boudreaux and his men, her rifle pulled from the scabbard and pointed at their heads. The men lay on their stomachs, hands and feet tied. Nichols' chest stuttered as he cried. Boudreaux wet himself.

"You can't get away with this." Will spit when she passed him.

"Don't talk." She had a set to her jaw that frightened me greatly. I reined the little mare over her way. "Pip, there's a whole group of people sitting in that wagon behind us. You really don't want to…"

"You're ruining the fun, Ruby."

"Cold-blooded murder is not fun, Pip, we have discussed this before."

"What should we do, then? Just shoot their legs?"

"Pip, you are not like them. We are not…" I swallowed then cut a glance back to the others. It was like having a peanut gallery watching and judging every move we made.

Martha Ruth held up the pocket watch she'd nicked from Boudreaux. "People need to catch trains," she called. "And I'm hungry."

I reached across my horse's withers and grabbed the barrel of the rifle. "Give it to me."

The men gave a collective sigh of relief when she released the hammer and handed it over.

I shoved the rifle stock to my shoulder. "If you go anywhere near my sister again, I swear to God—"

"Ruby!"

"This isn't your business, Rose." I looked over at her, hand to her throat and pale with shock. Then I lowered the gun.

"What the hell are you doing?" Pip asked.

"Seeing myself like Rose does. And I don't want to."

MARTHA RUTH LOOKED LIKE A CONQUISTADOR, WITH HER HEAD held high and Theodore high-stepping in front of the wagon. Paco rubbed his chin and stared a hundred miles out. Then he gave me a crooked smile. "I'm going to recreate that scene. Add a few more villains just to fill in the frame and really catch the audience by their collars. What do you think? We'll get to California and shoot the film there. Set up the laboratory—"

Marjorie and Horace both sighed.

"I'll need to do some deals, of course. Cameras don't come cheap, you know. But we can all lounge in the sand and gaze at the ocean as we wait."

I trotted around to Rose. "Listen, I know what you think of me."

She looked away. "You don't."

"Just let me talk for once." I scraped at the saddle horn with my thumb. "You've been good with the kids. I've never properly given thanks for you taking them in. So, thank you."

"I love them. I—wait." She dug the bills we'd retrieved from Will from her pocket and thrust them toward me. "I brought this for you. It's the last of...That's why I really came. To make sure..."

I held her hand in mine. "We probably won't see each other again."

"I know."

"But damnation, I would love to know what you tell Charles about this."

She slipped her hand back, leaving me just the money. "Be safe. Please."

Pip leaned into Dooley, resting a hand to his knee and saying something I could not hear. His jaw tightened and he nodded once.

She looked back at me and ducked her chin. "It's time."

I took in a breath. "Just one more thing, Rose."

"What's that?"

"Have the kids remember me like you write in the stories."

Pip yanked the whip from its holder and snapped it above the horses. "Haw!"

Bessie and Napoleon lurched so fast the front wheels of the wagon skimmed the road before smacking down.

Staying with the wagon would lead us into the handcuffs of two sheriffs. Going back to Vista Verde would have trapped us with the rangers combing the southeast of the state. Running was the only choice.

I lowered my head and put my heels to the horse. The yelling from the wagon disappeared in the stamp of her hooves to the hard soil. Then Pip and Satan drew up and galloped next to me.

"West?" she shouted.

"West."

"Hey! Hay hey ho!"

I glanced over my shoulder. Theo, big ears flat to his head and neck stretched out, gained on us. Martha Ruth urged him on and squeezed between us. Her eyes flashed. "I'd have appreciated some warning."

Pip slowed Satan to a canter, then a walk, and then stopped. "You're not going with us."

Martha Ruth's mouth dropped open. She looked at Pip with a stunned flitter of her lashes. "Yes, I am. I'm a full-fledged bandit, now."

"You get on the road back to your home."

"I will not. I am part of this gang."

"There is no gang."

Martha Ruth stuck out her jaw then spun Theo toward me. "What is she flapping her mouth about?"

"What are you flapping about, Pip?"

"You go on back to Gravette and see your family," Pip said. "You talk about them more than Ruby goes on about her damn kids."

"This isn't right, Pip."

"I thought we agreed, Ruby."

"No, we didn't—"

"Nobody knows who she is. She's still got a chance at a life." Pip gestured to me. "Not like us."

"Did I not just save your sorry ass?" Martha Ruth asked.

"I told you to do that."

"I believe I went above and beyond. You misunderestimate me."

"I don't under...mis...I estimate you highly. And I thank you for saving us, but you are no longer allowed to travel with us. So catch up with that wagon and get yourself a ticket back to Gravette." Pip looked at me. "Give her that cash you sister gave you."

"What? No. She's part of the gang."

"There is no gang. And if there was, I don't want her."

"You don't want me?" Martha Ruth's face fell.

"Pip—"

"That is exactly right." Pip's voice was hard. "We don't want you."

Martha Ruth's lip quivered. "All right." She stuck out her hand for the cash. I handed over the crumpled bills and waited while she licked her thumb and counted it out. "Here's what I owe you."

"Keep it."

"Nine dollars." Her lip stuck out as she shoved it back at me. "We'll go. But don't expect me to help you two when you find yourself in another stupid situation."

She touched a rein to Theo's neck and moved him into a trot.

"Wait." I stood up in my stirrups. "How did you get Theo?"

"I whistled."

❧

WE RODE UNTIL DUSK. THE FLAT LAND GREW LUSHER, WITH FIELDS of corn and melons and fresh painted farms evenly spaced along dirt and gravel roads. A lone train whistled in the distance.

"What happened with Jack?" I asked.

"He got a conscience. And money to pay the bank. And a kiss from me." Pip glanced back the way we came, her face soft and eyes searching. Then she shook herself and returned to normal. "I think we should drop south to Trinidad. Stick parallel to the tracks—"

"Maybe there's a Harvey House. Those roast beef sandwiches were some of the best I've had."

Pip peered at the corn fields, then twisted around in her saddle. "You see a corn crib?"

"There was one back there, before we hit that water trough."

"Let's tuck up there."

She stayed quiet as she took care of the horses. There wasn't much for me to do but take the saddles in and help her jig some hobbles with pieces of leather from the bridles.

I sunk down to the lip of the crib and rested my chin on my palm. "I'm feeling as sad as when we lost Theo the first time."

"We're not holding another funeral. Both Martha Ruth and the mule are alive and well."

"I know that, you fool. And I know it was the right thing to do. It's just how I'm feeling."

"You have a good heart, Ruby."

"You shouldn't have done it like that, Pip."

"It was the only way. You know that as well as me." She stepped by, slowing enough to rest a hand to my shoulder before ducking in. "Let's sleep."

❦

Pip wasn't there when the sun came up. I rubbed my face and shivered in the early chill. I knew when I went outside, it'd only be the pony waiting to greet me. No fire. No bubbling can of plums or asparagus stalks. No Pip.

"You have got to be kidding me." I kicked the dirt. "Pip, you are a no good, jack rabbit's ass, dirty dealing, snake breath, axle-oil tongued, pain in my..."

My stomach knotted. I thumped my hands to my thighs.

"You are the most exasperating woman I have ever known." I rubbed a knuckle under my eye to swipe off a tear. "Ever."

The pony raised her head, still chewing a tuft of grass she'd pulled up from the roadside.

"What's your name, horse?"

She flicked her ears around and watched me with her sweet brown eyes.

"Honey." I rubbed her nose. "I shall call you Honey."

CHAPTER 22

I Am All Alone

That first morning turned into a day and a half of fuming and looking for food. The night of the second day, I sold Honey to a melon farmer for a few dollars and a bottle of whiskey.

I found the rails and hopped a freight. I'd done it before—when Frank broke my arm and I first left him, then when I left him again and landed at the end of the line in Orinda, Arizona.

I'd been kicked awake later by another wanderer. He'd jumped on the box car at Timpas, too. We shared the whiskey and he promptly passed out in a visible haze of alcohol. I tried to keep awake, but the train swayed and I was about as beat as I'd ever been.

He nudged my arm with the toe of his boot.

"Leave me alone." I threw my arm over my face and rolled away to stare at the wall. Sunlight beat long slats against the wood. I sat up with a start. We weren't moving.

The man, whose pants and shirt were a patchwork of fabrics and stains, crossed to the door and dragged it open.

Tracks upon tracks lay outside. The stench of manure outweighed the tang of oil and coal. A line of cattle cars sat a few lines over, each car stuffed up with cattle lowing and stamping.

"Where are we?"

"Bull's coming."

"Who?"

"Rail cop. Welcome to Denver." He doffed his soft cap and hopped down. I scrambled over and peered out to see him cut across the tracks to a row of lean-tos and squat brick buildings. He squeezed through a gap in the fence and was gone.

The drop to the ground was an ankle-breaker. I clambered around to my stomach to slide off the bed, for a jump would be a losing bet. I let go of the door frame and landed in a heap.

One direction was a mass of trains and turnabouts, the city looming just beyond the railyard. The other direction was straight tracks, the land scorched yellow and, far out, mountains that seemed to cut the sky.

Then I saw the Bull's boots. He was on the other side of the train, stepping over iron rails, coming to do his job of finding people like me.

I tore off, jumping each of the rails and hoping not to catch the toe of my boot and end up face down in the gravel. Luck had never been much of a friend, but it pushed me now, and made the fence boards loose and easy to slip through.

There was no counting the streets I ran. I kept going until I couldn't.

A woman stood in a doorway staring at me. She had a grandmotherly bearing to her. Not grandmotherly like Grandma Ottoline, who looked more like a crow, but the kind you see in advertisements for cold remedies, rosy-cheeked and smiling. She poked a hairpin into her gray curls and leaned out to scan down the way I'd come.

I sucked in air and stared back at her.

"Who's chasing you?"

"No one."

"A lot of running for a 'no one.'"

"I'm looking for the Brown Palace."

"To meet a friend for afternoon tea?"

"Something like that."

"You got a long way up before you traipse in there."

The window glass next to her was stenciled in gold: *Barnett's Hattery*. In smaller print: *Hair Bought and Sold.*

"How much?" I asked.

"How much what?"

"For a hank of hair, how much?"

"I'm Nannie Barnett." She pulled a slow smile. "Come in."

🙠🙢

"Do you want to see?" Mrs. Barnett leaned a hip to the counter edge and crossed her arms. "You can still put your hair up. I sell a pack of pins for—"

"That's all right."

I gulped and turned the mirror I held to see myself. "Oh. Well. Better to nearly pass out here than outside and fall in front of a tram."

It wasn't the cut that shocked me; my hair just brushed my shoulder now and it'd grow out.

"It's very black," I said.

She shrugged then opened a tin box that had been squirreled behind her scissors and combs and mannequin heads. "Are you in need of a place of rest?" Her eyes stayed on the coins she counted out to her palm.

"I might be."

"There's a boarding house down on Larimer and 20th. Run by Dottie Meier, you can't miss it. No men. She doesn't mind dogs."

"Neither will be an issue."

"You all alone...?" One eyebrow went up.

"Valentina."

"Valentina, then." She took the mirror, hesitated a bit before setting it down. "Best avoid Market Street. The police have worn trenches into its sidewalk. Well, hell, so have the shady ladies who owned it before them."

I tucked the coins to my skirt pocket. "Any of those places need singers?"

The corner of her mouth turned up, lighting her face and showing off the beauty she once was. "You may look different at a glance, but I wouldn't trust that to hold under limelight."

My heart clenched up. I swiped sweat from the back of my neck and nodded. "Maybe a dishwashing job would be better."

She lifted the thick green curtain that separated the plain back room from her shop with its multitude of fancy wigs and mannequins with painted-on eyes. I gave a shiver as I passed them by. I shook my head at my own idiocy for thinking they watched me. I'd had little sleep since we'd all split up and all promised it was for the best.

"You've been kind, Mrs. Barnett."

"You call me Nannie."

"Nannie, then."

"Don't be a stranger. Denver's a hard town."

The bell on the door tinkled as I pushed it open. "I'll keep that in mind."

"Come by next Tuesday, Ruby Calhoun, so I can refresh—"

"My name is Valentina."

"As you say."

I shoved off the stoop and pushed my way into the crowd.

The noise pinched in on me. I took two wrong turns and then asked a fruit vendor for directions to Larimer and 20th. He laughed and pointed at the street sign. "You're here."

❧❧❧

DOTTIE WAS A FADED SORT WITH A VOICE THAT DRIFTED AWAY, SO I wasn't fully sure of my rent. She didn't complain about what I gave her. We climbed three flights of stale-air then she handed me a key and that was that.

I had a room with a bed, small chipboard dresser, washstand, and single window with a length of thin cotton folded over a metal bar. Tub and toilet down the hall. Breakfast from seven to eight, dinner extra. Day old paper free.

She eyed my closed fist as if she could see the quarter and dime I'd kept for myself. "Extra for guests. No men or cats. I do not like cats. But dogs are all right..." There went her voice. "You want a fan?"

"Is it extra?"

She drifted to the hall and returned with a tabletop fan. "Unplug it when you leave."

Then she stopped talking and stood there staring at me with her wispy blue eyes.

"Other rules?"

"Laundry goes down that chute."

"Okay."

"It's extra." She floated out of the room, closing the door with a soft snick.

I shook the coins in my palm, then set them on the dresser. The fan's braided cord was frayed as if a mouse had gotten to it. I chose not to be responsible for burning the place down, so dropped it to the floor. "Well, then. Let's instead have a little fresh air."

The window squealed as I shoved it open. I could just spy the street at the end of the alley and stepped out on the escape. The previous tenant had left a wicker chair with a precarious front leg, but I made it work.

ॐ

It was hotter in Denver than out in Vista Verde, what with all the brick picking up the heat, the paved roads soaking the sharp sun, and the buildings of commerce holding in the fumes from automobile exhaust pipes and horse manure. The road below me brimmed with both cars and horses working out who had the upper hand and right of way. There was quite a bit of honking and a few lumber wagons intent on blocking the path of the horseless carriages. But the drivers of the newest of conveniences simply swerved around and didn't mind taking up half a sidewalk as they did so. This led to people yelling and shaking fists, while others ignored it all and walked straight in front of the car and the wagon and then the streetcar as it screeched along, taking the other curb and not missing a beat of conversation with their friend.

The lobby of the Brown Palace was quiet. At least I assumed it was, as the only sound that came from inside was the whoosh of stratified air as the doormen gave the men in fancy togs and the women in soft linens a deferential nod. I was personally not allowed anywhere near the polished brass doors.

A doorman brushed past me to hail a horseless cab. "I told you yesterday not to idle."

"I need to find out if my friend is in inside."

"You have no friends in there, I can guarantee."

"Her name is Glorietta."

"No such person—"

"I could be a millionaire, you know."

"How'd you make the money?"

"Oil. Silver. Gold. Iron ore. All of the above."

But he didn't believe that and neither did the other doormen.

"I lied to you about that millionaire thing."

"Surprise."

The man trotted back and forth from the door to the street, letting guests out and whistling for cabs and carriages. During a lull in the spoiled crowd, I asked his name.

"Walter."

"Hello, Walter. I will note that down in my notes for future reference."

Five more sets of his servitude went by before he stopped in front of me. "Get away from the hotel entrance."

"Do you know why I lied to you, Walter?"

"I don't care."

"You don't have to, but you do need to know the truth about me. So you can be on alert."

His eyes narrowed.

I leaned in. "I'm a detective. From the Fillmore Blatt Agency in Milwaukie. That's in Wisconsin. The personage I am seeking—"

"Glorietta."

"Yes. You see her husband, well…" I tapped the side of my nose. "I do not need to expand." I held out a folded note. "She will ask for Valentina Holliday. Give her this. Here's a quarter for the trouble."

❧

EVERY TUESDAY, NANNIE DYED MY HAIR. SHE ASKED ME TO DROP A few envelopes through some mail slots along Wynkoop each week, which I did not ask about, and paid me enough for my next week's rent.

Thus it was I spent most my time bothering Walter, some time doing Nannie's bidding, and some other time wallowing in a bottle of hootch and reading the day old paper.

It all blended into each other. Until it didn't.

SURRENDERED
NOTORIOUS OUTLAW PIP QUINN SURRENDERS, RUBY CALHOUN'S FATE REMAINS A MYSTERY

THATCHER, COLORADO – SEPTEMBER 7. In a dramatic turn of events, Penelope "Pip" Quinn, the feared leader of the Quinn-Calhoun gang, has surrendered to local authorities in Thatcher, Colorado. Quinn's surrender came on the heels of a fierce altercation near Timpas, which has left her accomplice, Ruby Calhoun, missing and presumed dead.

Quinn, who had been on the run for months, walked into the Thatcher train depot yesterday evening. The notorious outlaw turned herself in to the station master without a hint of remorse.

Upon her surrender, Quinn vehemently denied that there was ever a third member to the gang. She claimed that it had always been just her and Calhoun. Authorities, however, remain skeptical, with some speculating that a third member may have played a role in their criminal activities.

Sheriff P.F. Clark took over custody of Quinn, expressing his relief at the capturing of one of the West's most disreputable outlaws. "This marks a significant victory for law and order in our region," he declared. "We will now work closely with Kansas authorities to ensure that Pip Quinn faces justice for her crimes."

I leaned from the wicker chair on the fire escape, hooked an arm over the railing, and sighed. A bit of a breeze made it through all the melee and ruffled my hair. I tucked it behind each ear then tugged the bobbed ends. My head felt light as a feather, all the weight of my locks long gone to Mrs. Nannie Barnett of Barnett's Wigs and Hattery.

"Oh, Pip."

CHAPTER 23

I Am Found

It was one week and then the next and then it was October. The decrepit little trees outside the boarding house dropped their leaves in one go. I had finished giving out Nannie's envelopes and thought I would find a sandwich and a soda somewhere, for the previous evening had been more hootch than sleep. A narrow diner around the corner from the Brown Palace called to me, so I trudged inside and sat at the counter. The fella next to me winced, crinkled his nose, and moved a couple seats over.

Nannie had gone overboard on her dye mixture and I had to admit that in the close quarters my hair had a stench I could not place.

"It's French," she'd said. "And South American."

"I can't help it," I told the man. He ignored me, so I read the menu card and gave my order to the waiter. "Ham and cheese. And a Coca-Cola."

The ceiling fan creaked above, giving off spits of air. A few people sat at tables, drinking steaming coffee and reading the evening paper. One man in a worsted suit and starched collar stood, took up his bowler from the hat tree and made to toss his news in the trash by the door.

"Excuse me," I said. "You wouldn't mind if I—"

He gave over the paper, a slight flicker of recognition on his face. But then a couple came through the door, and he must have changed his mind about knowing me. He mumbled, "Excuse me," to the two and left.

But then his step hitched and he looked at me again through the glass.

I turned back to the plate being slid across to me. "I need this to go."

⚜

THE BACK DOOR SWUNG OPEN TO AN ALLEY. TWO LIGHTS HAD BEEN busted out, the glass shattered across the cement. The man could be waiting at one entrance or the other. He might catch my arm and say, "You're her."

But I didn't look anything like myself. I was Valentina Holliday, which had a bright ring to it, and kept my spirits up when I said it aloud.

So I said it aloud, set my shoulders back with confidence, and strolled to the street. "I am Valentina Holliday taking a stroll," I said under my breath. I kept the paper rolled tight under my arm and tried not to squish the sandwich in my grip. "There is no one following me for I am a nobody to follow."

It was too early to go home. I'd eaten there enough on my own and the fewer hours I spent in the dank room that smelled disturbingly of cabbage and hair oil, the better. I took a bench in a small triangle of park with one measly-trunked tree. Light spilled from the saloons that bordered two sides and the nickelodeon along the other.

I unwrapped the sandwich, smoothing the corners of the course brown paper and setting it by my side. I unfurled the *Rocky Mountain News* and flipped the pages to the classifieds.

WANTED-SHIRT AND OVERALL MAKERS on power machines. Apply THE UNDEKHH.L MFG. CO.

A COMPETENT GIRL; MUST BE GOOD plain cook. 1107 9th St.

WANTED—YOUNG WOMAN TO SEW MATTRESS TICKS. Apply GEORGE J. KINDEL, 6th and Wynkoop.

LADIES WANTED, TO LEARN HAIRDRESSING TRADE; pay after 6 weeks, 311 14th St.

Valentina Holliday would apply for the shirt and overall maker's position. Ruby Calhoun, however, would not.

I sighed, took a pencil from my coat pocket, and circled the job. Maybe I'd cut it out and send it anonymously to Rose with a small note: *Not dead. Got a job. Love to you.*

"Mind if I have the rest of your sandwich?"

That voice. Half song and a bit of gravel.

I jumped up. The paper fluttered to the ground. The woman before me wore ruffles and lace and questionably appropriate attire, all of which dazzled and made me woozy. But I knew that voice. And I knew and had sorely missed those mismatched eyes. "Pip Quinn."

"I got your note."

"You're supposed to be in prison."

"Well, I'm not. I escaped."

"How?"

"Martha Ruth isn't the only sneak."

I gave her a side-eye. "I'm still mad at you."

She smoothed the back of her cloak and sat, allowing an emerald green skirt to peek out at the knee. "That's fair."

"Where'd you get such togs?"

"Here and there." She took a bite of the sandwich and looked about at the nightlife waking itself up. A barker had come out of the nickelodeon, set out a street sign, and gave a broad wink to three girls sashaying by. He took off his straw hat, spun it brim over brim, and tapped it back at a rakish angle.

"*Kidnapping on the Purgatory River*," he called. "Five showings tonight. Come see the true-life daring escapes of Horace and Marjorie Armstrong, starring as themselves."

"Huh." Pip finished the last bite and crunched the paper into a ball. "Shall we go see the first show?"

"You got a nickel?"

"We'll go in the side door once it starts." She stood and tossed the crumpled paper into a trash bin.

We waited for a streetcar to pass, then jogged to the other sidewalk. A line formed for the picture show. Pip stumbled into a group and gave a groveling apology as she backed her way out and bumped into me. She tucked my elbow tight against her ribs and took off at a clip.

"Hey," I said. "Slow down."

"I suggest instead you speed up."

A police whistle shrieked. People turned their attention to see what was going on.

Pip pulled me into an alley. She opened a wallet, clawed out the bills, then tossed the billfold behind a stack of crates. She licked her thumb and counted the money. "You need some?"

"Put it back."

"Why?"

"Because I said so."

"Don't tell me you've reformed."

"Maybe I have." I pulled a face thinking how I ran envelopes of bribes around town for Nannie without once asking her real business. "Maybe not. I'll take two dollars."

The policeman blew his whistle again, but it had a half-hearted ring to it. We continued down the alley, both holding up our skirts to avoid the questionable spots along the stone.

"You got a place you're staying?" she asked.

"Do you?"

"Of course I do. I'm just inquiring as to your health and welfare. I have been worrying—"

"You need a new hat. That is a silly monstrosity you have on. I can't concentrate on anything but the mound of feathers and dead birds upon it."

"This was the only choice."

"You should have passed on thieving that."

"You should have passed on that hair color. Gives your skin a terrible pallor."

I stopped at the boarding house door and took my key from my coat pocket. "It's supposed to frost tonight. You got any luggage?"

"I took it up already. Isn't that why you left an address with that Walter gentleman?"

"Dumb of me."

"I learned a new song. *Where the Morning Glories Twine Round the Door.*"

"I don't want to hear it."

"There is an excellent harmony, just made for your pretty voice."

I knocked the door open with my hip and hid a smile. "Well, get on in and teach it to me, Pip Quinn. And take that damn hat off on the way."

ACKNOWLEDGMENTS

Many thanks to Marc Wanamaker of Bison Archives for the invaluable information and hilarious stories on early silent film production and the pioneers of the birth of movie making; Library of Congress for Sanford Fire Maps; History Colorado; Missouri-Pacific Historical Society; Harvey House Museum; Kansas Historical Society; Bureau of Land Management Cultural Resources for "Land of Contrasts: A History of Southeast Colorado"; and Colorado Historic Newspapers Collection.

There aren't enough thanks in the world for the following individuals whose insights made this book so much better: Kerry Cathers, editor extraordinaire; the designers at ebooklaunch.com for another fab cover; Maryka Biaggio, empress of great ideas and an eagle eye; and Jacqueline Vick, who always figured a way to get me out of a sticky plot rut, or, as Ruby Calhoun would call it, a "dire situation."

So many thanks go to those who have cheered me on, kept me going through the Act Two swamp, and who inspire me in so many ways: Gail Lehrman, Tonya Mitchell, Robert Gwaltney, Alan Hlad, James Robert Daniels, the Morning Write crew, and the fabulous authors of Novelitics Writers Collective.

I could not have written this book or any other without the love and support of Dana Blakemore. You are my everything.

To readers: the biggest thanks. You are now a full-fledged member of the Quinn-Calhoun gang. I hope to see you on their next adventure. Until then, know that you are why I write.

ABOUT THE AUTHOR

K.T. Blakemore tells stories of women who venture beyond the lines history drew for them. In her *Good Time Girls* novels, the wide-open West becomes a proving ground for friendship, reinvention, and the kind of courage that grows quietly before it blazes.

A lifelong Westerner, she has hung her hat in California and Colorado and now calls the Pacific Northwest home, where gray skies make excellent writing weather. Her research has ranged from century-old railroad schedules to the fine art of wrangling an escaped horse—always in service of bringing the past vividly to life.

She is also the author of award-winning historical suspense and young adult fiction written under the name Kim Taylor Blakemore.

Learn more at kimtaylorblakemore.com